Making the Cut

Making the Cut

JIM LUSBY

VICTOR GOLLANCZ

LONDON

First published in Great Britain 1995
by Victor Gollancz
A Division of the Cassell group
Wellington House, 125 Strand, London WC2R 0BB

© Jim Lusby 1995

A catalogue record for this book is
available from the British Library

ISBN 0 575 05887 0

Photoset in Great Britain by
Rowland Phototypesetting Ltd, Bury St Edmunds, Suffolk
and printed in Great Britain by
St Edmundsbury Press Ltd, Bury St Edmunds, Suffolk

To Carl, Ciara and David

one

Under the shadows of the looming crane that carried the cargo containers between ship and shore, the river, roughened by a south-east wind gusting up the harbour, slapped noisily against the quay walls.

A plastic shopping bag had got itself trapped somewhere and flapped and billowed furiously every time the wind caught it.

And the wind, too, carried the sound of a lone singer from some nearby pub, his sweet, sentimental voice heavily amplified:

Were you ever in dear old Waterford, where flows the
silvery Suir,
Where grass is green the whole year round, and the
air is mild and pure?
I love the town and all around, and will love it
true till death,
But the hill of Ballybricken most, for there I first
drew breath.

Across the river a police car, its siren wailing and its lights flashing in the darkness, moved quickly through the crowded streets of the city.

It was ten-fifteen. Saturday night.

Outside the night-watchman's hut, two men stood close to each other without touching. One was the night-watchman himself, the other a down-and-out who'd been sleeping rough on the docks.

They stood outside, shivering in the harsh October night, even though there was a fire, chairs and hot drinks inside the hut.

The watchman, who wore a navy greatcoat over his heavy uniform, stamped his feet on the cold concrete and blew furiously into his cupped hands. The wino stood quite still, although his thin coat was held together at the waist only by string and his right trouser leg was slit from turn-up to knee.

They both looked down the river at the line of cargo ships that had been stranded in the port because of a strike the day before.

Then they both turned again and looked across the river at the lights of the police car travelling along the quay on the other side.

Even when the car went out of sight after crossing the bridge they tracked its progress up Dock Road by the glow from its flashing blue light against the dark night sky.

Still, they were almost startled when it suddenly appeared again, its headlights bearing rapidly down on them, less than a hundred metres away.

When the car stopped on the opposite side of the hut, its lights were killed and four got out. Two were in uniform, two in plainclothes. One, smaller than the others, wore a navy overcoat and black scarf. The last, wearing a brown woollen jacket over an open-necked denim shirt and light blue jeans, had two days of black stubble on his swarthy face.

The night-watchman and the wino looked only at the unshaven man in the light blue jeans as the group of four advanced uncertainly over the wet surface. They were still staring at him when he spoke.

'Detective Inspector Carl McCadden,' he said curtly, the strength of his voice without respect for either the stillness or the terror of the night. 'This is Detective Sergeant Liam de Burgh. Where is it?'

For some reason, perhaps because he felt disconcerted by McCadden's curt self-assurance, or perhaps because the inspector's appearance unsettled him, the night-watchman got suddenly nervous and started babbling while he was guiding the two detectives through the cargo containers squatting on the quayside.

'It should've been gone out of here yesterday,' he said. 'I mean, it shouldn't have been here at all last night. Do you know what I mean? They must've been getting ready to load it when the strike was called. That's what's held everything up. You see all of them ships there? They're all waiting to be loaded.'

The beam of his torch fell on a container close to the crane and settled there, although a bit unsteadily. The container's door was slightly open.

'That's it. That's the one.'

McCadden took the torch, stepped forward and shone the beam through the open door.

The container's cargo was peat moss. On the floor, between two packs of moss, McCadden could see the torn base of a black plastic sack with a dead man's head sticking out through the tear. It looked as if he'd just managed to burst through and then died from the effort. The rest of the body and the sack were still hidden from view. The body was lying face up and had a scar in the shape of a rough X or a cross cut into the right cheek, running from just under the eye down to the corner of the lips and stretching from the nostril to the ear lobe. The man was middle-aged. Probably forty to forty-five years old. He was gone a bit to fat and his black hair was thinning out. At a guess, McCadden reckoned that he'd laboured for a living and drank Guinness for his entertainment.

'A while,' McCadden said to de Burgh.

De Burgh nodded. 'Uh-huh.'

'What?'

'Two, three days,' de Burgh guessed. 'Maybe Wednesday or Thursday.'

McCadden shook his head. 'Not Wednesday, in any case,' he said. 'The face isn't swollen or discoloured yet. Maybe Thursday. Maybe even yesterday. Anyway. We'll tape this off, from there, across to there, right round the back, circle the

9

container. Have to wait for the technical crew from Dublin. They won't be travelling tonight, anyway.'

'And tomorrow is Sunday.'

'Doesn't matter,' McCadden said. 'Ready?'

De Burgh nodded again. 'Yeah.'

'Let's go then.'

The night-watchman's hut smelled faintly of brandy, and the wino's eyes were a little livelier and more alert than earlier.

The watchman sniffed once, very loudly, as he came in behind McCadden. The noise said he was surprised. The noise said he never kept alcohol in the hut and never drank while on duty. When no one else mentioned the brandy, he pretended he had a cold and blew once or twice into a cotton handkerchief.

The wino put another cigarette in his mouth and lit it while crushing the previous one under his heel. He coughed drily. His eyes wandered with the curling smoke up towards the roof of the hut.

'I lit a match,' he was telling Flynn, the uniformed guard. 'It was the last match I had in the world. I wouldn't have seen his face if I hadn't got it.'

McCadden said gruffly, 'That was *after* you tore the sack, was it?'

'It was the last match I had,' the wino said again, and again to Flynn. 'I thought he was going to throw me out. Would you credit that? I thought he was sleeping there as well. His eyes were open, you see.'

'Any idea what time you came in here tonight?' McCadden demanded.

'Hah?'

'Can you remember where you were tonight? Over in the city? Around here on the docks? Did you cross the bridge?'

The wino followed the ribbon of smoke back to its source and looked in amazement at the ash replacing the paper and tobacco between his fingers. He didn't draw on the cigarette any more.

'Poor Billy, hah?' he muttered disconsolately.

'What did you say?'

'But then,' the wino sighed, 'maybe he's better off out of it.'

'Out of what?'

'Poor Billy, hah?'

McCadden walked across the hut and drew a stool up to the wino and sat in front of him. 'Are you telling me you knew the man in the container?'

'Isn't that what gave me such a turn? Sure, I was only talking to him . . .'

The wino tailed off. At just about the same time, the tobacco in his cigarette burnt out and a last ribbon of unattached smoke climbed past his face, losing its shape against the roof of the hut. He didn't notice. He stared vacantly.

'When?' McCadden asked. 'When were you talking to him?'

'He kept dogs,' the wino rambled. 'None of them were ever any good, any of the ones he ever had. The best thing he ever had was a brindle bitch. Rockmount Cages, was it? No.'

'What was his name? What was the man's name?'

'Rockmount Ages! That was it. She couldn't break at all, though. She was always left going into the first bend and she still crossed the line third or fourth. She was always third or fourth.'

'Billy. You said poor Billy.'

'Billy, that's right. He was thinking of trying her over seven-fifty.'

'Billy what? What was his surname?'

'Power. Billy Power. John's Park. It went out of my head there for a while. That's where Billy was from. John's Park. I don't know what number.'

The wino had turned gradually away while talking, as if there was something unpleasant about McCadden, something that offended one of his senses.

McCadden moved to face him again. 'Why did they do it to him?'

'Hah?'

'To Billy Power,' McCadden said. 'Why did they do that to Billy Power?'

The wino's head came up sharply, the movement knocking

the curved ash from the filter he still held between his fingers.

'Who?' he asked dully. 'Who?'

'Was it the greyhounds?' McCadden asked. 'Did they do it because of greyhounds?'

The wino shook his head and lowered it again, a smile on his lips under the heavy stubble. 'Sure, no one ever got hurt much from the greyhounds, did they?'

McCadden sighed and got up and signalled the others to follow him outside the hut.

He said to Flynn, 'Keep chatting to him. Don't ask him questions. Just chat. See what you can pick up.'

The other uniform he sent with de Burgh to tape off the scene. Then he considered the night-watchman. A small man, used to kicking dossers and winos around, used to enjoying it too, but just as used to enjoying the bowing and scraping that went with the job as well. Convinced now that McCadden had got rid of the others just to be alone with him, but not too certain whether it was to praise or blame him, the expression in the night-watchman's eyes flicked between devotion and apprehension.

McCadden, slightly irritated, asked sharply, 'How did you find it?'

The watchman's shoulders moved inside the greatcoat as he drew a deep breath, a breath of great self-importance.

'Well,' he said, 'the way it is, the routine is not something I could break at this stage, even if I wanted to. You see, I — '

'Forget that,' McCadden interrupted. 'Did the old man come to you, or did you find him on your rounds?'

'He came to me.'

'He could've slipped away, could he?'

'I suppose he could,' the watchman conceded. 'I was in the hut. You see — '

'Yes, fine,' McCadden interrupted again. 'Did you touch anything?'

'No, I wouldn't, no. Just to look in, that's all.'

'How long has the container been on the docks here?'

'Well, there's so many of them, you see, and they all look the same, you know, and — '

'You don't know.'

'No, I don't.'

'Do you know where it came from, where it was headed?'

'I don't, no. You'd have to check with the office for that. And they won't be back until Monday. They mightn't even be back then because there's a strike on, you see, and —'

Exasperated now, McCadden walked away to stand at the edge of the open quay and waited for de Burgh. He listened to the river slapping against the wall underneath him, to the wind roaring down the channels between the containers behind, the plastic bag still flapping on the wires overhead, and the amplified singing from the nearby pub:

If the Sheriff was doomed with his hammer and nail,
  All those who frequent a bad house, to dovetail
How some gentry would tremble who're easily nam'd,
  What a crowd of respectable heads would be fram'd.

He didn't hear de Burgh coming back.

Until the Sergeant said, 'We're all ready now. Delaney and Flynn are staying here. They're off duty at twelve, so we can organize someone to relieve them then. Are we finished here?'

McCadden nodded.

De Burgh asked tentatively then, testing the ground in the darkness, 'Will you need me tomorrow?'

'Yes,' McCadden said curtly.

Without asking whether it was easy or awkward, possible or not.

Instead, as they were walking back towards the car, he said suddenly, 'Careless.'

'What is?' de Burgh wondered.

'The wino,' McCadden said. 'I was trying to think of his nickname. It's Careless.'

two

McCadden took a little detour the next morning.

A little after nine-thirty, driving from the station on Bally-bricken along Green Street and heading out towards John's Park, he said suddenly to de Burgh, 'Take the next right, will you, Liam. I'll tell you where to stop. I won't be long.'

Someone else he had to check on before talking to Billy Power's widow. Paul Hyland, a Detective Sergeant also stationed in Waterford. Hyland was more than just a colleague. Or he had been. Once.

Hyland should've been on duty the previous night. According to the roster, he was out sick. But McCadden had phoned his home and been told by his wife Tracy that he was working.

'This one, Liam,' McCadden said to de Burgh. 'I won't be long.'

An overweight, middle-aged man, all eighteen stone of him, and dressed only in striped pyjama bottoms, opened the door when McCadden rang the bell. His head, lengthened by a new spiky haircut, looked like an egg doing a balancing act, looked like it was balancing the wrong way round on his enormous torso and should really have been expanding sideways like the rest of him.

His name was Vinnie Foley. He worked as a bookie's pencil out at the greyhound track in Kilcohan Park, marking down the dogs and the odds, and the punters' stakes against their ticket numbers, then calling it all back on the winners.

Foley raised his eyebrows, but gestured McCadden in. 'Any news on Clarke, by the way?' he asked.

14

'No news on anything, Vinnie.'

'No?' Foley persisted. 'Peter Clarke, the chap escaped from Mountjoy Prison there on Tuesday. They say a murderer always comes back to the scene of the crime, don't they? I mean, like, he only killed her down the road there a bit. Poleberry, wasn't it, they were living in?'

'I'm not on that case,' McCadden said.

'You know the woman he killed, Theresa Cheasty? They say he's coming back to do in the fellow she was, you know, with. You know who she was doing it with, don't you?'

'His name wasn't Power, was it?' McCadden asked mischievously. 'Pass it on to Harry Boyce, will you, Vinnie. He's in charge of the case. I'm interested in something else.'

In the kitchen, Foley pulled on a black and gold Guinness T-shirt that left his paunch still exposed. He threw a stray fork from the draining board to the sink and picked up an electric kettle to fill it from the tap. 'Do you want a cup of tea or something? I'm only just after getting up.'

McCadden shook his head. 'Did you see Paul Hyland out in Kilcohan last night, Vinnie?'

'Paul Hyland? I did, yeah.'

'Was he betting with you?'

Foley plugged in the kettle and threw the switch. When his hands were free he put both thumbs down. 'Bad news too, boy. He was down about two hundred going into the last race.'

McCadden sighed. Hyland was a good detective, sharp witted and easy company, but he had a habit of chasing his losses, from dog track to race track, race track back to dog track again. It made him unreliable when he was on a slide.

Vinnie Foley was grinning. 'He had a good one lined up for the last race, though.'

'Did it win?' McCadden asked.

'Ah, Jaysus, a certainty, boy. Better than that, even. A dark certainty. A bitch be the name of Dondory. The outsider in the field at five-to-one and still drifting in the market.'

'Did it win?' McCadden repeated.

Foley took a teapot from the sink and fished two old teabags from inside it with his fingers. He tossed the sodden bags back in the sink and rinsed the pot, talking all the time. 'The dogs were out being paraded on the track before they put them in the traps and Paul was standing right there in front of us, waiting for the bitch to go out to six or even seven-to-one, when this fat Italian in all the clobber, one of those coats with suede on the collar and the cream silk scarf, and this redheaded bird in mink on his arm — '

'How did you know he was Italian?' McCadden interrupted.

'He had a heavy dark beard.'

'How did you know he was Italian?'

'I'd know them anywhere, sure. The sister's married to a man imports stuff from Italy, and the way it is — '

Annoyed with himself for even wondering, McCadden interrupted again. 'Hurry up, Vinnie. I've got somewhere else to go.'

'The Italian, anyway, steps up and puts five hundred straight win on Dondory and the price fell so fast, by the time Paul followed him all he could get was a hundred and fifty at six-to-four. He shouldn't have bothered. The bitch was no good, anyway. You should've seen the Italian and the redheaded bird after. Laughing their heads off. Have you ever come across them?'

'No,' McCadden said.

'It's not that you see all that many of them around now,' Foley persisted. 'Tourists. The end of October, like. Everything closed down out in Tramore and Dunmore East. Hardly any foreigners around at all.'

McCadden said impatiently, 'Hmm. Right.'

As if he had little interest in anything foreign, and none at all in Italians.

three

But an hour later McCadden and de Burgh were sitting in the living room of Billy Power's house in John's Park, talking to Power's widow and trying not to catch each other staring at an expensive Italian vase sitting on the mantelpiece.

The room was tiny and oppressively brown. Mary Power, a thin, haggard smoker, sat on one side in a bulky armchair, between a fireplace of cheap yellow tiles and some built-in chipboard shelves that held electrical equipment and more ornaments, but no books. McCadden and de Burgh sat opposite her on a matching fawn settee that stretched the width of the room. No one could've passed from the mushroom coloured door across to the thin ochre curtains on the small window without having to weave in and out of the three pairs of legs.

The place was badly maintained. The carpet was old and worn. The paintwork dirty and chipped. The woodchip wallpaper torn in places and lifting from the plaster in others. The coal scuttle was a caterer's plastic bucket. But the chipboard shelves held a state-of-the-art FST television, a twin-head VCR, a couple of remote controls and a high-tech computer games console.

The same contrast hit you from the mantelpiece, where the expensive Italian vase sat with two porcelain Dalmatians, a couple of porcelain leprechauns, a plastic rickshaw pulled by a plastic coolie and a red-combed wooden bird that bobbed up and down before dipping its yellow beak into a glass of dirty water.

There were four pictures hanging on the walls. Three were predictable. A posed family photograph bungled by some local snapper. A print of the Pope's visit to Ireland in 1979. Another religious print, this time of the Sacred Heart. The fourth picture, framed in unstained ash, was an original watercolour of the university in Padua by a talented artist. The artist's name was Perrugia. G. Perrugia.

So far the interview had been difficult. No, impossible. Neighbours kept poking their heads around the door saying, *I won't disturb you, but sorry for your troubles, Mary*, and Mrs Power kept sighing *Ah, Hannah* or *Ah, Bridie* and Hannah or Bridie kept edging further into the room, muttering *It must be a terrible shock to you* and *Do they know who did it yet?* and *It's the poor children I feel sorry for*.

Finally, McCadden had suggested either locking the door or doing the interview in the police station. Mary Power locked the door of the room, but left the front door of the house open and her eldest girl, Patricia, to welcome the stream of sympathizers.

'Your husband wasn't at home for the last few days, Mrs Power,' McCadden began.

'No, he wasn't.'

'How long?'

'Since Thursday.'

'Why didn't you report his absence?'

'Inspector, I don't know how many times Billy . . . If I had a pound for every night he didn't sleep under this roof I'd be rich enough to forget about him.'

'What exactly happened on Thursday?'

'Thursday night?'

'All day. What happened Thursday morning?'

Mary Power shrugged. 'Nothing. Billy got up the same time he always did, and after having his breakfast went off to work.'

'Where's work?'

'Byrne Plastics, out past Kilcohan there.'

'Is that Tom Byrne's place? The Alderman.'

'It is, yeah.'

'What did your husband work at?'

'A machinist. Any more, I don't know. They made sort of moulds for cases and things. I suppose you'll find out.'

'He went to work, then, and didn't come home?'

'No, he came home and had his food as usual — '

'I mean in the evening.'

'That's what I'm telling you, sure. He came home after work and had his tea. It must've been about seven when Martin O'Shea and Henry Barry called him. He was shaving himself, but they wouldn't come in. Stood there like Brown's cows on the doorstep.'

'O'Shea and Barry?'

'Two men worked with him.'

'Are they local?'

'They live a couple of roads down.'

'Where were they going?'

'Where do they ever go? Down to the pub, I suppose. He hadn't even walked the greyhounds that night.'

'Greyhounds?'

'There's three of them out the back, lying in sheds where the children's swings should be.'

McCadden thought of the Italian vase and watercolour, and the expensive stereo and video equipment and asked, 'Are they valuable? Do they win races?'

Mary Power laughed. 'Are you having me on? All they ever do is eat. That's what they're good at.'

'Did your husband ever have successful greyhounds?'

'The next one was always the good one.'

'Had he fed the dogs before going out last Thursday night?'

'He wouldn't feed them until after he'd walked them.'

'Did he say anything when he was leaving? Where he was going. If he'd be back later. Anything?'

'He'd hardly be likely to, would he, when he hadn't a civil word for me the past six months.'

'Can you remember what your husband was wearing when he went out last Thursday night?'

'Oh, God . . . No. Not really. I'm sorry.'

'Think about it, will you? Write down anything you

19

remember. Was he carrying anything distinctive? Anything in his wallet. Jewellery, maybe. Anything like that.'

'I suppose he would've had the Master McGrath keyring. He always carried that. I got it made special for him when we were going out, except it was on a chain for around the neck then. That'll tell you how young and innocent I was. He wouldn't be seen dead with a necklace, of course, so he got it done again as a keyring.'

'Gold? Silver?'

'It was silver.'

'Anything else?'

'I don't know. His driver's licence, I suppose. I can't think of anything else.'

McCadden got up to stretch his legs. But there was nowhere to go in the tiny living room. Still, he'd made the movement and de Burgh was looking at him expectantly, so he had to find something to justify rising.

He swerved past de Burgh's knees and studied the Italian watercolour hanging on the wall.

'Nice,' he said. Hoping he wouldn't have to ask where they got it. Hoping Mary Power would have memories of it she'd be eager to share. 'That's very nice, that.'

But Mary Power only shrugged and raised her eyebrows and sighed heavily.

'Italy, is it?' McCadden persisted.

'I couldn't tell you, now, to tell you the truth.'

'Must have been your husband's, of course. Any idea where he picked it up?'

'Benidorm.'

'Benidorm?'

'When we were on our holidays in Benidorm.'

'He bought it in Benidorm?'

'He came back to the apartment with it one day, anyway. Or I came back and he was already after getting it somewhere. That was it.'

'When was that?'

'This summer just gone. No, I tell a lie. That was Greece. Easter, it was. Benidorm was Easter.'

'Did you have a continental holiday more than once a year?'

'Billy was the one wanted it. It was he got the kids excited about it. I don't know how many times I told him I'd be happier for a fortnight on the beach in Woodstown. You might as well be talking to the wall.'

'But more than once a year?'

'In the last two years, I suppose we would, yeah.'

'That vase,' McCadden said, pointing to the item on the mantelpiece. 'Did you get that in Benidorm, too?'

'No, Tenerife.'

'Tenerife?' McCadden repeated.

And de Burgh nodded calmly and said, 'Tenerife.'

McCadden sat again, frowning. He said, 'If you wouldn't mind me asking, what sort of money was your husband providing for housekeeping?'

'The last ten years,' Mary Power said bitterly, 'everything else went up except what Billy put on the table in there Friday night to feed and clothe us for the week. That stayed the same. I had to go out and work meself to make up the difference.'

'Where was that?'

'Out in the hospital. Ardkeen. Helping in the kitchen.'

'Full time?'

'A couple of mornings a week.'

'Do you know what your husband's wages were?' McCadden asked.

'An awful lot more than he was giving up here to me, anyway,' Mary Power said. 'Other than that, I don't know. I never saw his wage-slip.'

'Did you never ask?'

'You wouldn't, if you wanted a bit of peace and quiet.'

'Right,' McCadden said. 'Right. Tell me. It was your husband paid for the holidays, was it? Organized them. Everything like that.'

'Like I said, I had nothing to do with it, I would've been happier here in Ireland. I went along because the children were going, though God knows why he wanted to bring the children because he never paid a blind bit of attention to them the whole holiday.'

'And the, ah, television and stuff,' McCadden probed. 'Your husband bought those as well, did he?'

'It wasn't me, anyway,' Mary Power snapped. 'Not on what you get working in a hospital kitchen two mornings a week. That's only enough to make sure the children have something to eat going out to school in the morning.'

four

McCadden and de Burgh had coffee and ham sandwiches for lunch at de Burgh's house on the Cork Road Estate. McCadden brought his own coffee, Chapman's Medium Blend from his local delicatessen, along with a filter cone and a packet of filter papers. Mostly, what people served as coffee he found undrinkable.

'Sunday,' McCadden said, walking up the footpath towards de Burgh's front door, carrying his coffee, cone and filter papers in a plastic bag. 'Sunday.'

He looked up and down the street while de Burgh was searching for his house keys. The wind had dropped overnight and there was nothing left of it now except a gentle breeze. Conditions were perfect for outdoor sport. One of those crisp autumn days when even the ailing sometimes feel active. People should've been striding about their business. Keeping up with the dog on the morning walk. Except it was Sunday. And because it was Sunday the place had the feel, the stillness, of a dull village. An elderly couple here and there, out for a sedate stroll. A few quiet teenagers hanging around a corner. Some older women coming back late from church and gossiping in clusters.

McCadden sighed.

He said, 'You ever get the impression everyone's marking time Sunday morning, Liam? You ever feel a sense of relief in the pubs in the evening, that everyone's glad it's all over and they can start enjoying themselves again? But then again, Monday morning traditionally represents the weary, reluctant return to the captivity of ordinary life. Saturday is the day of liberation. *Saturday Night Fever.* So, is Sunday the first day of the week or is it the last? And how many song titles or film titles or book titles can you name containing the word Sunday?'

De Burgh turned the key in the lock to open the door and asked dully, 'Sunday?'

'You know,' McCadden said. 'Like *Sunday, Bloody Sunday, Sunday in the Country.*'

'Oh, I see. Yeah.'

'*Saturday Night and Sunday Morning, The Sunday of Life.* Sunday is the best of days.'

'What's that?'

'Eh?'

'Sunday is the best of days. What is it? A film?'

'It's an opinion,' McCadden said. 'Hegel. The day of the sun, source of light, and therefore of life.'

De Burgh led the way to the small kitchen at the back of the house. He filled the electric kettle and took a sliced pan from the bread bin and milk, butter and ham from the fridge while McCadden lounged in the doorway and went on talking.

'As well as being the best of days, though, Sunday is also the worst of days. Charles Lamb, for instance . . . What was it? *There is a gloom for me attendant upon a city Sunday, a weight in the air*. A day not devoted to light and life at all, but the opposite. Still true. But maybe Sunday's only the day normality is suspended. Sunday driver. Sunday golfer. And of course, you can never get a soft-porn movie on any of the satellite channels on Sundays. Never. Anyway, best or worst of days, not great for starting a murder inquiry on.'

'Water's boiling,' de Burgh said.

'What?'

'The water's boiling.'

'Hmm. Right.' McCadden made a pot of coffee and followed de Burgh into the dining room. 'Talking about which, starting an inquiry, what *are* we talking about with this Billy Power murder?'

24

De Burgh, not used to working so closely with McCadden, muttered defensively, 'I'd rather wait for some technical reports.'

'Yeah, yeah,' McCadden said, killing the objection with a gesture. 'I guessed you'd rather wait. You always do, from what I hear.'

'I'd rather wait until I'm finished lunch, then.'

'No,' McCadden said, 'I'll tell you the results now. The autopsy will show the time of death as some time between Thursday noon and Friday noon, with all the usual precision of autopsies. I could get tighter on it than that myself. They'll tell us the weapon was a sharp instrument, probably a knife with a six-inch blade. Pierced the heart after a violent struggle. Bruising on the face and forearms, knuckles skinned. They'll identify fibres on the sack that'll eventually match fibres we'll find in the boot of the car that carried him to the docks. But it won't help us find the car, will it?'

'No, I suppose not.'

'So tell me, what do you think we're talking about?'

De Burgh reluctantly put down his sandwich and finished chewing. 'Money,' he said.

'Money,' McCadden repeated. 'Right! We're talking about money. We're talking about having money and about not having money. About having it and not having it at the same time. Here's a family house not properly maintained, the kids in poorish clothes, the mother working . . . Where?'

'She's a part-time kitchen help in Ardkeen Hospital.'

'The mother working for hardly enough to feed herself for the week. And yet they manage to run a new two-litre car, a new dishwasher, microwave, TV, video, two continental holidays a year . . . Two! You have two continental holidays a year, Liam? You have *one* continental holiday a year?'

'No.'

'Tell me, where are they getting the money?'

'Him,' de Burgh said. 'The woman would spend it on the kids and the house.'

'Where was *he* getting the money, then?'

'His wages?' de Burgh offered without enthusiasm.

25

McCadden shook his head. 'As a machinist? Can't be taking in enough. We'll find out tomorrow, but it can't be enough. Don't forget we're leaving out what he drank, and he looked like he was soaked in it, and we're leaving out what he spent on entertainment.'

'He won it gambling?'

McCadden shook his head again. 'Small-time punter. They don't win with the consistency you need to finance all that. And to gamble with the big boys you need a roll. Back to square one. Where did he get the money?'

'He bred and sold valuable greyhounds.'

'Possible,' McCadden conceded.

De Burgh smiled and picked up his sandwich again.

'But unlikely,' McCadden said. 'Remember what the old guy who found the body said last night?'

De Burgh looked sceptical. 'What? The wino? Careless?'

'You know why they call him Careless?'

De Burgh shook his head.

'Out in Kilcohan greyhound track one night about six years ago,' McCadden said, 'a dog named Careless Thoughts, with no previous form, ran away with a sprint at a price that hurt the bookies. A man called Ernest – of all things – Ernest Furlong, the track manager, had been doctoring its times. He'd been doctoring a lot of others' as well, but Careless Thoughts was the one he got caught on. And that's why Ernest is now called Careless. If the man says Power isn't making any money from greyhounds, we'd better look elsewhere.'

McCadden's coffee pot was empty and there was nothing left in his mug either. He stood up.

De Burgh said, 'I put another kettle on. It'll be boiled by now.'

'No,' McCadden said. 'Can I use your phone?'

'Yeah, sure. Go ahead.'

The telephone was in the hallway, on a small, unsteady table just inside the front door. There was nowhere to sit. McCadden bent to dial Paul Hyland at his home and then leaned back against the front door, listening to the tone.

It was Tracy Hyland who answered. She sounded as if she'd

26

been crying before coming to the phone. She sniffed a couple of times to clear her nose and swallowed noisily.

'Hello?' she said anxiously.

'Tracy? It's Carl McCadden.'

'Oh, hello, Carl. I'll get him for you now.'

McCadden held the receiver loosely on his shoulder, regretting the call a bit, thinking that the job seemed to take a heavy toll on relationships. McCadden himself was separated from his wife, Jenny. Five years now. De Burgh, too, was separated from *his* wife. And the chief superintendent's wife, Nora Cody, had just gone into hospital for tests on a suspected tumour.

And Tracy Hyland? One of those beautiful, intelligent, capable women who felt ugly and dumb and incompetent when their husbands looked at them critically. Had everything except confidence, belief. Everything. McCadden hadn't met her alone, without her husband, the past few years. For a year or so after he'd separated from his own wife Tracy had helped him through, meeting him for drinks, a couple of meals, coffee in his flat, until they'd talked one another to the edge of his bed, into an embrace that was more than just mutual sympathy. Just once. And they'd managed to keep their clothes on and their feelings unspoken. So. They hadn't been alone together after that, the past few years.

Funny expression, McCadden thought. Alone together.

Without warning, Hyland barked impatiently on the other end of the line.

'Yeah?'

And McCadden started. Guiltily.

'Paul? Carl McCadden.'

The swing was instant, back to charm and concern and interest. 'Oh, hi, Carl! Tracy didn't say who it was. Anything wrong?'

'There's a briefing this afternoon, Paul. Two-fifteen. I'll need you there.'

'What's it about?'

McCadden explained, as quickly as possible, and broke the connection with his fingers immediately afterwards. He held the receiver absently in his hand for a while, but then put it down and forced a smile before going back into the dining room to bother de Burgh with the question: 'Why do film stars, Liam, American film stars, find it impossible to sustain sexual relationships?'

De Burgh gazed at him blankly, chewing over something else. 'Who's Master McGrath?' he asked.

'What?'

'Master McGrath,' de Burgh repeated. 'The keyring Billy Power had. Who is he?'

'No, hang on,' McCadden said. 'I was listening to a radio programme the other day on . . . Who was it? I can't remember. Some writer. Anyway, they were praising his supreme dedication to his art. Do you remember the renowned Cyril Lamond, who set up the highly regarded drop-in centre for the despairing here in town and whose wife committed suicide from loneliness?'

'Yeah,' de Burgh said. 'But Master McGrath. Master McGrath.'

'Master McGrath?' McCadden said. He sighed and sat again at the table, conceding the choice of topic to de Burgh. 'Master McGrath was a famous Waterford greyhound. Unbeatable, like all Waterford greyhounds. He won the Waterloo Cup in eighteen sixty-eight, I think, and the year after that, and two years later again. Three times in all. Had an audience with Queen Victoria once. They wrote a ballad about him. I can't sing, but it goes, *And when they arrived in big London town; The great English sportsmen they all gathered round, And some of the gentlemen gave a ha-ha, Saying is that the great dog you call Master McGrath.* Pretty lousy rhymes, aren't they? They also built a statue to him and put it up outside Cappoquin in the county, where the punters still come in their droves every day to kneel and pray at the shrine.'

'An awful lot of greyhounds on this case,' de Burgh grumbled.

'Isn't there?' McCadden sympathized. 'What time is it?'

'Just five to two.'

'We'd better head. Cody will be inside already by now, waiting for us.'

28

five

McCadden's chief superintendent, Daniel Cody, was standing absently in the centre of his immaculate office with the door wide open behind him when McCadden shoved his head in. Cody, his hands stuffed deep in his trouser pockets, was saying quietly to himself, 'A good thing. A good thing.'

McCadden coughed.

Cody swivelled and exclaimed, 'Ah, yes!', and sat behind his desk and gestured McCadden into the hard chair on the other side, all in the one embarrassed movement. He took a pipe from the ashtray and searched his pockets for matches.

Cody was a tall man, a little over six-one. He looked older than the fifty-eight he was. His hair had greyed and thinned into two carefully trimmed patches above and behind his ears. Usually, like now, his mouth was clamped firmly around the stem of a pipe, concealing what he felt.

Still searching for his matches, he asked McCadden, 'Well? Has Carroll arrived yet?'

Leonard Carroll was the state pathologist. For homicides, suicides, other suspicious deaths in the provinces, he usually travelled from Dublin to do the autopsy.

'He got here about half an hour ago, apparently,' McCadden said. 'I haven't seen him yet.'

'What about the Technical Bureau?'

'Much the same. Half an hour ago. They're over on the docks now.'

It was three-thirty, Sunday afternoon. Somewhere else in the near-deserted building, a portable radio was tuned in to the

29

afternoon sports programme. The programme was switching between two commentaries, one from a hurling game in Dublin's Croke Park, the other from a League of Ireland soccer match in Cork. Even without hearing the words distinctly, you could always tell which was which. The hurling commentator was in a continuous state of high excitement, the soccer man was measured and analytical. The sounds were carrying fairly clearly to the chief superintendent's office. On a weekday the radio wouldn't have been heard; the bustle inside the building and the noise of traffic outside would've drowned it out. It wouldn't have been heard anyway on a weekday, because it wouldn't have been tolerated. But this was Sunday. And Sunday was unreal, McCadden had decided.

Cody had found the matches and got his pipe going. He stretched back in the swivel chair and puffed and asked, 'How much of a problem is this one going to be?'

'I don't know yet,' McCadden admitted. 'All I really know is that probably on Thursday night, maybe Friday morning, Billy Power was stabbed after a fight. Normally you'd say a brawl, over a woman, an insult, money. Except they removed all his clothes and all his personal possessions. You'd say robbery, then. Except they took the trouble to carve a cross or an X on his face, probably after he was dead, too neat to have been done while he was conscious. So you'd say the cross was a sign, the death some kind of warning. Except they concealed the body in a sack, and hid the sack and the body in a cargo container where no one could see it, all with the intention of shipping it out of the country. In normal circumstances that would've given them a week or so before the container was opened in France. It was bound for Lyon, by the way. Funnily enough, because of the strike, they would've had much longer if the wino hadn't stumbled into it. So, whoever it was needed a week or so before the body was discovered and they didn't particularly mind after that. It's odd.'

'You keep saying *they*.'

'Well, yeah,' McCadden agreed. 'You see, it's possible that a single man could've overpowered . . . overcome Power in a fight. I mean, a straight fight, in the open, man to man. It's possible. But somehow I can't see one man tidying the corpse in a sack, getting it into the boot of a car, then forcing the locks on the cargo container and getting the body in there. It's possible, of course, but I can't see it. I think a man alone would've thought of some other way.'

'How do you intend proceeding?'

'Well, I'll keep Liam de Burgh with me, if that's all right with you.'

Cody leaned forward, placed his elbows on the desk. 'Not Hyland?'

'No,' McCadden said. 'Not on this one.'

Cody said, 'Hmm. A good man.'

'Well,' McCadden said, 'de Burgh started with me last night, so I won't ditch him now. Paul Hyland was on sick leave. He was at the briefing earlier today, but he didn't look the best.'

Cody was reluctant. Didn't like changing winning patterns. But he said eventually, 'Yes, all right then, all right. If Hyland's ill. Who else will you need?'

'I thought myself and de Burgh would interview Billy Power's two friends, Barry and O'Shea, this afternoon. To-morrow I'd like John Widger and some uniforms to hit the area around the docks, look after the ferry company, check out the history of that container, the strike on the docks, the wino's movements that night, see if they can pick up anything happening around the estimated time of the murder.'

'Ah, Widger,' Cody interrupted suddenly. 'A neat lad. Quiet. Nicely turned out ...'

McCadden stopped listening, letting it exhaust itself. For five days, ever since Tuesday, ever since Cody's wife was admitted to hospital, he'd been having trouble with the chief superintendent. The man was inclined to drift into irrel-evancies, sometimes to ramble into nonsense.

'Anyone else?' Cody was asking.

'Yes,' McCadden said. 'I'll need Andy Laffan and Jerry Tobin for the first few days, more or less full time.'

Cody frowned. He separated the stem from the bowl of his pipe and considered the parts.

31

'Hmm,' he muttered. 'We can't stretch ourselves too thin, you know. We're under a lot of pressure as it is with this local chap escaping from Mountjoy.'

'Peter Clarke?' McCadden said. 'He hasn't been sighted back in Waterford yet, though, has he?'

'People are worried, Inspector.'

They get like that watching the police overreacting, McCadden thought. But he said, 'I'm not asking for any of Harry Boyce's people. He's got Frank Ryan, he's got — '

'I'm aware of who he's got,' Cody interrupted. 'I'll consider your request. Is that clear?'

Like that for five days now, Cody. Confusing discussion with insubordination. Thought the rest of the world was going to hell because his own home was coming apart. Touchy. Sentimental. A local's jail break hitting some raw nerve and fouling up every other investigation in the district.

McCadden said patiently, 'Yeah, that's fine. Yeah.'

Cody, putting the parts of his pipe together again and wondering where his cleaning knife was, waited until McCadden was getting up. He then said, 'Oh, and, ah, before you go — '

'Yes?'

Cody cleared his throat. 'I know it's Sunday and you didn't expect to be in here, no more than myself, but — '

'Well, Sunday,' McCadden interrupted cheerfully. 'Sunday depends on where you're coming from, doesn't it? Charles Lamb, now — '

'Yes,' Cody said impatiently. 'Quite. But while you're on duty, possibly something a little more . . . something a little less casual . . .'

McCadden, dressed in jeans again, this time with a white T-shirt and a blue cotton jacket, kept his irritation still in check. The man's wife might be seriously ill, he thought. Possibly dying. The man was looking for comfort. Neat haircuts and respectable clothes will rid the world of cancer. Modest dress will deliver us all from Aids. Uniforms will keep crime off our streets.

McCadden's mind flicked back over four hundred and fifty

years, back to Martin Luther warning the German princes
that extravagance in dress was a sign of corruption, and Calvin
railing against slashed breeches because he thought the gaps
let devils in.

McCadden tried not to smile.

Cody was muttering, 'A suit, for instance . . .'

A suit, McCadden thought. A suit. Efficiency. Rectitude.
Restraint. Statesmen, politicians and gangsters wouldn't be
seen dead in anything but a suit.

McCadden said, 'Yes, of course,' as convincingly as he could
manage and got out of there as quickly as he could move. He
walked briskly through the echoing corridors, the voice of a
sports commentator getting louder and louder, until he
opened the door to the office he shared with the other
inspectors and saw that the noisy ghettoblaster tuned to
the sports programme belonged to Paul Hyland, who was
sitting at McCadden's own desk, waiting for him to come
back.

Hyland held up an index finger to forestall interruption
while an attack was in progress in the featured hurling match.
Then, with a gesture of disgust when the team didn't score,
he lowered the volume.

He asked, 'Why didn't you put me on the investigation?'

'You can answer that one yourself, Paul,' McCadden told
him.

One last chance to come clean. Nothing to do with their
friendship. Nothing to do with ethics or duty or honour or
principles. It just came down to whether you could depend
on someone or not.

But Hyland refused the chance. Refused even to recognize
the offer.

Instead he complained, 'You needn't have phoned me. Why
did you ring if you didn't need me? I could've stayed at home
instead of disrupting the whole day, putting Tracy and the
kids out.'

During the briefing, McCadden had said repeatedly,
'Foreign. Foreign. I want you to think about foreigners. We've
got a freight container bound for France. We've got an odd

33

selection of Italian artefacts in Billy Power's house. Think foreigners.'

Hyland had kept his mouth shut about the Italian at the dog track.

Now McCadden walked across to the desk and switched off the ghettoblaster and in the sudden silence said, 'You were at the dogs last night, Paul.'

Hyland smiled. A perfect set of gleaming teeth in a shining, almost a polished face. Always too clean to be wholesome, really.

'I was at the dogs, yeah. You go there yourself. You know the score. A bit of fun, a bit of excitement, a bit of relaxation. So what?'

'How much did you lose?' McCadden asked.

'Oh, ye of little faith! I didn't lose anything. I wasn't up anything either, of course. I had five winners in the first seven races, Carl. Five winners! I was ahead nine points.'

'How much were you staking?'

'Couple of quid,' Hyland said dismissively. 'But you know me, I don't give a shit, really. I put the whole lot on this sure thing in the last race. A brindle bitch. Dondory.'

Hyland laughed, the noise echoing around the empty room. You'd swear he hadn't a care.

He said, still laughing, 'The story was she'd been held back a bit in her first three races. Not many were in on it. Her connections. The owner. The trainer. *Moi*. I know the trainer. She was in trap three. She broke reasonably, second or third, and picked up speed going into the first bend. On the bend the dog inside her swung wide and bumped her haunches. She spun round. She was still facing the wrong way when the rest of them finished.'

Hyland's laughter died out kind of reluctantly in the silence.

McCadden said, 'Let's cut the shit, Paul. You're gambling again. A couple of pounds, a couple of pence. It doesn't really matter. You're gambling, and you're looking over your shoulder, waiting for Cody or Tracy or someone else to catch you. No good. You only fuck up, not watching where you're going.'

Hyland snorted. 'I see. Is that what you brought me in here for? Just to tell me that?'

'More or less.'

Hyland stood up and took the ghettoblaster by its handle and said, 'Thanks,' adding with heavy irony, 'pal.'

He was at the doorway when he turned and asked, 'Who've you got with you? Liam de Burgh?'

McCadden nodded.

'Liam's reliable,' Hyland said. Making it sound like a failing. 'Liam's solid. You know what you get with solid, reliable people? You get solid, reliable results.'

He sighed heavily. The prospect too boring even to contemplate.

And then he was gone, switching on the ghettoblaster as he left.

six

Henry Barry and Martin O'Shea both lived in the same cul-de-sac in John's Park, a couple of rows behind Billy Power's house.

When the estate was first built, in the mid-nineteen fifties, the local authority had housed city workers and their families there in a tight, intimate community. Almost forty years now. The tail-end of one depression. Right through the booming sixties and early seventies. Back into another recession. Every shift leaving its own mark behind it. And yet the place still had that old-fashioned feel to it, still kept something of its origins.

At five that Sunday afternoon, some youngsters were playing soccer in the cul-de-sac where Barry and O'Shea lived, using their sweatshirts as goalposts. Women were standing in their small front gardens, gossiping to next-door neighbours or calling across the street to others. Teenage girls were imagining romances in one far corner and some younger girls were skipping in the other.

Then a clock struck somewhere and a police car rolled into the cul-de-sac and it altered the life of the place.

Sitting in the front passenger seat, McCadden caught the transformation as de Burgh pulled the Ford Sierra into the footpath outside Henry Barry's house. It was always the same. Always the same defensive cessation of ordinary life. Always the same cautious silence. Always the same guarded waiting.

It never really bothered him.

He opened the door and stepped jauntily out.

'Come on, Liam. Let's go.'

The Barrys had red and pink roses and a little Sweet William growing in their front garden and they had paint instead of wallpaper on their interior walls, but otherwise their house was almost identical to the Powers' place. The cramped rooms cluttered with heavy furniture. The many, too many, silent, inquisitive kids. The visiting neighbour, a thin, nervous woman from next door, standing awkwardly in the narrow hallway, just on her way in or just on her way out, you couldn't really tell, and she hardly knew herself any more. The knick-knacks on every available shelf space. The porcelain animals. The sports trophies. The souvenirs from holiday resorts. And then, of course, the nicely framed watercolours of Italian universities hanging in the small front room. The terracotta figure of a peasant and his donkey in the centre of the mantelpiece. The concert keyboard. The camcorder ... The signs of a welcome, but inexplicable prosperity.

Henry Barry, overweight, sweating heavily even in light grey slacks and a white Levi 501 T-shirt, was sitting at the table in the kitchen, half-way through his tea.

Coming into the room to meet him, McCadden thought he spotted an easy explanation for all the mysterious wealth. On the melamine dresser, between some garish ornamental plates, there was a large, hand-cut piece of Waterford Crystal glass. A woman's arm and a man's arm intertwined, the hands joined at the top. Obviously an original. If Barry and Power had worked in Waterford Glass and taken one of the company's voluntary redundancy schemes, you were talking about fifteen thousand pounds. Maybe more. Anyway, enough to account for all the gear. It still left an unusual taste for Italian art and artefacts unexplained, but still ...

'It's a detective inspector, Henry,' Barry's wife was saying.

It was a statement of fact, without either anxiety or awe.

'Carl McCadden,' McCadden supplied. 'This is Sergeant de Burgh.'

Barry nodded amiably. 'Come on in. I'm Henry Barry. That's the wife there, Annie.'

McCadden pointed to the glass sculpture on the dresser

37

and said, 'You must've worked in Waterford Glass, did you, Henry?'

Barry forked egg and rasher and fried bread into his mouth and chewed while talking. 'Naw,' he said. 'That was a wedding present for the sister, but she got cold feet and pulled out before the father could drag her up the aisle. Sort of left it on me hands. I couldn't give it to her. You know. Only remind her of something every time she looked at it.'

Some present, McCadden thought. He nodded and said, 'Disappointing.'

Barry shrugged, the rolls of flesh across his breast wobbling when he dropped his shoulders again. 'That's the way it goes, isn't it? More disappointing for her than it was for me. Do you want to go inside, in the front room? Might be a bit more comfortable. Take them into the front room, Annie. Throw them children out. Watching television,' he explained apologetically.

'No,' McCadden said. 'No. We're OK here. You finish your tea.'

Annie Barry, overweight and breathless too, and overworked on top of it, sat heavily at the table beside her husband. Then, immediately, she pushed herself upwards again, groaning with the effort. 'Would you like a cup of tea or something?'

When McCadden and de Burgh shook their heads, she sat once more and took up her own mug of tea and a heavily buttered thick slice of fruit brack.

McCadden asked, 'Do you know why we're here?'

'Ah sure, we do, we do,' Barry said. 'Poor Billy Power, hah? The Lord have mercy on him.'

Annie Barry's right hand flickered briefly in front of her slightly bowed face making a vague sign of the cross.

'When was the last time you saw Billy Power, Mr Barry?' McCadden asked.

Barry put his knife and fork on to the empty plate and washed down the last of the food with a swig of tea. His wife got up again to bring the teapot from the top of the cooker to the table. She poured silently for Barry and herself.

'Thursday night,' Barry said, using his tongue to scoop the

38

particles of food from between his gums and upper lip. 'The last time I ever saw Billy alive was Thursday night.'

'Could you tell us what happened that night, please?'

'Well, I got home from work the usual time, half-five — '

'Where do you work?'

'Byrne Plastics. Do you know it? It's out the road there. Tom Byrne's place. The Alderman.'

'What exactly do you do?'

'Machinist. They do moulds, casings, like that. Billy and meself were machinists.'

'You were saying. You got home at five-thirty.'

'Had me tea. Put the feet up in front of the box. No intention in the wide world of going out again. Had I, Annie?'

His wife shook her head. 'Henry is not a great one for going out.'

'But then Martin O'Shea called across,' Barry explained, 'about quarter to seven I think it was, and said we'll give Billy a shout. By the time I got the shoes back on and the overcoat on and Martin had a cup of tea, it must've been after seven when we finally called to Billy's.'

'I heard the clock going there,' Annie Barry put in. 'Seven. The two of you hadn't left then.'

'Was that usual?' McCadden asked.

'What?' Barry asked.

'Calling each other at that time on a mid-week evening.'

'Well, it wasn't out of the blue anyway. If the evening was any way fine, like, we'd go for a walk early, maybe give Billy's greyhounds a bit of gallop before feeding them.'

'Where did you go last Thursday night?'

'Out the back road to Tramore.'

'What was the route? Exactly.'

'Well, we went down through the houses on the estate here, on to Ballytruckle Road, took a left, straight out past Kilcohan Park, past the factory, Byrne Plastics, and straight on.'

'Anyone you know see the three of you?'

'Ah, they did, yeah,' Barry said quickly.

Too quickly, McCadden thought. Too much on cue.

Barry was saying, 'Mossy Fennelly. He lives next door to

us. You saw his wife there in the hallway. Mossy passed the three of us going the other way that night.'

'How far out?'

'A fair bit, I'd say. Hard to tell now.'

'Had you brought the greyhounds?'

'Billy was after walking them already, sure.'

'You walked all the way to Tramore, did you?'

Barry laughed easily and slapped his gut with the palms of his hands, the idea of carrying that weight on a round trip of fourteen miles amusing him. 'Naw, not at all. Just out the road a bit, you know.'

'Then what?'

'Well, we turned around and came back. It must've been about quarter to nine, I'd say, we got back here. I was all on for a few large bottles of Guinness, and so was Martin. Billy wasn't, though.'

'That unusual?'

'Well, it was something to pass a remark on, anyway. He liked his bottle, Billy did.'

'Why do you think he didn't want to drink that night?'

Barry shrugged his shoulders and blew air from his puffed cheeks. 'You have me there. I suppose he must've had other business. I didn't press him on it, like.'

'So you parted from him then?'

'Well, we left him about nine, outside Shefflin's pub in the Manor.'

McCadden frowned. Manor Street, linking the Cork and Tramore Roads to the centre of the city, was almost two miles from where they were sitting, in the opposite direction to the walk the three had taken that night.

'How did you get to Manor Street by nine?' he asked.

'We picked up Martin O'Shea's car on the way back.'

'Oh,' McCadden said. 'I see. You walked back here, got Mr O'Shea's car, and drove to Manor Street.'

'That's it.'

'Did you call in to any of your homes?'

Annie Barry scoffed. 'Them?' she cried. 'They'd be terrified they wouldn't be let out again.'

Barry laughed with her briefly. And then he was serious again. 'Anyway,' he said, 'meself and Martin went into Shefflin's and poor Billy, God help him, went off wherever he was going.'

'He didn't say?'

'We didn't ask him, sure. You wouldn't go prying into a chap's business like that.'

'Anyone you know see yourself and Mr O'Shea in Shefflin's?'

'Sure, all you have to do is ask any of the barmen there.'

'What direction did Mr Power go?'

'In towards town, along, ah, Parnell Street.'

McCadden nodded sympathetically. 'You and Mr Power were close friends, were you?'

Barry held up his right hand and showed two plump fingers squeezed together. 'Like that,' he said. 'Meself and Billy. Like that.'

'Did your families holiday together?' McCadden asked.

'We did, we did. Annie and the kids, and Mary Power and her kids, and poor Billy and meself, we'd all go off down to ... What's the name of that place in Cork, Annie?'

'Trabolgan.'

'We'd go off to Trabolgan together. Long weekends. That sort of thing. Sometimes we'd go camping in the summer if the weather was holding up.'

'No,' McCadden said. 'I meant, abroad. Continental holidays. Spain? Greece?'

Barry shook his head. 'No, no. You see, Billy's holidays wouldn't be the same as mine. The factory didn't close down for a couple of weeks like some do, so the holidays were always staggered.'

'Do you holiday on the Continent yourselves?' McCadden asked.

'You'd have to, wouldn't you?' Annie Barry exclaimed. 'For the kids' sake. If you could afford it at all.'

'When was the last time you were away?'

'What is it now?' Barry wondered. 'October. It was August. Last August. Where were we August, Annie?'

'Oh, God, don't ask me to tell you the name, Inspector. Some place in Greece, now. I'll get the brochure for you if you want.'

'No,' McCadden said. 'It's not important.'

McCadden and de Burgh got up then. Henry and Annie Barry stayed sitting at the table, looking upwards at them expectantly.

McCadden said, 'One last thing. You don't have to answer it now. Think about it. Did Mr Power have any enemies that you know of?'

Barry threw his hands in the air. 'That's the mystery, isn't it? The whole thing's a mystery, that's what it is. You wouldn't find anyone round here anyway to say a bad word about Billy Power, even *behind* his back. He was that type of chap.'

In the hallway on the way out, with the Barrys trying to squeeze either side of him to see him off, McCadden stopped and gestured through the open door at the two paintings hanging in the front room. 'You must've been in Italy, were you?'

Barry looked blank. 'Italy?'

'That watercolour in there,' McCadden said.

Barry raised a finger to point at a muddy depiction of some local scene. 'That? That's the pier out in Dunmore East.'

'No, the other one. That's the university in Rome, isn't it?'

Barry's slack and troubled face brightened into a smile. 'Sure, we were all over there for the World Cup in ninety. Meself. Martin. Poor Billy.'

'Oh, yeah,' McCadden said weakly. 'The World Cup. Right. Right.'

'Were you there yourself?'

'No. No. Working.'

And McCadden left, muttering to himself. He felt foolish. Why the hell hadn't he thought of it before? Why hadn't *de Burgh* thought of it? Italia 90. The Republic of Ireland in the quarter-finals of the World Cup after beating Romania 5–4 on penalties, going out unluckily to a Schillaci goal against the hosts. Half the fucking population had been over in Italy that summer.

seven

Across the road an hour later, after listening impatiently to
Martin O'Shea's description of the stroll out the back road to
Tramore, the return to collect the car and the parting of the
ways outside Shefflin's pub, McCadden was starting to feel a
bit more positive, a bit more like an intruder and less like a
sympathetic caller. Because this time McCadden struck lucky.
This time he had a couple who hated each other.

The O'Sheas had knocked down the wall between their
kitchen and the tiny front room. The result was uncertain. It
wasn't a kitchen any more. It wasn't a living room. It wasn't
a dining room. It wasn't even a combination of all three. The
only thing it did, it allowed the pair more space to express
their relationship.

Evelyn O'Shea, dark haired, sharp featured, sharp witted,
sharp tongued, still physically attractive in her late thirties,
was sitting at the dining table in the old kitchen area, smoking
heavily and aggressively. Her domain. Neither of the O'Sheas
had offered the visitors anything to eat or drink and it looked
like little food had been cooked in the place recently. But the
kitchen was still Evelyn's domain. In possession of it, she could
simultaneously deny her husband food and accuse him of never
helping with the cooking.

McCadden had an idea their life was coloured by such little
psychological power plays. He had an idea Evelyn was way
out in front in that department.

O'Shea himself, his black hair now greying rapidly, his face
becoming slack and veined from the alcohol, the remnants of

handsomeness still visible for another year or two, was sitting at the furthest possible point from his wife, in the armchair beside the front window. He too was smoking, but moodily.

The contrast in styles was fascinating.

She snapped at the cigarette like a bad-tempered terrier, filling her lungs only after numerous lunges. He sucked lengthily on the filter tip, wearing out the cigarette with two or three long visits, like a sedated vampire.

Her posture and movements said of him that he was stupid and lumbering and childish, a typical man. His posture and movements said of her that she was neurotic and two-faced and dangerous, a typical woman.

McCadden's posture said only that he was enjoying himself. But no one except de Burgh, sitting beside him on the comfortable settee, could have noticed that.

'You were both very good friends of Mr Power's, weren't you?' McCadden was deliberately representing the pair as a couple, wanting them to explode apart from being forced together. Because Evelyn O'Shea hadn't yet contested any of her husband's statements. And McCadden was uneasy with some of them. She'd questioned O'Shea's intelligence. She'd dismissed his judgement. She'd ridiculed his virility. She'd demeaned his sex, without even apologizing to McCadden or de Burgh. No good. Entertaining, but useless. Because she hadn't contradicted his account of that night on a single, solitary point.

'You were both very good friends of Mr Power's, weren't you?'

Evelyn O'Shea tossed back her head and threw out a short, exaggerated laugh of derision. She snapped the flint on the lighter and put the flame to the cigarette dangling from her lips.

'Billy Power,' she said venomously, drawing sharply on the filter and blowing out the smoke, 'was the greatest fucking eejit I ever came across.'

'He's dead, girl,' O'Shea snarled at her. 'Let the man rest in peace.'

'Billy Power tried to pick a fight with every man in John's

Park when he had drink on him. Am I right or am I wrong? Tell me I'm wrong.'

O'Shea looked away from her.

McCadden looked from one to the other with apparent bewilderment, not saying anything, letting the two of them get on with it.

'The hard man,' Evelyn O'Shea scoffed. 'Billy Power, the hard man. Every little Irish boy's dream of what it's like to be a man.'

She put the cigarette in her mouth and held up her left hand as a calculator, and with the index finger of her right counted off the accusations. 'The large bottles of Guinness, six or seven of them every night of the week. The dogs, Kilcohan Park twice a week. The horses. The pitch and putt in Tramore, Saturdays and Sundays. The rubber of thirties every Friday and Saturday and Sunday nights —'

'He enjoyed himself, anyway,' O'Shea cut in.

'More than can be said for his wife and children.'

'He got the most out of life. Not like some.'

'He had a good innings,' Evelyn O'Shea scoffed. 'A good innings. And anyone says he didn't, Billy Power, the hard man, will get up from his grave and have half a dozen large bottles in Shefflin's and give him a dig in the face. Unless it's a woman, of course.'

'Shut up, Evelyn.'

'If you're a woman,' Evelyn O'Shea went on, 'Billy Power, the hard man, will get up from his grave and have half a dozen large bottles in Shefflin's and try to ride you whether you want it or not, and only then give you a dig in the face when he can't get a horn. The hard man! Hah!'

'Shut *up*, Evelyn.'

She crushed the cigarette in the ashtray, wildly, leaving half of it smouldering. She stood up suddenly, knocking over the chair behind her. She pulled up the short black skirt she was wearing, settling it untidily around her waist, and rolled down her black tights and displayed the inside of her left thigh, holding the flesh bunched between her hands. The area had a greenish, circular bruise from a recent injury.

45

'You see that? You see that? That was my present from Billy Power just for sitting beside him in the pub last week and finding his great big spawk of a hand up my skirt.'

The tears came to her eyes then, as she shouted, 'And the fucking hard man trying to make out I was bawling because I was enjoying it.'

There was silence in the room for a while, except for Evelyn O'Shea's hard breathing and her efforts to hold the sobs. She rolled back her tights, more self-conscious now, her fury dying a little. She adjusted her skirt and sat down. She snatched a cigarette from the box on the table and snapped the lighter into action again. After drawing in the smoke three or four times, she said more quietly, 'You know what Rambo here did?' Pointing at her sulking husband with the burning cigarette, 'Rambo here went up to the bar to order another round until the all clear was sounded.'

She drew sharply again on the cigarette and looked vacantly out the kitchen window on to the overgrown back garden, away from the three men. She didn't turn again as she said, 'Listen, Inspector. If you want to find out who killed Billy Power, ask any man with a bit of gumption in John's Park who had a wife or a daughter pawed by the hard man. And when you find him I'll go down on my bended knees to thank him. Ask any man here with a bit of spunk in him. And ask Tom Byrne as well.'

'Evelyn,' O'Shea pleaded.

This time, McCadden really was surprised. 'Tom Byrne?' he repeated.

'The Alderman,' Evelyn O'Shea said. 'Byrne Plastics. Where they all work. Ask Tom Byrne what the hard man did to his daughter Tina.'

eight

McCadden's flat was on the top floor of a tall Victorian building in Manor Street, opposite Railway Square and just a little away from Shefflin's public house.

Twelve years before, when he'd been promoted to detective sergeant and transferred to Waterford, a colleague already stationed there had offered McCadden a choice between accommodation near the Clock Tower, or close to the old Lunacy Hospital or opposite Railway Square. McCadden had gone for the square, where they'd built the railway in 1845 to replace the stagecoach that ran between Waterford and Kilkenny, thirty miles away. Less of a journey to hump the luggage on the way in, he reckoned, and a much quicker exit when the time came to leave.

The irony was, they'd moved the railway station across the river and under Mount Misery in the late nineteen sixties, then pulled down the buildings and torn up the old track in the square.

McCadden had a car of his own now, of course. Didn't have to rely on the railway any more. But he didn't have the urge to leave any more, either.

His flat had a spacious living room facing on to Manor Street, a small kitchen-cum-dining room behind that and a bedroom in the loft, up retractable stairs. In the main room, McCadden had had the pine floorboards stripped and sealed and then partially covered with hand-woven rugs. The furniture he'd collected over the years was nearly all light oak pieces from the Arts and Crafts period. A carver. A coffee table. A writing bureau. The only exceptions were a futon and a comfortable modern armchair.

The books, in the alcoves either side of the tiled Victorian fireplace, along the opposite wall and in the loft, were mostly paperbacks, mostly politics, philosophy and fiction, and mostly well read. A small video library – all classics except for Peter Weir's modern thriller *Witness* – took up a shelf in the bedroom. *Some Like it Hot*, the 1938 version of *The Adventures of Robin Hood* with Errol Flynn and Olivia de Havilland, *Citizen Kane, The Discreet Charm of the Bourgeoisie*. Under it there was a bewildering collection of LPs and compact discs. Bach and Scarlatti, Dizzy Gillespie and Louis Stewart, Ewan McColl and Peggy Seeger, and Fairport Convention, Neil Young and Paul Simon. Otherwise the walls held nothing but framed black and white photographs; nineteenth-century shots of urban Irish scenes and contemporary newspaper snaps of public figures caught unawares. There were no prints, no reproductions, no watercolours. Nothing else. Except, that is, for a framed 1920 Russian poster showing a muscular hand holding a writing quill and pressing a stack of old books down on a curved chain that was just about to snap and shatter into the legend at the bottom that said in Russian: *Knowledge Will Break The Fetters of Slavery*. Taken together, the image, the caption, the historical context, they just about summed up everything McCadden felt about most things.

Later that evening, a little after nine o'clock, McCadden and de Burgh were sitting in the candle-lit kitchen of the flat, putting away the last of a lasagne, a salad and a bottle of tough Italian red wine from Piedmont.

McCadden was saying, 'So, there were two Billy Powers. Two. One the men loved. One the women hated. Loved is probably the wrong word. Maybe hated is, too. We need a woman, Liam.'

De Burgh, mopping up sauce with a slice of crusty bread, asked with characteristic literalness, 'Where's Sarah, by the way?'

'Ah,' McCadden exclaimed.

The half-bottle of red wine was getting to him a little bit, luring him into lechery and sentimentality the way too much alcohol always did. There wasn't much point in the present company. De Burgh was usually too impassive to get anywhere near sentiment. And he was the wrong gender.

'Sarah,' McCadden said. 'Sarah left to take up a teaching job in Dublin seven or eight weeks ago. At the beginning of September.'

'Permanent?'

'Permanent.'

'You applying for a transfer?'

'No,' McCadden said. 'No, I don't think so. Let's get back to the point, though. There's only two Billy Powers. The big question is . . .'

'Which is the real one,' de Burgh offered.

'They're both real, Liam.'

'Well, I know that.'

McCadden put back the wine glass he'd just taken from the table. 'You'll just have to give up longing for absolutes, Liam. You'll have to give up thinking there's only a single truth. You'll have to renounce your faith in experts. Especially now that Communism has just evaporated.'

'I was joking,' de Burgh said desperately.

It was impossible to believe him, though. His face was glum, almost contrite.

'No, no,' McCadden went on, 'the big question is, which one was murdered. Billy, the man's man, doing with other men what a man has to do, and getting killed in the process. Or Billy, the ladies' man, victim of a jealous husband or out-raged father. Well?'

'I don't know,' de Burgh admitted.

'Neither do I,' McCadden said. 'You want to open another bottle of wine?'

'I don't know,' de Burgh said again. 'In a while?'

'Open it now,' McCadden insisted. 'Let it breathe. Drink it in a while.'

McCadden got up and took the last bottle of wine from a small wooden rack beside the door to the living room. After

49

uncorking the bottle and leaving it on the table he sat down again.

'What about Barry's next-door neighbour, Fennessy?' he said.

'Fennelly.'

'Fennelly. Get anything from him?'

De Burgh shook his head. 'Nothing there. He said he met the three of them some time between seven and when he got back home himself at a quarter to eight. It wasn't very far out the road, though.'

'Despite what Barry would have us believe.'

'Only a ten-minute walk from John's Park.'

'Which means Fennelly met them at seven thirty-five.'

'No. He stopped to talk to someone else.'

'Great. What about the barman across in Shefflin's?'

'Barry and O'Shea came in about the nine mark. Maybe half-past. That time of the evening, two hours away from closing time, nobody's looking at the clock in a pub. The barman didn't notice anything unusual about either of them.'

'Tomorrow we'll get to the rest of the customers in there Thursday night and put out an appeal for anyone who saw Power alone. Do you think those two are telling the truth?'

'Barry and O'Shea? No.'

'Neither do I. It means there was something else going on that night, long before Power was killed. Whether it had anything to do with the murder or not is another thing.'

'It'd be a bit of a coincidence if it hadn't, wouldn't it?'

'Wouldn't it. What do you think's wrong with their stories, by the way?'

'Well,' de Burgh said, 'the most obvious thing is the greyhounds. I can't see Power going out on a brisk stroll with the two lads, just on a stroll, and not taking his beloved greyhounds along. The dogs hadn't been walked yet that day.'

'But Power,' McCadden said, 'obviously told the other two that they *had* been walked. It's not something they'd lie about. Too easy to check with Power's widow. No need, anyway. You see? They were setting out for a stroll, but when they

50

left the house only Power knew that something else was involved. Only Power didn't want the dogs along.'

De Burgh, hitting the same line of thought, added, 'As well as that, the dogs hadn't been fed and Power didn't leave any instructions with his wife about feeding them. Which suggests to me that he was anticipating going out for a while, an hour maybe, finishing some bit of business, coming back, walking and feeding the dogs, and *then* going out for a few jars. Something happened to change that.'

'Right,' McCadden said. 'Right. I don't think the *women* are lying, by the way.'

'No, I don't, either.'

'So the lads definitely left home — '

'That's another thing,' de Burgh cut in. 'I don't think they would've come back to John's Park to collect O'Shea's car without letting someone know what they were doing.'

McCadden raised his eyebrows. 'Why not?'

'The wife looks out the window and sees the car gone. Panic button.'

'O'Shea's wife?' McCadden exclaimed.

'Well, you know what I mean.'

'You must be joking, Liam,' McCadden said. 'You only panic if you care for someone. Evelyn O'Shea would've tossed a coin between the car having been stolen and crashed and the car having been stolen and burned, either way a couple of weeks' grief and inconvenience for the husband. But not for her. No, no, I wouldn't see that as a problem. These characters are independent spirits. They hardly ever tell their wives anything.'

De Burgh persisted. 'Power and O'Shea, maybe,' he said. 'Not Barry. Barry and his wife are close. Did you notice the way they've gone to seed together? Power's wife and O'Shea's wife are thin and haggard, while the two lads are nice and plump. I think Barry would've dropped in to let the wife know where he was going.'

'I take your point,' McCadden said. 'But you're leaving something out. Peer pressure. That's what usually keeps us warriors away from soft little gestures like that. What I'm more interested in, though, is where the three were getting all that extra money. What were they into?'

'We could always ask them.'

'We will. We will. Like to guess before we do? Drugs? Industrial fraud? Industrial espionage? Black market? House breaking? Like to guess?'

De Burgh said firmly, almost stuffily, 'No.'

McCadden laughed. He said, 'OK, OK, we'll ask. First, though, we'll have a look round where they worked. In the morning. Byrne Plastics. You know Tom Byrne?'

De Burgh shook his head. 'No.'

'Friend of Cody's. They drink together in the Munster Lounge. Sing light opera together. Gilbert and Sullivan. A policeman's lot is not a happy one. Rodgers and Hammerstein. William Vincent Wallace, the local bard, born just down the road from us. He wrote "Maritana" and "Desert Song" and "Amber" something. "Witch", is it? "Amber Witch"?'

'I don't know.'

McCadden shook his head, gave up the chase. 'I've never had the pleasure of meeting Byrne, either. Anyway, we'll take the factory in the morning, the two of us. Widger on the docks. Tobin and Laffan can organize the leg-work around John's Park, see if they can trace the movements of the three amigos.'

'Right. What about Paul Hyland?'

McCadden shook his head and looked straight and hard into de Burgh's eyes.

De Burgh asked quickly, 'What about Tina Byrne, the Alderman's daughter who's supposed to have attracted Power's attentions?'

McCadden's eyes softened again. He took up the fresh bottle of wine, sniffed at the neck and poured into de Burgh's glass and then his own and said, 'I've already met her.'

'What? About the case?'

'No, no. About five days ago.'

McCadden laughed, but de Burgh was concentrating too much on his own line of thought.

McCadden said, 'I met her out in Woodlawn Grove. The

funny thing about street names in housing estates is that the Crescent is always a straight line, the Rise always leads you down a shallow valley, and there are never any trees or shrubs in the Grove.'

De Burgh sighed. 'Yeah,' he said impatiently, 'but what about Tina Byrne?'

'Tina Byrne,' McCadden said slowly, taking a mouthful of wine afterwards and refilling the glass. 'Tina Byrne. There was a protest outside John Kirwan's house in Woodlawn Grove last week. You know Kirwan? Brother of Patrick, the county councillor – the two of them are the other side of the political tracks to Tom Byrne.'

'I've heard of him, yeah.'

'There was this kid,' McCadden remembered, 'twelve or thirteen, huddled up in an old anorak and holding up a placard his mother must've made for him with NO DIVORCE scribbled on it. About twenty or thirty others, late teens, early twenties. More placards. Anti-abortion. Anti-contraception. Someone had thrown a stone through one of Kirwan's windows and hit his old mother on the head with it. The old woman wasn't divorced and had never had an abortion, so she must've been well into safe sex.'

'Come on,' de Burgh urged.

'Right at the front of the group,' McCadden said, 'there was a young couple, obviously the leaders. The youngster had red hair, really cold eyes – intelligent cold, though – and a very bruised face. Must ask him whose fist he ran into. Name of Ian Wilkins. Ever come across him?'

'No.'

'I didn't even have to ask him his name. He told me while he was demanding my own. I did have to tell him to shut up, though. You know the sort of thing. We're not breaking any law. There's no legislation against picketing. Abortion is murder. We have a right to protest against that. The girl who was with him was a blonde, sharp features.'

'And?'

McCadden took up his glass and gently swirled the wine around. 'She wouldn't tell me her name at first. But this is the interesting bit. Wilkins went off to restrain someone, and while he was away she fell into . . . well, you'd have to call it a coquettish pose. You know the way the body kind of leans backwards a bit to receive you, the way the head is tilted at a little angle, the way the hair is sort of languidly brushed from the eyes. Frail and feminine, sexually alluring and maiden in distress. That was Tina Byrne.'

McCadden remembered.

De Burgh dismissed it with a gesture, saying, 'You were imagining things.'

McCadden shook his head. 'No, no. I don't even like that sort of thing.'

'Uh-huh.'

'I wouldn't even have noticed it, really — '

'Women are always affected like that with you.'

'. . . except when Wilkins returned, she suddenly clicked back into defiance. And that was Tina Byrne, too. Two Billy Powers. And two Tina Byrnes. She was like a child's doll with a couple of standard positions.'

'You were imagining it,' de Burgh said again. 'How long since Sarah left you? Two months? You were imagining it.'

McCadden leaned back in the chair and said, 'I wonder who Wilkins was fighting with? And which one of the two Tina Byrnes he was probably protecting.'

nine

The technical crew from headquarters and the state pathologist had come and gone and left their opinions and promised speedy reports.

Andy Laffan and Jerry Tobin were slogging it out around John's Park, looking for anyone who'd seen Power and O'Shea and Barry on the night Billy Power was knifed, the two of them knowing their informants wouldn't remember back that far with any accuracy, wouldn't be certain it wasn't Wednesday instead of Thursday, wouldn't have noticed much anyway. Unless someone had seen something remarkable, something that had lived on through gossip and was still fresh, if a bit coloured now, in the mind. Long odds. But you had to play them.

John Widger and a couple of uniforms were covering the docks on the other side of the river, looking for witnesses there. Widger had just finished negotiating with a trade union official on the picket line about gaining access to the office files on the container's movements.

And about mid-way between these points, in the Garda station on Ballybricken Hill, McCadden was sitting at his desk in the inspectors' office, waiting for Liam de Burgh to turn up. The only other person in the room was a uniformed inspector tapping away at a computer terminal.

It was ten o'clock on a grey, drizzling Monday morning.

McCadden, feeling the effects of the wine the previous night, got up gingerly and eased himself across to open the window slightly for a little air. But there was no breeze, only a heavy stillness that threatened to break into a storm, and the persistent, miserable, debilitating drizzle that was falling softly. Like every other cop and every fireman in the city, McCadden was hoping for heavier and more prolonged rain. Not for today. For tomorrow. Tuesday 31 October. Hallowe'en. Rain to quench the bonfires. Rain to keep the lunatics off the streets.

Not a very sporting wish.

But every Hallowe'en for the last five years, someone had died or been seriously injured in the city.

Because everything ended up on the bonfires. Car tyres. Pressurized containers. Wooden palettes. Gas cylinders. Unwanted furniture. Sometimes even wanted furniture. After dusk, in the more troublesome areas, teenagers might add a stolen car to the pyre. Someone would panic then and call the fire brigade. The firemen would inevitably be stoned by the kids and just as inevitably they'd call in the cops for protection and just as inevitably . . .

More than just a game, though. Half-way through a night like that you got a weird feeling the flames were threatening everything, everywhere.

McCadden closed the window and glanced at his watch – eight minutes past ten – and was just turning to write a note to leave for de Burgh when Michael Terry, in a flowing black cape and white scarf that made him look like an acolyte of Dracula's, and had to mean he was collecting money for something, swept into the office and swooped down towards McCadden's desk.

Terry was a local auctioneer and valuer who sometimes advised on stolen antiques.

'Carl,' he said, deliberately caressing the roundness of the sound. He stopped and held a sheet of paper at arm's length to study it. 'No,' he said. 'No, you're not on my hit list.'

'For what?' McCadden asked suspiciously.

'The Friends of the Brockenshaw Collection Annual Fund-Raising Dinner.'

'The what?' McCadden asked.

'Next Saturday night,' Terry went on, 'in the Tower Hotel.

Is your chief superintendent at home? He *is* on my hit list. And is your Inspector Boyce about? Also on my hit list. And your Sergeant Hyland? Also on my list.'

He turned without waiting for an answer. In the doorway he almost collided with de Burgh, who was hurrying inwards, and had to whip the billowing cloak away from the sergeant's feet.

De Burgh passed him without a second glance.

'Sorry I'm late,' de Burgh apologized.

McCadden shrugged and shook his head, then grimaced. He had a slight headache and it wasn't wise to move too suddenly.

De Burgh went on, 'I was talking to Jerry Tobin earlier and he put me on to something I had to go and follow up. The thing is, I've dug up something interesting on Wilkins.'

McCadden repeated vacantly, 'Wilkins?'

'The youngster with the red hair and the bruised face who was with Tina Byrne last week on the picket outside John Kirwan's house. You told me about him last night.'

'Oh, yes,' McCadden muttered. 'Wilkins. What about him?'

'You wanted to find out who he'd been fighting with.'

'I know that, Liam,' McCadden said irritably. 'What else?'

De Burgh sat and said triumphantly, 'He has a history of violence on demonstrations.'

McCadden's attitude softened a little. He leaned forward to put his elbow on the desk and rest his chin in his palm. 'Has he, now?'

'You remember the anti-abortion march last year where they hired the thugs with baseball bats to walk in front and clear the path of any dissenters?'

'Uh-huh.'

'Well, there was our Ian, right in the middle of them, with his bat. Got his picture in the paper and all. Two weeks later he was charged with causing an affray when himself and a few mates barrelled into a pro-divorce march, leaving a couple of hospital cases behind, including an old man with a split fore-head and a ten-year-old girl with a broken arm. In March this year he was acquitted of assault, claiming self-defence, after

57

putting away – two broken ribs, multiple bruising – a forty-year-old man who just happened to be a campaign worker for Tom Byrne.'

'I thought they were on the same side.'

'Not when it comes to tactics, no. Or to Byrne's daughter.'

McCadden asked, 'He's never used a knife, I suppose, has he? Wilkins.'

'No, he's never used a knife.'

'And he's been quiet since March.'

De Burgh grimaced. 'Well, suspiciously.'

McCadden grunted.

'No,' de Burgh insisted, 'Jerry Tobin, who's dealing with these things, has a list as long as your arm of night-time attacks on pro-divorce activists, pro-abortion activists, liberals, left-wingers, anyone not enrolled in either the Knights of Columbanus or the Legion of Mary. Broken windows. Slashed tyres. Dead cats. You can only speculate about who's involved.'

'Why did he murder Billy Power, then?' McCadden asked. 'Since that's where your speculation is leading.'

'Ah,' de Burgh exclaimed happily. 'I have a theory about that.'

'No,' McCadden pleaded. 'I'm sorry I asked. I wasn't serious. It's too early. We'll go and grill Wilkins later. OK?'

'OK. But before we go.'

'What?'

'Have you ever heard of the Young Salamanders?'

'The what?' McCadden asked for the second time that morning.

'The Young Salamanders,' de Burgh repeated.

'What are they?'

De Burgh consulted his notebook. 'They're small dragons, usually depicted as living in flames of fire.'

'Yes, Liam,' McCadden sighed wearily, 'but – '

'In the old myths,' de Burgh pressed on, 'a dragon sat on riches, so it became a symbol of a guardian of treasure. In this case the treasure is obviously the moral character of the nation.'

'*Who* are they, Liam?'

'They're the young, conservative, Catholic pressure group, anti-Durex, anti-divorce, anti-abortion, that Tina Byrne and Ian Wilkins belong to.'

'Thanks,' McCadden muttered ironically.

'They're using a Corporation house in Ballybeg as their headquarters and offices. I wrote the address down for you. It's where you'll find Tina Byrne.'

McCadden took the sheet of A4 paper with the address on it and gazed at it blankly, things still moving too fast for him. He usually wrote off the hours before eleven o'clock. He said, 'I wonder what Tina's old man thinks about it all.'

He'd once heard Tom Byrne described, quite seriously, as a strictly middle-of-the-road, all-things-to-all-men type of politician who'd strenuously resist any attempt to smear him with character or principles or policies. Any hint of extremism would bring him out in a rash.

'Must be some conflict there,' McCadden mused.

De Burgh said, 'Harry Boyce met him last night, you know.'

'Met who?'

'Tom Byrne. At a function in Jurys Hotel. He didn't think much of him.'

'Did he think he had enough in him to kill a man?'

'He thought he was dishonest.'

McCadden sighed. 'There are two types of people in the world, Liam,' he said. 'Those who profess to believe that we should practise what we preach and those who profess to believe that we should preach what we practise. I'd put you right in the middle of the first group and I'd just about squeeze myself into the second group. But Detective Inspector Harold Boyce is an exception. Harry Boyce really *does* believe that we should practise what we preach.'

'I don't think it's that,' de Burgh said earnestly. 'I think Harry's already in bad form as it is. He's probably not in much humour for politicians, you know, and official functions. Cody's riding him about this Peter Clarke case.'

McCadden flicked a hand impatiently. 'Cody's riding everyone right now.'

'No,' de Burgh said, his enthusiasm getting a grip on him.

'No, this Peter Clarke thing is interesting, you see, because Harry Boyce himself — '

De Burgh looked up, caught McCadden's stare, and suddenly broke off. 'Sorry,' he said, quietly. 'I forgot.'

'Let's go,' McCadden said wearily. He pushed back the chair, stood up and checked his pockets for nothing in particular. 'Let's go. Fresh ground. Alderman Byrne is waiting for us.'

ten

As it turned out, Tom Byrne struck McCadden the way all politicians struck him. Byrne, he decided, was a chancer.

Not that Byrne had said a word to McCadden yet. But here he was now, advancing on McCadden across the floor of his office in Byrne Plastics, like a disciple winding up to having an audience with the Messiah, his right arm fully extended in greeting, a look of – you'd have to say, ecstasy – on his face.

Physically, he reminded McCadden of Tina. Not the sandy-coloured, lifeless hair, but the thin, severe mouth and the prominent cheekbones. His face gave an impression of something a little anaemic, a little washed out. What character and presence he had were expressed through his body. Like his daughter, too. He was a tall man, powerfully built, no more than a few pounds overweight. Even at fifty-three, he obviously kept himself fit.

'Detective Inspector McCadden,' he was saying now with easy familiarity. You'd never guess he'd just heard the name for the first time, from his secretary over the intercom. 'And Detective Sergeant de Burgh, isn't it? How are you? Come in. Come in. Take a seat, won't you.' His voice dipped suddenly from cheerfulness to gravity, hitting the note just as the others were bending to sit. 'I understand why you're here, of course. Poor Billy Power.'

McCadden decided to cut the bullshit. The false sadness, the timing of the mood swing, that politician's *understand*, all tipping him over into bad humour.

'Yeah,' he said sharply. 'Poor Billy Power.'

Byrne caught the animosity, but he smiled anyway. It was the kind of smile that hung in there, a smile peculiar to politicians who were elected by proportional representation. *If you can't see your way to giving me your number 1 vote, don't forget me for your number 2. Number 3? 4? 5?*

McCadden asked, 'Power worked here as a machinist, didn't he?'

Byrne sat on the opposite side of his desk. 'That's right, yes,' he said seriously, again crowding the words with more feeling than they were worth. 'We manufacture plastic moulds. Camera cases, doctors' cases. Anything holding instruments or equipment. Precision work. Billy was one of our best machinists.'

'How long had he worked here?'

'Ten years. Since the day we opened.'

'Was he a good worker? Reliable?'

'He was very skilled at his own job. Very reliable. Very good socially. Well liked.'

'You never had any trouble with him?'

'What kind, Inspector?'

'Any kind of trouble, Mr Byrne.'

'No, none at all.'

'It seems he was killed Thursday night,' McCadden said. 'Did you see him that day?'

'I suppose I must've seen him in here, at work. I can't really remember that distinctly.'

'Did you see him at any time afterwards? When you were driving home from work, for instance. Or later in the evening, if you were out.'

'No,' Byrne said slowly. Thinking hard. 'No. We had a family dinner that night, so I wasn't out again after arriving home at six. I can't remember seeing him as I was driving home.'

'Don't mind me asking this, but would you describe the wages here as poor, or average, or good?'

Byrne laughed. 'There's no secret, Inspector. I pay union rates for all categories and all grades. You'll appreciate that as a politician I couldn't pay less and retain the popularity of the voters, and also that I couldn't pay more and retain the credibility, in these difficult times, of the economists and the party strategists. With union rates, everyone is content. You'll find his current rate of pay and copies of recent pay-slips in Billy's file.'

'No one's going to earn a fortune here, then,' McCadden remarked.

'No one's going to starve either, Inspector.'

McCadden said, 'Hmm. Was Power often absent, by the way?'

'No, very rarely.'

'Did he usually contact you with an explanation when he was out?'

'As far as I remember, yes. My foreman would deal with that directly, of course. You can ask him. He never complained to me on the point.'

'Why did nobody follow it up when Power was absent without explanation last Friday?'

Byrne frowned and mused. 'Did Martin O'Shea mention something to me in passing?' He looked at McCadden and then at de Burgh for guidance on that one. He found none, but left the question hanging there all the same. 'I can't really remember now. In any case, the foreman probably assumed that Power was late and then probably forgot about the matter. Friday is a busy day. If Billy had been absent for two consecutive days, it would obviously have raised eyebrows; but because of the weekend, you see — '

'He was also absent this morning.'

'Oh, by then, of course, we were all aware of the terrible tragedy — '

'Yes,' McCadden said. 'Would you mind if I asked a few questions about your daughter?'

'Which one, Inspector?'

McCadden blinked, caught unawares for the first time. 'Sorry?'

'My elder daughter Catherine, or my younger daughter Tina? I have two.'

'It's Tina I'm interested in.'

Byrne laughed heartily, much louder than the occasion merited. 'Yes,' he said, 'I really knew that without asking you, you know. It's always Tina everybody is interested in, whether it's the police or the Revenue Commissioners, the press or the boyfriends. Always Tina. You're no doubt aware that she's a leading light in one of the stronger Christian fundamentalist movements at the moment. But she's always been like that. As a child she was full of it. Much more rebellious than Catherine. But she's always come round to agreeing with me in the end. By her own route, of course. By her own route.'

He might have been laughing, but there was something chilling about his assurance of control. His daughter was twenty-two years old, not a moody twelve-year-old.

McCadden said, 'I was more interested in finding out if she knew Billy Power, actually.'

Byrne stopped smiling. He looked with raised eyebrows at McCadden. The expression was exaggerated. 'I beg your pardon?'

'I was wondering if your daughter Tina knew Billy Power.'

'Well,' Byrne said smoothly, 'Tina worked in the office here last year, helping with wages and accounts. She would've known him as a fellow employee, although from the other side of the desk.'

'Did she know him otherwise? Socially.'

'No.'

'Are you sure?'

'Of course I'm sure.'

There was a silence.

The two of them let it hang there, McCadden letting it say *You're lying, aren't you?* and Byrne letting his negative hold the floor, saying *I don't give a shit whether you believe me or not, Inspector. If I say it's the truth, then it's the truth.*

There was a silence.

But Byrne broke it first.

'Would you like to have a quick look around, Inspector? See where Billy worked. If you want to question any of the workforce, my office is at your disposal, of course.'

He was on his feet, gesturing through the glass partition at the side of the office that gave him an overview of the factory floor below.

McCadden got up too and went across to look down. Like whipped mongrels, Martin O'Shea and Henry Barry were looking furtively up at him. Well, maybe one whipped mongrel and one dim St Bernard.

But there was someone else watching McCadden as well. In a far corner of the factory floor, pretending to be sweeping rubbish into a tidy pile, there was a tall, black-haired youngster in his late teens, his eyes darting uncontrollably between the office upstairs and the dirt at his feet.

'Who's the young chap sweeping?' McCadden asked.

'His name is Eddie Hayes,' Byrne told him. 'He's here on an FAS scheme, gaining work experience for six months. His time's nearly up now. Next week, I think. I may keep him on.'

Now that you've got a vacancy, McCadden thought.

'He's a good worker,' Byrne explained.

eleven

Tina Byrne snared a stray lock of her blonde hair between the
thumb and forefinger of her right hand and curled it delicately
behind her right ear, inclining her head to do it, so that she had
to look upwards with shy, darting blue eyes at Carl McCadden.

'I saw you last Tuesday, didn't I, Inspector?'

'So you did.'

She was out in front of her desk in the living room of
the house in Ballybeg that the Young Salamanders used as
headquarters and offices, her hips resting against the edge, but
not so heavily that the natural curves were distorted. Most of
her weight was supported by her left hand on the desk's surface. The rest was taken by her right leg, bent at the knee,
the toes pressing into the carpet. Her other leg was stretched
fully out, its heel resting on the ground.

A classic pose.

Another classic pose, McCadden thought unkindly. De
Burgh and himself had already been treated to the seated one,
the one with the torso thrown back against the rear of the
swivel chair behind the desk, the open fingers of her raised
hand running rhythmically through her blonde hair, her
breasts alternately raised and lowered by the movements. And
he knew there'd be more. Especially now that de Burgh had
left to chase up Ian Wilkins and McCadden was alone.

Tina Byrne was quite a tall young woman, more than five
foot eight. Facially she wasn't beautiful, at least not in the
glossy style she searched for. Her cheeks and chin were too
prominent and her lips too thin to make the whole striking.

But she had a marvellous figure and she was dressed superbly, today in a startlingly white, wide-collared blouse and eye-catching orange baggy trousers with a broad black belt between.

A bit reluctantly, McCadden looked away from her as she was adjusting the lock of hair. He hadn't much objection to a private, temporary viewing of a woman as sexually desirable. Even while on duty. But he resented the attempted bribery, the invitation to close his eyes to anything that wasn't delectable.

He walked across to the window and rubbed a clear circle into the condensation with his forefinger and looked out. The view, the same as from every other front room in this local-authority housing estate, was depressing. Your own cramped and featureless front garden, the road, the backs of house after house after house, all exactly like your own. Patches of open ground that must've been designed as play areas were all waste-land now, choked by weeds and litter. A few of the houses were vacant and vandalized. Others were crumbling with neg-lect. Above all, it was the monotony of the place that got to you, made you indifferent about its condition.

And this morning, with the thin drizzle falling, it was even bleaker than usual. There was hardly anyone about. A kid, who couldn't have been more than eight, was struggling to roll a huge tractor tyre down the middle of the road, presumably towards the bonfire pile for the following night. A skinny, muddied kid in cheap, threadbare clothes. Both parents prob-ably unemployed, probably only in their mid-twenties, but already beaten. The type of kid about whom you habitually said that he didn't have a chance, until you finally booked him for mugging an old woman and all your sympathy seemed to have gone.

The sight, and the thought, made McCadden even more irritated with Tina Byrne.

When he turned to face her again, though, he saw a different person, a sad, uncertain young woman, her body limper, her eyes staring vacantly at the floor; and he understood that what she'd sought from him was assurance, that she used her body to boost her self-esteem. A dangerous habit. Much worse than her father's. He used his body too, but only to advertise his self-confidence.

'Can't we sit down?' McCadden asked, gesturing her towards her own swivel chair and taking another chair and putting it in front of the desk for himself.

While she was moving, she picked up a white trilby hat from the desk and stuck it jauntily on her head. She said, 'This was my father's, you know. He gave it to me as a present because he thought it looked better on me than on him. Do you know him, Inspector? Tom Byrne, the Alderman.'

'I know of him,' McCadden said.

She laughed as she sat. 'Oh, *every*body knows *of* him.'

Said without any irony, even with pride. Now that she was convinced she'd have to deal with a cold fish, she was falling back on the importance of her social position.

'What do you want to see me about, Inspector?' she asked.

The way she used his title, too, making herself weaker than it, vulnerable enough to be protected by it, bending their relationship again along conventional lines. And he couldn't stop her, couldn't risk making things worse by inviting her to use his first name.

McCadden said, 'I was wondering where you were last Thursday night. After, say, six o'clock in the evening.'

'I should ask you why, but I suppose you'll tell me anyway. Let's see. Last Thursday.' She frowned, crinkling her nose. 'I know. I was out at my parents' home for a meal. I got there around six-thirty and my father drove me back here some time after midnight.'

'You don't live there?'

'No, I live here.'

'Alone?'

'No. The house is rented by the president of the Young Salamanders.'

'Who is?'

'His name is Ian Wilkins. You met him last Tuesday, too. He was standing beside me.'

'Yes, I remember now.'

'I share the house with Ian.'

'Who else was at the dinner that night?' McCadden asked.

'My father. My mother, of course. My sister Catherine and her husband Robbie. Robbie Hearne. And myself. We don't have any other family.'

'You didn't invite Mr Wilkins?'

'Inspector!' she admonished him coquettishly, looking away in mock dismay. 'My father wouldn't be able to eat properly with Ian in the room. And anyway, myself and Ian are not like that.'

'Not like what?'

'We're not lovers, Inspector. We're allies.'

McCadden said, 'Hmm. Right.' Then he went on, 'Last Thursday a man was murdered here in Waterford.'

'Do you think I had anything to do with it?'

'No, that's not the point. Depending on where you were at the time, you might've seen something relevant. You might know something helpful. We have to question anybody who knew the victim. Do you know who it was, by the way?'

'Yes,' Tina Byrne said. 'Billy Power. He worked for my father. I read it in *The Irish Times* this morning. It got a small paragraph on page four.'

The local provincial papers didn't come out until late in the week, Thursday and Friday. The current editions couldn't have known of the story.

McCadden asked, 'Did you know Mr Power well?'

'Not any better than I knew any of my father's employees. I worked in the office out at the factory myself. For a while last year. What are you suggesting, Inspector?'

McCadden looked her silently in the eyes for a few moments, getting nothing but flickering eyelashes, so he said bluntly, 'I'm suggesting that he sexually assaulted you.'

Tina Byrne laughed thinly, but whether from embarrassment or fear it was impossible to tell. She lost herself for a moment, adjusting that stray lock of hair again, finding an excuse to lower her eyes. Then, shrugging her shoulders, she asked, 'Why would anyone sexually assault me?'

McCadden looked again, almost tempted to answer, but asked instead, 'Did he?'

She took a breath. She held it a second. The breath said, unpleasant as this was, she was going to get it over with, it was her duty.

'No,' she said firmly. 'He didn't. He made a suggestion once, that was all.'

'What kind of suggestion?'

She closed her eyes, wearily. 'Please, Inspector.'

'When did he make this suggestion?'

'About a fortnight ago.'

'Where?'

'Outside my father's factory. I was visiting my father.'

'What was your reaction?'

'Outrage, of course. I didn't answer him.'

'Did you tell your father?'

'No, of course not.'

'Why not?'

'Inspector, my father and myself don't always see eye to eye on political matters and I think he'd prefer if I was one of his campaign workers instead of being secretary to the Young Salamanders, but I can assure you that he loves me dearly and that he's still very protective towards me. We have a very special relationship. He would've sacked Mr Power on the spot.'

'Were you frightened of Power?'

'Of course I wasn't. I didn't want him to lose his job over a silly suggestion, that was all. He had a wife and children to support, hadn't he?'

'Had he?'

'Well, I assume he had.'

'Did you ever give Power presents?'

She laughed, and talked while laughing. 'What?'

'Were you ever in his house?'

'No, I wasn't.'

'Let me get this straight. You didn't tell your father about Power's proposition because you thought the incident too trivial to make a fuss of. Is that right?'

'As I said.'

'But you did tell Wilkins, didn't you?'

70

She started, and looked for a moment very frightened. Then she lowered her head and said quietly, 'No, I didn't tell Ian. Why should I? It was a personal matter.'

'Did you tell your sister, Catherine?' McCadden asked.

'No, I didn't tell anyone.'

'You didn't tell anyone.'

'No.'

'And it happened outside the factory with no one else about.'

'Yes.'

'Then how come I know of it?'

'What?'

And McCadden repeated, 'How do I know about it if you told no one and no one saw it?'

twelve

Tina Byrne's older sister, Catherine – 'Catherine *Hearne* now', as she kept reminding herself – had this odd habit of starting a sentence as an independent woman and rediscovering half-way through that she was only somebody's wife, somebody's mother.

'I wonder, Inspector, if you'd like . . . What do you think, Robbie?'

Watching her, McCadden could see the child she once was, the enthusiasm spontaneous, the timid caution learned the hard way from someone or other. The child she still was, in many ways, even though she was in her late twenties now.

Her features weren't as sharp and her figure wasn't as neat as her sister's. Three kids and a delinquent hand with the cakes and chocolate had softened almost everything about her. Even the anxiety. It came to her eyes for only an instant before being banished again with a reassuring look at her husband.

'I'm glad you called when you did, Inspector,' she said to McCadden. 'With Robbie home to lunch.'

And she meant it.

They sat in the kitchen of the Hearnes' enormous bungalow in Glenview, one of the better locations for property in the city. A model couple. Catherine, looking as if she'd expected and prepared for visitors, her blonde hair newly cut to shoulder length, the mauve necklace and earrings matching the dress, her face a little pale from make-up, was on one side of the large mahogany dining table. Her husband Robbie, the origin and the centre of all the valuables, including his wife, was

72

opposite her. Robbie was tall and powerfully built, probably a second row or number eight on the rugby pitch when he was younger. Now he was thirty, but looking, in style, a decade more than that, looking like a middle-aged man who'd settled on a lifestyle a long time before and hadn't come round to feeling bitter about it yet. Like most redheads, his skin was naturally pallid.

Sitting between them at the head of the table, dark-skinned and still a little rough from the night before, McCadden thought he must look like a coarse cut of overdone beef between two slices of white bread.

McCadden said, 'I'm sorry. I didn't mean to interrupt your lunch.'

'No,' Hearne told him. 'I've finished.'

'What do you work at, by the way, Mr Hearne?' McCadden asked.

'I have my own business. I have several, as a matter of fact. A couple of mini-markets, a café, and a steel manufacturing plant. We do cutlery, kitchen implements, some tools — '

'And knives,' McCadden supplied.

'And knives,' Hearne confirmed.

He didn't seem to get the point, though.

Catherine Hearne said suddenly, 'I wonder, Inspector, if you'd like . . . What do you think, Robbie? Coffee?'

'No,' McCadden lied, 'I don't drink coffee.'

'It's Java, from Bewley's Café. We grind the beans ourselves.'

'Ah,' McCadden said.

'He'll have coffee,' Hearne predicted. 'What was it you wanted to see us about, Inspector?'

Catherine Hearne had left the table and walked across to the presses. She poured the rich roasted Java beans into an electric grinder and turned the machine on.

McCadden sniffed. Marvellous aroma.

'Sorry?' he muttered. 'What did you say?'

'Why did you want to see us?' Hearne repeated patiently.

'Well, a man was murdered in the city last week. Probably last Thursday night.'

'Ah, yes. Billy Power.'

'Did you know him?'

Catherine Hearne spilled a little water over the side of the coffee-maker and glanced suddenly at her husband.

Her husband said, 'We never met him, no.'

'I —'

'Yes, Mrs Hearne?'

'We know he was employed by Catherine's father, of course,' Hearne put in. 'Don't we, Catherine?'

His wife nodded and concentrated on the coffee again.

McCadden didn't even bother looking from one to the other. He said to Hearne, 'This is purely routine, to confirm information already given. Could you let me know where you both were last Thursday evening?'

'Thursday? We had dinner at Catherine's father's house.'

'Do you go there often? Socially.'

'Very rarely.'

'When was the last time?'

'Last Christmas Day.'

'Hmm. Right. Any special reason why he invited you last Thursday?'

'Not that I know of, no.'

'You didn't, ah, mix socially, then. Yourself and your father-in-law.'

Catherine Hearne came back to the table and put a mug of coffee and a plate of biscuits in front of McCadden and another coffee before her husband and said, 'Robbie . . .' Pretending to draw attention to the drink, but really pleading with him. Her turn to object to some disclosure. But she hadn't the strength to sustain it.

Hearne looked into the black coffee and said, 'I'll be honest with you, Inspector. I haven't a great deal of time for Tom Byrne. And I'll tell you why. Tom Byrne is full of pious shit.'

'Robbie . . .'

Hearne's accent grew flatter, more local, his language less restrained, as he angered. 'No, Catherine, this'll only do good. I'll give you an example, Inspector. Catherine was wearing a new dress she'd bought in Dublin when we went along to this

74

farce last Thursday night. The minute we walked in the door Byrne says to her, the colour suits you, Catherine. Nothing in the world wrong with that, you might say. The man was only paying a compliment to his daughter like any decent father would. But it was the cutting way he said it. You wouldn't get it and Icky-Ocky wouldn't get it.'

Icky-Ocky? McCadden wondered.

'But myself and Catherine got it, all right. What he was saying was a slap in the face. What he was saying was that the colour was the only thing about the dress that *did* suit Catherine. It didn't fit right and it was the wrong length and it was the wrong pattern and we probably paid too much for it anyway, and if he'd had anything to do with it she'd be looking better than she had a right to deserve instead of worse. Do you see what I mean? Always the bitter word. Always putting Catherine down, though you couldn't put your finger on it exactly how he was doing it, until you got to know him.'

Hearne drank his coffee and glanced at his watch at the same time, both with sharp, angry movements.

McCadden asked conversationally, 'What time did you leave the dinner on Thursday night?'

'Early. About ten.'

'Just the two of you?'

'That's right.'

McCadden, who'd been steadily drinking Java and eating chocolate sandwich bars during Hearne's outburst, now finished the coffee and got up. 'Well, you've been very helpful. Could I have your telephone numbers in case I need to contact you again? Home and work.'

Outside the house he waved back merrily towards the slightly parted curtains in the downstairs front room and got in his car and drove away. He took a left, out the Dunmore Road, past Ardkeen Hospital, about three miles out to the Woodstown junction, where he did a U-turn and drove back, past Ardkeen Hospital again, and back into Glenview. He parked outside the Hearnes' house, this time a little closer to the front door because Hearne's car was no longer in the driveway, and rang their doorbell. Catherine Hearne, her eyes still slightly moist with the tears, opened up and stared at him in dismay.

'Sorry to disturb you again,' McCadden said breezily. 'It's just that I forgot to ask you something.'

He could see in her eyes the burden of what she was concealing from him.

'Has your husband left?' he asked with apparent surprise. 'It doesn't really matter. You'll be able to help me yourself.'

He slipped past her immobile figure into the hallway and sniffed.

'Any more of that great coffee?'

In the kitchen he watched her fumbling with the coffee beans and the electric grinder and the filter paper. When the coffee was dripping into the glass jug she finally said, 'What was it you forgot to ask?'

'Icky-Ocky,' McCadden said.

'What?'

'Your husband said Icky-Ocky wouldn't know what your father, Tom Byrne, was up to. What did he mean?'

She stared at him. She looked as if she was going to laugh, from relief, from the sudden snapping of a tension.

'It's only a saying, Inspector. I think he was a local character who imagined he was a horse. The sounds he made galloping in the street got him his nickname. Icky-Ocky. People say it when they want . . . when they mean you can't understand something.'

McCadden took a mug of coffee from her and added milk and stirred slowly, frowning all the time. 'I see, yes. Bit stupid of me.' He drank a little, exclaiming appreciatively. And then asked suddenly, 'What was it you wanted to tell me about Billy Power that you didn't want your husband to hear, or want him to hear you saying?'

And again, McCadden could see the child she'd once been. She stood with her head bowed, not wanting to meet his eyes. Hoping he'd go away if she didn't look at him. Knowing that he wouldn't. Uncertain of her duties and her allegiances.

McCadden felt no pity for her. Pity was a useless emotion. But he wasn't going to add to her discomfort.

He said, 'It was that Billy Power sexually assaulted your sister Tina, wasn't it?'

She looked at him then, her eyes widening. 'Yes.'

'I already knew that,' McCadden said. 'Your father told me when I met him earlier this morning.'

The eyes widened a bit more. 'My father?'

'You did tell him, didn't you?'

'Yes, but — '

'And you thought that he might've taken the law into his own hands and hustled up some quick revenge, or at least you were frightened I might think that. Not to worry. Your father has more sense. Who told you about Power's assault, by the way? Tina herself?'

'No.'

'Was it Wilkins?'

'Ian Wilkins? No.'

'Who was it, then?'

'It was one of my father's employees who saw what happened.'

'Ah! Right.'

'Hayes,' Catherine Hearne said. 'Eddie Hayes. The young chap on the FAS employment scheme out in the factory.'

McCadden nodded and lifted his coffee mug, but the coffee, untouched since he'd first tasted it, had lost its attraction for him.

thirteen

Three o'clock in the afternoon, and Tina Byrne might've been a different person to the version McCadden had been treated to earlier. Almost everything around her was the same as before. She was still in the house in Ballybeg Estate that the Young Salamanders used as headquarters. She was still in the front room of that house. McCadden and de Burgh, who'd come back together an hour before, were again her audience. But now she was severe. Now she was hard and unfriendly and efficiently secretarial. Now she made it clear she disliked and distrusted men, particularly flirtatious policemen. And the only addition to the earlier scene was that now Ian Wilkins was standing in the room as well.

De Burgh had spent three hours trying to trace Wilkins, finally tracking him down at a lecture in the Regional Technical College, only for Wilkins to give him the slip again by dodging through the crowded corridors as soon as de Burgh had introduced himself. Untypical, according to Wilkins' teachers. Uncharacteristic. Hard to believe of the lad. Apparently Wilkins was an excellent student, academically one of the brighter lights, a natural organizer, always present, never late for lectures . . .

McCadden had listened patiently to de Burgh's detailed account, although he had no interest in the information and considered most of it irrelevant. The thing about Wilkins was his fervour. His determination to declaim the truth. Above all, his conviction that he knew what the truth was. Didn't make him unique, of course. No more than his belief that most other people were mostly wrong made him unique. It was the fervour that made him unusual, the commitment to fists and baseball bats as instruments of persuasion.

All a bit of an irony, McCadden thought, with Tina Byrne reverting to form or deviating from form or slipping from one invention to another, right under Wilkins' nose. So much for truth. And absolutes. And knowing them. But then, irony was always lost on people who couldn't see more than one side at a time.

'You're going to ask me why I ran away from your sergeant,' Wilkins predicted, even before McCadden could greet him. 'It's quite simple. I wanted to see Tina before talking to either of you. I wanted to find out what you asked her and what she told you.'

His face set around the cuts and bruises after delivering that. The expression said, *What are you going to do about it?*

McCadden said, 'Hmm. Is that room upstairs free?'

An upstairs bedroom, visible through its open door from the bottom of the stairs, was obviously used as a meeting place. Five rows of hard chairs faced one comfortable armchair at the top of the room.

McCadden stood behind the chairman's seat with his hands on its back, not wanting to concede the dominant space to Wilkins, but not wanting to sit either. Wilkins sat in the front row opposite him. De Burgh stayed near the doorway.

'Did you know Billy Power?' McCadden asked.

'Yes, I did.'

'How come?'

'I made it my business to know him, Inspector.'

'Better explain that one for me.'

Wilkins sat stiffly in his chair, neither relaxed nor nervous, just alert and confident. 'Billy Power was guilty of sexually harassing Tina,' he said. 'I know — '

'Harassing?' McCadden interrupted.

'He suggested having sex with her, only in much cruder language than that.'

'Where did you hear this?'

'From Tina herself.'

79

'Right. You were saying?'

'I know Tina misled you by saying that she *didn't* tell me. The fact is that she did. She was simply frightened that you'd come to the wrong conclusions.'

'No doubt,' McCadden observed drily.

'Particularly,' Wilkins went on, 'as I had a fight with Billy Power on Monday night, the Monday before his death. I challenged him to apologize to Tina and — '

'Where was this?'

'I met him when he finished work. We fought on a piece of wasteground near the factory.'

'Anyone watching?'

'No, no one. In any case, I made a mistake. I shouldn't have gone alone. He was much stronger than me. As you can still see,' he added, using both hands to indicate the bruising and cuts around his eyes and mouth, 'I lost.'

'But you made your point,' McCadden suggested.

Wilkins snorted. 'The purpose of the exercise wasn't to make a point, Inspector. If I wanted to make a point, I would've sent him a letter. In any case, people like Billy Power never see anyone else's point. Even if they do, they can rarely understand it. The purpose of the exercise was to hurt him and warn him off. I failed.'

Monday night, anyway, McCadden thought.

'At least I failed to hurt him,' Wilkins corrected himself. 'I may have succeeded in warning him off, if only because he knew there were many more of us.'

McCadden asked, 'Would you mainly or exclusively see your role as defending Tina Byrne's honour; or would you consider yourself like a medieval knight, champion to *all* Christian women?'

Wilkins puckered his lips before he answered, but he gave no other indication of being annoyed. 'You're trying to be facetious, Inspector.'

'No, Mr Wilkins, I'm not, actually.'

'It doesn't matter,' Wilkins said dismissively. 'I'm quite used to it. What you probably cannot understand, Inspector, is that Tina is a very hurt young woman. Very traumatized. It can't

80

have escaped your attention that she's very beautiful. I mean, physically. What you won't have noticed, of course, is that she's also very modest.'

De Burgh shifted on his feet at the doorway.

Wilkins went on, starting to declaim now, the voice getting louder, 'The pressures our society puts on women, the way it treats them as objects, as sexual possessions, and Billy Power's obnoxious behaviour was an example of that . . . The point is, Inspector, we need to return to the values of the family, when women can be seen, not as playthings, not as objects of gratification, but as worthy of our veneration, the cornerstone . . .'

McCadden let the homily ramble on, entertaining himself with thoughts of Tom Byrne's family, where the women came out of it with such low self-esteem that they either hid behind solid husbands or else had no confidence in anything except their figure. The values of the family. Home. Also a euphemism for the grave, an asylum, an infirmary and a madhouse.

But finally McCadden grew tired of the sermon and tired of the entertainment and asked, 'How do you deal with all these issues, Mr Wilkins?'

'I beg your pardon?'

'Do you lobby for your point of view?'

'Yes, of course.'

'Street protests?'

'I think you know the answer to that already.'

'Violence? Well, I know the answer to that, too, don't I?'

'Just because in one specific case — '

'All right. Murder, then?'

'Inspector — '

'What's your attitude to the law, Mr Wilkins? Do you think the system is doing enough for you, or do you consider it part of the whole sinful corruption? Would you go outside it? Of course I mean further outside it than you've already gone. Would you kill?'

'You're obviously referring to Billy Power.'

'Obviously,' McCadden confirmed. 'What were you doing Thursday night while Tina Byrne was at her father's house?'

'I was here, working.'

'Anyone with you?'

'No. I was alone.'

'Anyone call? Anyone phone? Anyone see you here?'

'I have no alibi for Thursday night, Inspector.'

'A last question, Mr Wilkins. You said you shouldn't have gone alone to confront Billy Power. Is that what you revised for Thursday night? Is that what you did? Gather a few of the more muscular faithful around you, armed with their baseball bats, and head off to look for the infidel.'

'I didn't kill Billy Power, Inspector,' Wilkins said calmly. 'I would've liked to, God forgive me, but I didn't.'

fourteen

Eddie Hayes, the worker on the youth employment scheme taken on by Tom Byrne, lived with his parents in a small two-bedroom house in Poleberry Street in the south of the city. The houses on the road had no front gardens. You came off the footpath on to a single step and you were standing at the front door.

At six o'clock, after tailing Hayes in from Byrne Plastics, McCadden had used the door knocker and was studying its raised design – an escutcheon with the three gallies from the city arms and the Waterford motto *Urbs Intacta Manet* underneath – when a stout middle-aged woman opened up and found herself staring into his brown eyes. Hayes' mother. She brought him fussily to the front room – a cold, unused place that seemed to have been preserved in anticipation of such a visitor – and went off in search of her son.

Hayes himself came in a minute or so later. Reluctantly. His cheeks a little red, probably from the effort of trying to convince his mother that he hadn't done anything.

McCadden was standing by the hearth, his back to the unlit fireplace.

He said, 'I suppose you've been expecting me, have you?'

'I suppose I have,' Hayes conceded.

'Sit down, son.'

There were two lumpy old armchairs and a straight-backed mahogany dining-room chair in the room. None looked comfortable. Hayes went for the chair, sitting erect on it, but with his head lowered. His thick black hair, dropping untidily over his forehead, gave the impression of concealing his eyes even more than he intended.

'Why were you expecting me?' McCadden asked.

'What?'

'You said you were expecting me. Why?'

Hayes raised his head to look at him with haunted eyes. 'I . . . ah . . . I suppose because you must've heard I saw something, is it?'

'Is it?' McCadden enquired. 'What did you see?'

Hayes struggled. 'Well . . . it couldn't be anything else, I suppose, could it?'

'I don't know,' McCadden said. 'You tell me. Could it?'

'It must be Billy Power, then, is it?'

'Is it?' McCadden asked mercilessly. 'I don't know.'

'Well, like, I saw Billy Power attacking Tina Byrne, didn't I. I told Tina's sister about it. Catherine. Catherine Hearne she is now. She must've told you. That's all I saw. So it must be that.'

There was a silence. Hayes, his head hanging, waited nervously. He seemed used to expecting blame, whether he'd done anything or not.

'When did it happen?' McCadden asked then. 'This attack.'

'Last Thursday week, it was.'

'Eleven days ago. Where?'

'In the factory. After work.'

'Right,' McCadden nodded. 'Go on.'

Hayes spoke more easily now, his head rising and his eyes meeting McCadden's every so often to emphasize a point: 'Work was finished. I was down on the factory floor, tidying up. There wasn't anybody else there. The foreman, Richie Morrissey, he was up with the owner, Tom Byrne, up in the office. The daughter was there as well, Tina, visiting her father. Anyway, about ten past five Billy Power comes back suddenly for something, just after Tina Byrne is after coming down the stairs on her way out. Power, he's standing there blocking the door, so she can't get out. I could hear him asking her for a kiss, you know, then she could pass. When I looked up from behind the machine he was after grabbing her round

84

the waist and turning her round, so he was pressing himself into her, with his hand down the front of her trousers.'

Hayes stopped and shrugged.

'How long did the struggle go on for?' McCadden asked.

'It wasn't very long. Only a couple of seconds. He let her go then. Laughing, like. She wasn't, though. She was crying. Power went up the stairs to the office and she ran out the door.'

'Did either of them see you?'

'Power didn't, anyway. I don't think she did, either.'

'Why did you tell Catherine Hearne?'

'I knew she was Tina's sister. I seen the two of them together when they came visiting Byrne.'

'Catherine Hearne visits her father? At the factory?'

'That's right, yeah.'

'How often?'

'I'd say, maybe once every two weeks. Like that.'

'Tell me. Why didn't you tell Tom Byrne what you saw?'

Hayes shook his head, a smile playing on his lips now. 'Ah, well, you'd have to know the story out there, you know. You'd have to know the form.'

'Tell me.'

'I'm only there meself six months now, that's all. Other fellas would know a lot more than me.'

'You look bright enough,' McCadden said, the irony being wasted on its victim again. 'I'm sure you could pick up more in six months than others could in six years.' Then, more sharply, he said, 'Let's hear it.'

'Well,' Hayes said, 'Power, you see, Billy Power, he was the golden boy out there. Power was the white-haired boy. Even though there was a foreman for the rest of us, Power could do whatever he liked. Most of the time he did, too. Very pally with Byrne, you know. Up for chats every chance he got. So the way it was, you wouldn't know whether you'd be doing yourself any favours telling the boss man anything about Power. And if Byrne passed it back, Power'd be after you then, wouldn't he? You were better staying out of it.'

'But you didn't stay out of it.'

'Hah?'

'Why didn't you just forget about the incident? Why tell anyone?'

'I kind of like Tina Byrne, you know.'

'Hmm. Right.'

Thinking hard, McCadden held his open palms behind him and towards the imaginary warmth of an imaginary fire. He asked, 'Did Tom Byrne talk to Power after the attack you described?'

Hayes thought. 'No, not that I know of, anyway. Not until Thursday, anyway.'

'Last Thursday?'

'That's right, yeah.'

'In the office?'

'That's right. I thought Byrne called him up to give him his cards, after hearing the story. Maybe he did, and all. Maybe he tried to. But I'll tell you something, Power came out of that office laughing his head off and went back to his machine the same as if he'd got a pay rise.'

'Hmm,' McCadden said.

fifteen

Liam de Burgh, Jerry Tobin, Andy Laffan and John Widger were all sitting around McCadden's desk in the inspectors' office. No one was talking very much. It was seven-forty in the evening and they were too tired, too wary of adding another five minutes to the day with idle chatter. Most of them should've been elsewhere already. Tobin was married and had a five-year-old who would still be awake and arguing and a two-year-old who'd hopefully be asleep by the time he got home. Laffan and Widger had girlfriends. For the moment, anyway.

Behind the desk, McCadden was studying some papers, among them a list of the clothes Billy Power was wearing the night he'd disappeared. Jeans, denim jacket, an Ireland soccer T-shirt, Adidas sports shoes. All mass produced. The combinations so popular they might've been parts of a uniform. Put out a description with that lot and you'd have a few hundred reported sightings for the Thursday night.

McCadden sighed and put the papers away. He picked up a note the duty sergeant had left on his desk. Paul Hyland's wife, Tracy, had been looking for him earlier. He'd ring her later, see what it was about. If he had time. If he remembered. If he still felt like talking to someone.

He rubbed his eyes and said, 'We'll keep this short. Jerry?'

'Uh-huh?'

'You kick off.'

'Right,' Tobin said. 'Well, we did a house-to-house in John's Park around the area Power lived and I suppose we

87

struck fairly lucky. We got one helpful statement. Mrs Marsh, who lives across the road from Martin O'Shea, same side as Henry Barry, was out weeding her garden Thursday night. It had to be Thursday, because she was expecting her sister from Dublin. The sister didn't make it until ten. It had to be after eight o'clock, because she'd just finished watching a soap on television. It could've been a quarter past eight, half-eight, a quarter to nine. She's not so sure about that. It had to be before nine, though. At nine she went back in to watch the main evening news on RTE1 and didn't go back out again. Anyway, she was coming out her door with her gardening fork — '

'Quarter past eight,' McCadden interrupted.

'What?'

'It had to be quarter past eight,' McCadden said. 'Or earlier. She was coming from the house. Ten minutes at most to get organized and get the gear together after watching the TV programme.'

'Well, she moved between the house and the garden a lot.'

'With a fork?' McCadden asked. 'No. You want to go back to the house, you leave the fork leaning against something in the garden. You don't carry it with you. What did she see?'

'She saw O'Shea's car driving away,' Tobin said. 'O'Shea himself was driving. Barry was in the front passenger seat. She didn't notice if anyone was in the back.'

'Let's say Power *was* in the back,' McCadden said. 'Quarter past eight. Five minutes at the outside to drive to Shefflin's pub. That's forty minutes more before they actually show in the pub. If he *wasn't* in the back, they're still lying. No one corroborating the green fingers, I suppose?'

'No.'

'All very iffy, really. Anything else?'

'No, that's it. Otherwise not a sausage.'

'Right,' McCadden said. 'John?'

Widger assembled his notes.

Widger had been assembling his notes for ten minutes. Noisily. And with impatience.

He said, talking quickly, 'I've got something interesting.

The container of peat moss was loaded in Kilkenny on Thursday afternoon. Fine. But wait. It didn't leave Kilkenny to travel the thirty miles down here by road on a truck *until seven o'clock on Friday morning.*'

A chorus from the others: 'What?'

'It was unloaded in Waterford about nine o'clock Friday morning,' Widger continued. 'Unloaded intact. The locks all secure. It was due to leave for France on Saturday morning, but the stoppage on the docks around lunchtime on Friday escalated into an official dispute in the afternoon. No one could move it. The thing is, as you can see, the container wasn't on the docks on Thursday night.'

'The time of death,' de Burgh said, 'was between seven and midnight Thursday. Officially. Off the record, Carroll put it personally at eight, eight-thirty.'

McCadden said, 'Killed on Thursday. Hidden on Friday.'

'Solomon Grundy,' Andy Laffan muttered.

McCadden looked at him wearily.

'If Carroll's guess is right,' de Burgh said, 'eight, eight-thirty, then Power never walked back with O'Shea and Barry and Jerry's witness . . .'

'Mrs Marsh,' Tobin said.

'What Mrs Marsh saw fits that, too.'

'No, wait,' McCadden put in. 'Don't get carried away on Carroll's opinion. Don't firm it up into fact. It's another possibility, that's all. We've got two major questions. Why wait until Friday, obviously Friday night, to move the body, when the same conditions existed the previous night? That's one. Secondly . . .' He lowered his head and rubbed his closed eyes again, muttering, 'What the hell was the second one?'

'Tom Byrne?' de Burgh suggested.

'Byrne!' McCadden exclaimed. 'Yeah. We know that Byrne was aware of Power's attack on his daughter. Now, whether Byrne did or didn't do anything about that attack, it still leaves us with a problem. If he did, what did he do? Did he kill him? If he didn't do anything, why did he hold off on something as serious as that? What frightened him off?'

'It seems to me from everything that's been said,' Tobin offered, 'that Byrne went out of his way to arrange an alibi with the dinner while he set up Billy Power to be killed.'

'Killed by who?' McCadden asked.

'Well, O'Shea and Barry, I suppose.'

'I can't see it,' de Burgh objected. 'I can see the Byrne alibi – the whole family dinner thing, it's a bit too convenient – but I can't see O'Shea and Barry killing what was really their best mate, when it comes down to it.'

'Unless there was an added ingredient,' McCadden suggested. 'Something personal. The assault on O'Shea's wife, maybe. It would hardly drag Barry in to that level of commitment, though. Doesn't Barry have a teenage daughter as well? A sequence of assaults might bring them together. Either that or money.'

De Burgh, like a machine with a programmed response, said instantly, 'We still haven't asked them where they're getting all that extra cash.'

McCadden sat upright in the chair and said, 'OK. This is what we do tomorrow. We'll put some pressure on O'Shea and Barry. Obviously they're making something up. Obviously they've agreed on what they're making up. So we'll worry them. We'll worry them together and we'll worry them separately.

'Jerry, you question O'Shea's wife. First, O'Shea's movements. Second, how they can afford the luxuries. Everything you can bring in. Go in with the attitude that you know O'Shea has been lying, even that you know what he's lying about. But without saying anything definite. And get there early. Wait until O'Shea is leaving for work, then go past him and make sure he sees you, make sure he knows what you're up to. So he spends the whole day worrying in work.

'Andy, team up with Jerry later on and pull in O'Shea as he's leaving work. Five o'clock. Leave him to stew here for a few hours. We'll leave Barry to stew, too. All day. All night. We won't go near him.

'Right, that's that.

'Now, we've got a list of customers the barman in Shefflin's is certain were in last Thursday night. John, you look after that.

'Also, we've got to switch the time period on anything suspicious going on in and around the docks from Thursday night to all day Friday. Friday, possibly Friday evening, probably Friday night, someone opened up the container and tossed the body in. Andy, you take that. And Jerry, too, once you've finished with O'Shea's wife. The two of you spend the rest of the day on the docks. And don't forget you need to be out at Byrne Plastics for five or a little before.

'I'll have another go at Byrne myself. Myself and Liam. We'll face him with the evidence. See how his media consultants have taught him to handle being caught with his lies in the open. Any questions? Any points to raise?'

There were no questions, no points.

They said good night to each other and got up. But afterwards they left the room silently. There was nothing to get excited about, nothing to discuss, nothing to argue over.

The feeling was that the case was going nowhere.

McCadden sat on at his desk for a while, not able to add anything to the investigation, not able to leave it at that either. Feeling tired and helpless.

He couldn't believe Tom Byrne had hired hands to protect his daughter's honour. He couldn't believe O'Shea and Barry had turned to knifing, either as agents of someone else or for obscure reasons of their own. And he couldn't believe in Wilkins at all.

But still, he knew too that all four of them were lying to him.

Only he didn't know how or where, about what or how much.

He stood up to tidy the papers on his desk and found the note from Tracy Hyland still among them, so he sat again and punched out the Hylands' home number on his phone station. Tracy herself answered. Instantly. As if she was sitting by the phone. She sounded odd. Timid. Or anxious. Or ill.

'Hello?'

'Tracy? Carl McCadden. Were you looking for me earlier?'

91

'Ah . . . no, Carl. No, I wasn't.'

'Must've got the wrong message. Was it Paul?'

'Carl . . .'

'Yeah?'

There was a silence. A silence so strained, so *loaded*, that McCadden was reminded of another silence between the two of them, almost four years ago now, when they'd sat on the edge of the bed in the loft of his flat and wondered what to do and what the hell to say next.

But Tracy Hyland said now, 'Paul . . . Paul didn't leave any message, no.'

'Is he there now?'

'No. No, not at the moment, Carl.'

There was another strained silence then, all of six seconds, until McCadden said, 'Tell him to give me a ring when he gets a chance, Tracy, will you?'

'Good night, Carl.'

And the line went suddenly dead.

That was eight-fourteen. McCadden didn't have much time to dwell on it all. A minute later, quarter past eight, Frank Ryan, another detective sergeant, bustled into the room in much the same disgruntled humour as McCadden.

Ryan was a big, broad man who always had a crumpled look to him. People said he slept in his grey suits and grey soft hats – they were that creased, that battered, you were inclined to believe it. He smoked continuously, the nicotine heavily staining his fingers, the ash gathering in the creases of his clothes, the butts stuck to the soles of his shoes. Whenever he took the stand to give evidence in court, his appearance always sent the judge's nose a bit higher in the air.

'Hi, Carl!' Ryan called. 'How's it going?'

McCadden shrugged, not inviting discussion.

Ryan was working with Harry Boyce now, trying to catch up with the Waterford man, Peter Clarke, who'd escaped from prison the previous Tuesday. And McCadden didn't want to get involved in opening old wounds made by that case.

No. The wounds were still open. He just wanted to avoid infecting them again.

You could trace what troubles McCadden had with his job back to the day in March 1990, three and a half years ago now, when Peter Clarke had killed his own lover, Theresa Cheasty, slicing her cheeks and then her throat with a blade of a cut-throat razor. Even though McCadden himself had been on holiday at the time. The start of his troubles with the new Superintendent, Daniel Cody. Because it was the start of his troubles with Cody's protégé, Harry Boyce.

That spring, the Peter Clarke case had fallen to Harry Boyce. Boyce had put Clarke away for a life sentence and he'd been highly commended for it by the chief superintendent. But Boyce had never discovered the reason for the murder.

When McCadden came back from holiday, the station was alive with black jokes about the Baby Killer. Peter Clarke had claimed in his own defence that the woman he'd killed was timid and clinging, that she was too weak to survive by herself, and that she cried all the time. And McCadden, unable to resist, foolishly threw his hat in the ring.

'Yeah, well,' he said once, in front of others, after a long dispute with Boyce, 'someday you'll find out what the motive was, Harry. Too late.'

Harry Boyce had him disciplined for the interference.

'Jesus!' McCadden exclaimed. 'It was an opinion, Harry. Meant to be helpful.'

'I won't be laughed at, McCadden.'

'So what was he doing with a cut-throat razor, then?'

'Shaving himself, McCadden. Shaving himself.'

'Every day?'

'Every day.'

'So what was different about this particular day that he cut her instead of himself?'

'Wait for the trial, McCadden.'

Three and a half years now and that little thing between McCadden and Boyce, that quiet jostling for dominance in the station, that difference in the angles they looked at the world, they were all more prominent than ever.

No, McCadden didn't want to get involved in the Peter Clarke hunt. Not with problems of his own piling up.

But Frank Ryan didn't need an invitation, didn't recognize reluctance.

He ambled across to McCadden's desk and sat ponderously and complained, 'It's shit, Carl! You know that? Pure shit! We don't even know if Clarke is in Waterford or not. We go out in the mornings and follow our arses. No leads. No sightings. No clues. No ideas. I hate wasting time. I know the pressure is coming straight down from Cody, I know Cody is under pressure himself, people worrying about Clarke coming back swinging a razor, but Jesus, Carl, Harry Boyce is just as bad as Cody himself on this one.'

Given the opening, McCadden quickly changed the line of the conversation. 'Well, Frank,' he said, 'you'll always find that the character who's looking for the boss's job eventually gets round to behaving like the boss. That's why our democracy will never work, you know. The qualities you need to grab a position of authority – selfishness, the ability to ape and please, no originality – are exactly the opposite of the qualities you need to lead properly.'

'You know what your problem is?' Ryan said. 'You're too full of shit to be a sergeant.'

McCadden got up, smiling. 'No,' he said. 'My problem is that I'm too intelligent to be a superintendent. I'll see you.'

'Good luck.'

McCadden was in the doorway when he turned. 'You seen Paul Hyland around, Frank?'

'He's out sick,' Ryan said. 'On sick leave.'

'He call in himself? Or did his wife do it?'

'Jesus, I don't know. What does it matter?'

'Depends.'

'Probably himself. You know the story with Paul. Sick leave means he doesn't have to go into work or go home for two or three days.'

'Yeah. See you.'

'Good luck.'

sixteen

Ten o'clock on Tuesday morning, McCadden took the note from the desk sergeant and walked briskly to the station car park, took out the Ford Sierra and hit the siren once he was on the road. The first real break in the case and he wanted to get there quickly.

He kept the foot hard on the accelerator most of the way, along much the same route as he'd travelled with de Burgh the day before, thinking about what he might find when he got there. Maybe a kid who'd picked it up from where it had fallen after Billy Power had struggled and died. Maybe a barman from a pub. A cinema usher. Maybe even the character whose knife had snuffed out Billy Power.

The house was supposed to be at the back of Ballybeg Estate, furthest away from the main suburban road and facing the uncultivated fields at the beginning of the country-side.

McCadden slowed and killed the siren when he reached the turn into Ballybeg. With the schools out on mid-term break, there were too many wild kids who ran without looking. And too many jittery teenagers.

He dropped down to second gear and crawled and started checking through the side windows for street names, finding nothing he needed at first. Then, passing an opening, he found something he hadn't expected at all. At the end of a long road, maybe five hundred yards away, there was a crowd and there was an ambulance with its flashing blue lights and there were some squad cars with their own flashing blue lights. A

Hallowe'en crowd? A bonfire out of control? Hardly. It was eight hours too early for that.

McCadden reversed and turned down the street and found that he was following the desk sergeant's directions after all. He rolled to the back of the crowd and braked gently. No one turned to look at him. No one moved to let him pass.

Some of the crowd were kids and teenagers who'd obviously drifted down from stacking the local bonfire when word had passed round. Some were adults, men and women, who were probably just curious. But they seemed to be curious in a tense, resentful sort of way. And they were quiet. Very quiet.

The ambulance got its siren going and pulled away from where it was parked. The crowd parted reluctantly. McCadden let the ambulance pass and then squeezed through the gap that was still there.

The address the desk sergeant had given him was the last house in a sequence of three vacant houses on the corner of the estate. The whole section was derelict. The gardens and hedges and grass margins were wildly overgrown. Weeds were sprouting through the concrete on the footpaths. The street-lamps were damaged. The area was littered with empty cider bottles, crushed lager cans and broken glass. There was graffiti spray-painted on to every surface.

The doors and windows of the vacant houses had been sealed, not with the concrete blocks that were sometimes used, but with removable steel plates. On the last house, the plate had been taken away from the door.

And in that open doorway, behind a line of uniformed guards and beside a young detective with a barely concealed Uzi sub-machine-gun, stood Detective Sergeant Frank Ryan, his overcoat unevenly buttoned and his hat sloping off the back of his head.

Seeing him, McCadden should've twigged. But he didn't.

He got out of the car and walked towards the house, thinking of something else. Thinking of the low, disgruntled murmur that came suddenly from the crowd behind him.

Ryan greeted him with a wave and a laugh. He said, 'More of the shit, Carl, hah?'

McCadden smiled and passed him, but the way you smile and pass someone who's just made a comment you're supposed to understand and don't, don't have a clue what they're talking about. Better to smile. A smile has a better chance of conveying intelligence.

Someone had run a cable from the battery of a patrol car to bring a lighted bulb into the dark interior of the house. McCadden followed the cable; then, once he was inside, the light itself. He ended up at the back of the house, in what must've been the kitchen once. Except for an isolated press that was hanging from the wall by a couple of screws still clinging to the loosened Rawlplugs, there was nothing left of the kitchen's fittings.

A young guard holding the lighted bulb was standing in the centre of the room on the bare concrete floor. And beside him, squat and scowling, stood Detective Inspector Harry Boyce.

And McCadden still didn't understand.

Boyce was a dour man happily married to a woman with a piercing laugh. That seemed the only thing he was content with, though. Otherwise he was glum. Only six years older than McCadden, at forty-one he already looked in late middle-age. He was bald and wore a heavy, gloomy moustache.

McCadden walked across the room and saw then, behind the others, that the back windows of the house had been forced.

He said to Boyce, 'Someone said you found the Master McGrath keyring.'

Without a word, with a melancholy expression, Boyce reached into a pocket and took out a small, self-sealing plastic bag and handed it over.

The silver model of the greyhound Master McGrath, which was all that was left of Billy Power's keyring, was inside the bag. The ring itself and the keys were no longer attached. The loop that had once held them was split and broken, probably from being stepped on. WP was engraved on the reverse of the dog's left forepaw. William Power. William. That slight formality courting couples like to maintain, at a time when you're certain that life is not going to reduce you to being a mere Billy. MM was engraved on the reverse of the right hindpaw. Mary McGrath. Her maiden name.

MM. Master McGrath. Mary McGrath.

The dreams of a young working-class woman, must be seventeen, eighteen years ago now. She'd be the greatest love of his life. Not the only love, nothing could be that, but the greatest. But Power's love for the dead dog had stayed on better than his love for the woman.

'Ryan found it,' Boyce grunted suddenly.

Boyce moved to leave, the young guard with the light moved to follow him, and McCadden, left in the darkness, was forced to go with them. He caught up and passed the guard, intending to ask Boyce something else, but then, suddenly, in the hallway of the house, just before they reached the doorway of the front room, he flung his arms sideways to stop the other two advancing. Boyce sighed and went to remove the barrier. But McCadden stepped in front of him and crouched. And after a moment the guard with the light crouched as well, bringing it down to illuminate the concrete floor. A dull, red stain was visible in the rough concrete by McCadden's feet, under his pointing finger. Blood. Obviously blood. Dried for a few days or more. The stain was circular, but smeared on one side a little, towards the doorway of the front room.

McCadden followed the direction of the smear, over the threshold, into the room, gesturing for the light as he went. On the bare ground inside, over to the left of the doorway and almost under the boarded window, the concrete had been scrubbed clean and then partially dirtied again with rubbish and dust from the rest of the room.

'That's where Ryan found the keyring,' Boyce said from the doorway. 'By the window.'

And suddenly, McCadden understood that this was where Billy Power had been killed.

This house, *this* was where Power was killed.

'Did you take the plate from the front door?' he asked Boyce. 'Or someone else?'

'We took it,' Boyce said. 'But access was possible before that.'

Yes. Yes. Billy Power, coming in the front door that Thursday night. Someone waiting for him in the pitch-black hallway. He'd walked right into the lunging knife, impaling his heart on the blade. And even then he'd struggled, although the skinned knuckles were probably from the wall or the floor. Afterwards the corpse had been dragged, just a little, and then lifted into the front room.

Whoever moved Billy Power from this house to the cargo container, had cleaned-up where Power had bled under the window in the front room.

But whoever moved him hadn't killed him, hadn't even talked to his killer. Because they didn't know where he'd died. They didn't know about the bloodstain in the hallway. They'd walked right over it. Twice. Once on the way in to collect the corpse, and again on the way out carrying a black plastic refuse sack.

But what time on Thursday night had Power been killed? After nine o'clock, when O'Shea and Barry were already in Shefflin's pub? Or before? And who'd moved the body? And why? And why on Friday?

McCadden stood up and turned into the light to ask Harry Boyce a question. He shielded his eyes, but still couldn't see Boyce.

'Who was in here?' he asked. 'Who were you after in here?'

The silence lasted a long time. So long that McCadden thought Boyce had already left. When he stepped past the light though, Boyce was still there, standing in the doorway, staring at him with mournful, defensive eyes.

And then McCadden twigged.

Then McCadden understood.

Harry Boyce, the senior inspector at the station, had made all the right moves so far in his drive for promotion. All except one. Three and a half years ago. Putting away a murderer without understanding the motive. A murderer who'd sprung himself and come back home to Waterford.

'Peter Clarke,' McCadden said quietly. 'It was Peter Clarke, wasn't it?'

Frank Ryan and the young detective with the sub-machine-gun had come in from the street to stand in the hallway just inside the front door.

Ryan said, 'We found his prison clothes in the back garden under some blackberry bushes.'

'I'll tell you what he's wearing now,' McCadden said impetuously.

'Five seconds ago you didn't even know who was here. Now you can tell us what he was wearing,' Boyce said sarcastically.

In the tense silence, Ryan looked from one inspector to the other, waiting for the next play.

McCadden made it. 'Denim jeans. Light blue, less than a month old. An Opel Ireland T-shirt. Denim jacket. Adidas runners.'

Boyce laughed. A short, unpleasant laugh.

McCadden said, 'Peter Clarke killed or helped to kill Billy Power here. He put on Power's clothes and hid his own. That's what Billy Power was wearing the night he died.'

'You've got a couple of bloodstains,' Boyce said, counting off on his fingers. 'You've got part of a keyring. You've got a set of prison clothes. If I was you, I'd learn to wait for more evidence before jumping to obvious conclusions. Otherwise it can be embarrassing.'

He swivelled and left, careful not to step on or near the bloodstain in the hallway. Once he was outside he called back impatiently, 'Sergeant!'

Frank Ryan turned to McCadden. 'What business would Peter Clarke have with Billy Power in a place like this?'

He put the question, but he didn't wait around afterwards. It was obvious McCadden didn't have the answer.

seventeen

One of the drawbacks of being a detective, McCadden decided about eight o'clock that evening, was that you had to put in quality time with characters you didn't like and not be there for the ones you enjoyed.

By then, McCadden had punched in five and a half hours between Henry Barry and Martin O'Shea, ever since he'd had them picked up from Byrne Plastics that afternoon. All in all, he would've traded a week in a holiday resort with O'Shea for a couple of hours standing in the rain with Barry.

Barry just sat there in front of you. The man was a little dull. A little slow. Not quite sharp enough to keep to the pitch of the questions and not even in the game when it came to judging strategy. But he was comfortable. He knew he could depend on his wife back home. She'd see him through. If you told him you'd grilled her for hours and she'd finally cracked and sold him down the river, he simply wouldn't believe you. The wife and himself were partners.

So McCadden changed the angle of attack.

'You don't really want to let her down, do you, Henry?' he said softly.

Barry frowned and crossed his arms over his fat chest. He said seriously, 'I wouldn't, sure.'

'You know we're going to have to charge you with obstruction, don't you?'

'I don't see why.'

'Because you misled us. You told us lies.'

'What lies?'

'About Billy Power. Last Thursday night.'

'Somebody else's been telling you the lies, Inspector, not me.'

'And it might be a lot worse than just obstruction. What's your wife going to say when we put you away for a few years?'

'I suppose she'll say what she always says,' Barry muttered, without a trace of irony. 'Am I ever going to knock any sense into that head of yours?'

McCadden sighed.

The wife was Barry's strong flank. His weak flank was Martin O'Shea. But then, Barry knew that it was weak. He accepted that it was weak.

McCadden went out for a coffee at one stage and when he came back he said, 'A bit of trouble, I'm afraid, Henry.'

Barry hadn't moved in the meantime. He didn't seem to know what restlessness was. He turned his head now to look easily at McCadden again.

'You don't say.'

'O'Shea has started telling the truth,' McCadden said. 'He's changed his story, Henry.'

'Is that so?'

'He's blaming you now. All of it on you, Henry.'

'Go on.'

The trouble was, McCadden liked Henry Barry. The man had figured out the two or three most important things in his life and he was happy holding on to them. Which was more than McCadden himself had managed. Barry was good company. So McCadden left him to Jerry Tobin after half an hour and went to concentrate on Martin O'Shea instead.

O'Shea, who'd seen detectives visiting his house that morning, had, as McCadden had predicted, sweated out the day wondering what his wife had said to the police. And now he'd sweated another half an hour wondering what Barry was saying.

O'Shea sweated because O'Shea distrusted everyone. He distrusted their loyalty. He distrusted their nerve. He distrusted their intelligence. No one else was quite as bright, no one was quite as steady, no one was quite as comfortably on the inside track as Martin O'Shea. What problems he had, someone else was always to blame for them. His neurotic wife. His dim friends. His unavoidable family. He was one of those characters who constantly reached for the phrase, *If you want something done, do it yourself.* He was also one of those characters who never seemed to take his own advice.

Coming up from the waiting room with a uniformed guard, O'Shea looked physically unwell. Underneath the greying black hair his scalp was dry and flaky from days of tension. The veins stood blue and prominent on his flushed face. His hands were restless, shaking slightly whenever he wasn't clenching and unclenching them.

The first thing he said to McCadden was, 'Could I have a smoke?'

McCadden replied, 'Later. When we're finished. This is a No Smoking area.'

In the small interview room, McCadden sat opposite O'Shea, with a desk between them. Liam de Burgh hovered.

Without saying anything else, McCadden started reading the sheet of paper de Burgh had just handed to him. Sometimes he went back to de Burgh to clarify a point. Sometimes he mumbled to himself. Sometimes he shared a silent look with de Burgh.

It was all a sham. The piece of paper was an internal bulletin about overtime from Chief Superintendent Cody.

But the sham was wearing O'Shea down a little more. The man didn't like being confined to a seat. He liked to express himself in sharp, nervy movements. Dramatic things, like slamming a door at work or toppling a chair in his kitchen. Things that made plenty of noise, that showed what he thought of you, that demonstrated his strength and his recklessness. All he could manage here was crossing and uncrossing his legs, folding and unfolding his arms, clasping and unclasping his hands. The sort of things that went unnoticed by an audience.

Finally, McCadden put away the sheet of paper, face down, and looked hard at O'Shea until O'Shea's eyes came furtively up to meet his and darted away again. McCadden was frowning.

He said, 'Mr O'Shea, a few, ah, discrepancies have cropped up in your statement that we need to iron out.'

O'Shea licked his lips and cleared his throat. 'Discrepancies?' he repeated.

'That's right.'

'How do you mean?' O'Shea asked. 'How do you mean, discrepancies? What sort of discrepancies?'

'Well, we'll go into the details later,' McCadden said casually. 'Right now, maybe you could describe for us again exactly what happened last Friday.'

'Friday?' O'Shea repeated. He swallowed again. 'You mean Thursday.'

McCadden addressed de Burgh by raising a finger. 'Wasn't it Friday Henry Barry said, Liam?'

But he didn't turn away from watching O'Shea. O'Shea's mouth hung open and his eyes were narrowed. There was nothing but bewilderment on his face.

De Burgh said, 'Friday, that's right. That's what Barry said.'

'Look,' O'Shea said. 'I don't know nothing about Friday. I don't know what Henry was talking about. It was Thursday we called Billy Power, and to tell you nothing but the truth I'm sick, sore and sorry going over that.'

'Why *did* you call Billy Power, now that you mention it?' McCadden asked.

O'Shea rubbed his nose with the back of his hand, looking warily over the fingers. 'What?'

'You called Barry,' McCadden said. 'Is that right?'

O'Shea nodded cautiously. 'Yeah.'

'And then you both called Power.'

'That's right, yeah.'

'So, it must've been your idea, since you started the ball rolling. What had you in mind?'

O'Shea smiled then, with relief, taking the hand away from his face to show it. 'Sure, Billy himself asked me to call over.'

'Any reason?'

104

'You don't need a reason for calling on a friend, do you?'

'Not a *friend*, no,' McCadden emphasized. 'You don't need a reason for calling on a friend. What *did* you do on Friday, by the way?'

O'Shea laughed nervously. 'Friday?' He shifted in the seat, untangling his legs, and said again, 'How do you mean, Friday?'

'As a matter of interest,' McCadden said. 'All day Friday.'

O'Shea frowned and had to search his memory for the answer. Never had to search like that for Thursday night's details. They'd come rolling off his tongue like a tape recording of Henry Barry's account being played back.

'Friday,' O'Shea said again, without the question this time. 'Friday I left for work at the usual time in the morning. I got in at the usual time. I had lunch out there. I left at the usual time. I had the dinner. I watched the telly. And then I went into Shefflin's for about nine o'clock again. I stayed there until closing time. What about it?'

'You tell me,' McCadden invited.

'I can't tell you what I don't know, can I?'

'No,' McCadden said, 'I suppose not. Let's get back to Thursday night, then.'

O'Shea obviously reckoned he'd gained some ground. He sat back in the chair and asked cockily, 'Are you sure, now?'

'Thursday night,' McCadden repeated, 'you and Henry Barry called Billy Power at seven o'clock.'

'That's right.'

'You walked out the road with him.'

'That's right.'

'But you came back without him.'

This time, McCadden didn't have to look to know that his guess was accurate. O'Shea's silence told him the truth. Henry Barry would've asked where he'd heard that sort of nonsense. But O'Shea was asking himself the questions. Who'd ratted? Who'd double-crossed him? Who'd grassed? Had his wife seen him coming back to John's Park to get the car and had the bitch squealed to the police? Had Henry Barry cracked and had the shaking bastard spilled everything?

105

Just then, O'Shea's world was populated with nothing but traitors. Counting them off, stacking the allegations against them and sifting through the evidence, they all left him no time to answer McCadden's question. And it was his own silence, not anyone else, that exposed him.

When he'd got through the renegades and come up with a possible culprit, he finally started to say something. McCadden cut him off.

'Listen,' McCadden said sharply. 'Listen very carefully. You can answer to a murder charge, you can answer to accessory or you can answer to obstruction for trying to lead me up the garden path. It's up to you which one. But don't get yourself stuck in the wrong groove. I know you walked two miles out the road with Billy Power and then came back without him. Two miles. No more. No less.'

O'Shea made fists of his hands and drummed them rapidly on the table. He breathed hard, his mouth contorted with anger. His fierce eyes said it was Barry, it had to be Henry Barry who'd broken. Only two others knew the distance the three of them had travelled that night, and one of those was dead.

It wasn't Barry, though. Only McCadden himself, a little simple calculation, and a guess. O'Shea and Barry had been back in John's Park by eight-fifteen that Thursday night, when Mrs Marsh had seen them from her garden. McCadden was certain of the time now. So, half an hour out, half an hour back. Walking pace advanced you a mile or so every fifteen minutes.

McCadden said, 'What I want you to do now, and you only get this chance to do it properly, I want you to confirm exactly what happened last Thursday night before you turned back without Billy Power.'

Confirm?

De Burgh glanced at him, making a dubious face.

McCadden winked, happy with the word. A nice word, confirm.

It wasn't needed, though. And neither was the threat. Because O'Shea was already gone. There'd never been a great

106

deal to him anyway, mostly bluster, mostly shapes and noise, but it was all gone now. He sat back from the desk with his head hanging and his hands dangling limply between his parted knees. When he finally looked up again, his dead eyes and his wry grimace excused himself.

They said, *Well, since you already know it anyway, I suppose . . .*

He said, quietly, slowly, 'We went out a bit the back road to Tramore where we met Mossy Fennelly, all right, but then we cut down to the main Tramore Road and from there across the fields and into the back of Ballybeg Estate. That's where Billy told us we were going to meet this Peter Clarke chap got out of Mountjoy jail a Tuesday and he wanted us along to back him up, like.'

'Back him up? He was expecting a fight?'

'He must've done, yeah. That's the impression I got, anyway.'

'Did you know Peter Clarke before this?'

'Only what I read in the papers about him killing that girl he was living with, Theresa Cheasty, and him getting out of jail last week.'

'Did Billy Power know Clarke?'

'I wouldn't swear on it now, but I don't think so, no.'

'Did he ever talk about him before? Ever mention him before?'

'He didn't, no, not that I remember.'

McCadden nodded. 'Go on with what you were saying. You'd reached the back of Ballybeg Estate.'

O'Shea said, 'Henry Barry wouldn't go along at all, for love or money and, to tell you nothing but the God's honest truth, I was a bit doubtful about it myself. Anyway, we argued it over for a while out there, just at the back of the estate, and it ended up with me and Barry going back without Billy. That's the last we ever saw of him. We walked back to John's Park to get the car. But then we felt kind of bad about leaving Billy by himself, so we drove back down to Ballybeg, out the main road now, because you can't drive into it from the back, thinking we'd meet up with Billy there again. When we didn't see him, we headed in for Shefflin's, thinking we'd meet up with him there. We got to the pub about nine, all right.'

'Had you arranged to meet Power in the pub?' McCadden asked.

'No, we hadn't, no.'

'So,' McCadden said. 'When was the first time you started thinking something had gone seriously wrong?'

'Well, in the morning, the next morning, Friday morning, like, when Billy didn't show for work, you know.'

'So,' McCadden said again. 'What did you do? Did you ring Power's home? Did you drive back there at lunchtime? Did you check with the office to see if Power had called in sick? Did you go back out to Ballybeg to look for him? What did you do?'

O'Shea shook his head, hiding his eyes again. 'No.'

'You didn't do anything?'

'No.'

'Why not?'

Obviously O'Shea hadn't really thought about that one. He couldn't think much about it now, either.

He said, 'I don't know. I don't know.'

McCadden shrugged and said, 'This story of yours, about leaving Power outside the pub at nine. Who concocted that?'

'No one concocted it.'

'Who told you to spin it?'

'No one. No one told us anything.'

'Us?' McCadden repeated. 'What that says, it says someone told you and Henry Barry at the same time. Who? Where?'

'I didn't mean it like that.'

'Last chance. Who's idea was it? And why?'

O'Shea blurted suddenly, 'It was all Billy Power's own idea, that's what it was.'

'Power's?' McCadden repeated sceptically.

O'Shea said, 'Just when we were going to leave him before he went to see Clarke in Ballybeg, he turns and says to us, he says, if anyone asks you anything about tonight, no matter what happens, we went out for a walk out the back road to Tramore and came straight into Shefflin's.'

'What about the car?' McCadden asked. 'Going back with Power to pick up the car. Who put that into your mind, and into your story?'

'Well, we had to, didn't we, the way things went for us?'

McCadden said wearily, 'Power knew he was going to die that night, did he? And he wanted to protect his own murderer, so he fed you a story to pass on to us that would leave the killer's identity a mystery.'

'I'm telling you the truth,' O'Shea insisted.

McCadden sighed. 'No doubt, but you were telling the truth last Sunday, too.'

'Sunday was for Billy,' O'Shea said fiercely, as if responsible for some heroic gesture. 'The way Billy would've wanted it.'

'Listen,' McCadden said slowly. 'If *Clarke* had died last Thursday night instead of Power, I could believe in you holding on to your story. You'd be protecting Power. If Power had been *wounded*, I'd believe you. You'd still be protecting him. But Power died. By Friday you suspected he was dead. By Sunday you knew he was dead. You couldn't protect him. So who *are* you protecting?'

'It was the way Billy wanted to tell it, that's all.'

'OK, OK,' McCadden said, 'have it your own way. So tell me instead. What did you think yourself and Power and Barry were going out for last Thursday night?'

'What?'

'The three of you were at the back of Ballybeg Estate, opposite the house where Clarke was hiding, before Power told you the real purpose of the outing. Right?'

'That's where I said he told us, didn't I?'

'Up to that, you obviously thought you were involved in something else. But what? Walking the greyhounds?'

'Billy didn't take the dogs that night.'

'Exactly,' McCadden said. 'And you said to him on the doorstep, are you not taking the dogs, Billy? And he said, no, I'll tell you on the way. So what did you expect him to tell you?'

'Nothing. I just thought we were going for a walk.'

'Without the greyhounds?'

'Yeah, without the greyhounds.'

'Had you ever done that before, gone for a walk without the greyhounds?'

'Well . . .'

'Had you or hadn't you?' McCadden insisted.

O'Shea was silent.

'Look,' McCadden said sharply. 'You have to understand something. I know what wages you're on. I know what the recent refurbishing of your home cost and I know the cost of the equipment you have there. They don't add up. You can't afford your lifestyle on your wages. Now, you'd better understand something else as well. I even know what racket you three were involved in. What I *don't* know is whether you were doing it locally or not. Whether Clarke was in on it or not. Whether it was big enough to kill for.'

O'Shea gave him a straight, slightly derisive look, not chancing much, too afraid of the reaction, but letting his lips twist into a little sneer anyway. So that McCadden thought, no. Not Peter Clarke. That was a mistake. Not as far as O'Shea was concerned, anyway. If Clarke had been involved, O'Shea knew nothing about it. And not Waterford, either. Somewhere else? Abroad?

But O'Shea was saying, 'I don't want to embarrass anyone or anything, Inspector, but when it comes down to me and someone else's reputation, I'm not going to hold back any more. Myself and Billy Power and Henry Barry were all getting it under the counter from Tom Byrne. The way it was, you'd sometimes get a large rush order from a big company that wouldn't wait maybe longer than the ten days. Get them done inside that or forget about it. You didn't want to leave your regular small customers at the bottom of the pile, so you got your best people back in after hours. No sense looking for someone else, taking someone else on, because you'd have to train them; and no sense putting it through the books because fellows wouldn't work for what was left after the taxman had his cut out of it. There was a lot of money for all of us in that type of thing.'

'Well,' McCadden said, 'we can always check that with Mr Byrne.'

'You'd better do that, yeah.'

And McCadden's confidence, on that particular point, was just starting to drain a little when someone knocked on the door of the interview room.

De Burgh answered, muttered for a while outside, and then came back to tell McCadden that the desk sergeant wanted a word with him. Urgently.

McCadden went outside.

The desk sergeant said, 'They've found Peter Clarke, sir. Sergeant Ryan asked me to let you know.'

'Thanks,' McCadden said. 'Where is it?'

'It's out in Ballybeg again, sir,' the sergeant said. And then added, almost as an afterthought, 'And he's after taking himself a hostage this time, sir. It's a young woman.'

eighteen

That morning, McCadden had come back into daylight from a darkened, blood-stained house in Ballybeg. Now he left the artificial light of the station to head for Ballybeg again and found it was dark outside.

It hadn't rained yet, even though the sky had been grey and overcast since morning. In the darkness, it was impossible to tell what it was going to do now. But it hadn't rained yet.

From outside the station on Ballybricken Hill, McCadden could see the glow of Hallowe'en bonfires and their rising black smoke dotted around the city. Noisy children, dressed as witches and devils and skeletons, swarmed around the hill like ants, collecting anything on offer. Coins. Nuts. Fruit.

It was the same on the journey to Ballybeg, along Green Street, down Manor Hill, out the Cork Road. Smoking bonfires. Noisy children. Loud teenagers with cans of beer. Cheap fireworks occasionally exploding in the sky.

Along Green Street. Down Manor Hill. Out the Cork Road.

But not in Ballybeg itself.

There were lights in Ballybeg. But they weren't the lights of bonfires or the lights of fireworks. They were floodlights from police cars.

And Ballybeg was quiet. Frighteningly quiet.

A group of teenagers, maybe twenty in all, was hanging around the main entrance to the estate from the Cork Road. They weren't exactly blocking the road. They weren't stretched across it in single file, or two, or three deep. But they were lounging here, spread out there, ambling somewhere else, never leaving a space wide enough for a car to fit through. So if you wanted to get past you had to run them over or stop and press the horn and take your chance on how they'd react.

De Burgh, driving the Sierra, rolled down the window and called across to one of the lads. Just his name, just in greeting, but the rest of them melted away from the front of the car.

'Soccer,' de Burgh explained, taking the car into the estate. 'I manage a youth team out here.'

'Hmm. Right,' McCadden said. 'Good player, is he?'

De Burgh shook his head. 'No,' he said. 'The good players don't have to be polite. He's looking for a place in the team.'

Earlier, coming back to the station from his previous visit to Ballybeg, McCadden had learned the reason for all the hostility, all the tension, on the housing estate.

A couple of days ago, Cody had ordered a crackdown on local joyriders. An unmarked squad car had chased two lads from Ballybeg out the Tramore Road the previous night. Both lads had been badly injured in a crash. And they'd been legally driving their own car.

De Burgh drove slowly and carefully through the estate, heading for the address they'd been given and the inevitable crowd surrounding it, but keeping an eye on the shadows at the same time. The streets were almost deserted. Every so often a lone youngster, coming late to the action, darted out of the shadows and ran and quickly disappeared again.

'There,' McCadden said suddenly, pointing down a road towards the floodlights.

They rolled gently towards the siege, not wanting to excite anybody. When they got there, McCadden noticed immediately that there was only a scattering of teenage girls in the big crowd and that otherwise there were no women, no children. Men only. Men and youths, dressed in jackets and hooded sweatshirts, standing silently side by side. Most of them were unarmed. Some were holding walking sticks or hurleys, the kind of weapons you could make an easy excuse for carrying. But there were no women. And there were no

113

children. Because the women had already taken their children home, knowing there was going to be trouble.

And McCadden could see the reason for their fears, too. He could see what was going to set this one off. In the centre of the police cordon, to the right of the house where Clarke was obviously holed up, stood the local Hallowe'en bonfire. It wasn't lighting. Ribbons of smoke rose upwards from charred wood at the base of its pile, but there were no flames. It must've been lit, and then quickly put out again.

They had few jobs out here in this housing estate. They had little money. They had hardly any voice. They'd just been pushed into open anger by the car crash involving the two youths from the area. And now their discontent had finally crystallized around an unlit bonfire.

It was obvious to McCadden too, that the time for discussion, the time for pleas, was long past. Because there was no noise from the vast crowd. No slogans. No catch cries. No catcalls. No abuse. No humour. Nothing. Just a resentful silence.

Here and there youths with distorted faces pushed aggressively against the police cordon, testing their own resolve and the resolve of the guards.

As de Burgh drove through the channel of uniforms and on to the other side of the cordon, the first thing McCadden noticed was a squad of police in riot gear over to his left. Over to the right, directly opposite the house Clarke was occupying (a neat house with a tidy garden and bright red windows and door), stood Chief Superintendent Cody and Detective Inspector Boyce. Beside them was Alderman Tom Byrne and Alderman Patrick Kirwan, two other local politicians, a couple of priests and some community leaders from the area.

De Burgh was directed left by a uniform doing point duty. It suited McCadden. He stepped out the front passenger door and slipped away to find Frank Ryan before any of the others saw him.

Ryan, eating a greasy hamburger that was wrapped in tissue paper covered with ketchup, was standing behind a patrol car with two other detectives. Both the others were heavily armed,

114

one with an Uzi sub-machine-gun, one with a high-powered sniper's rifle. Ryan greeted McCadden with the same phrase he used that morning: 'More of the shit, Carl, hah?'

Only McCadden understood it a bit quicker this time. 'What happened, Frank?'

Ryan took a bite from the hamburger and talked while chewing. 'Well, we were doing house-to-house, the usual questionnaire, on the estate here after finding Clarke's old hideout this morning. Particularly looking at any unoccupied houses. People away on holidays. No tenants. You know. Anyway, we were just coming into this area, just starting at the first house on that block there, when we noticed this woman, and she seemed to be going from house to house as well, except coming from the opposite direction.'

'What? Political canvass? Church collection? Something like that?'

'Don't know.'

'What did it look like?'

'Funny enough, the kids had just lit the bonfire there and she was passing it. Otherwise we wouldn't have got such a good look at her. She might've had something in her hand. Leaflets. I don't know. She's probably mid-twenties, not much older. Tall. Red hair. Dressed in jeans and a black leather jacket. Anyway, she looked like she was canvassing, or collecting, or distributing leaflets. That sort of thing. We tried to head her off. I shouted at her myself. She musn't have heard me, or else she rang the bell or knocked just a split second before I called out. We were heading towards her when the door opened. And Jesus, there was Clarke, standing right there in the doorway, lit up by the bonfire.'

'Why did he open the door?'

'I was thinking that. You see, I thought at first he didn't see us. But he must have. He must've known we were on the way. He dragged the woman in and closed the door. So we thought, we'll knock too. I got a couple of uniforms round the back to head him off if he was trying to make a run for it out the rear. What we were thinking was, if he opens up, we'll grab him. But he must've known who we were, like I said.

When he opened up again he had the woman in front of him, his arm round her neck and a knife to her throat. He made as if he was going to come out with her. We backed off, letting him come. But then he changed his mind. Maybe the fire and the noise confused him. There were still some bangers and some fireworks going off. Or maybe he thought his back was vulnerable, we'd shoot him from behind or something. I don't know. Anyway, he reversed in, still holding the woman.'

'Anyone else in the house?'

'No, no one.'

'Is it vacant?'

'No. It belongs to people called Donovan. He's away working in Spain. She's got the two kids with her mother in Dublin the last three weeks.'

'Any contact with Clarke yet?'

'The phone in there is live and they've hitched up a direct connection to the superintendent out here, but he hasn't talked to anyone yet.'

'What happened to the bonfire?'

'When we radioed through, the superintendent got the fire brigade out. I'll tell you, it was looking dicey there for a while. Just me and Walsh here and the fire brigade, trying to convince those kids it'd be better if we knocked their bonfire out.'

'But then Cody himself rode in to rescue you.'

'Huh!' Ryan exclaimed, stuffing the last of the burger in his mouth and trying to clean his hands with the tomato-smeared tissue paper. 'Yeah.'

'Any trouble yet?'

'Not yet, no. Everyone else got here too quickly. Everyone's armed. Jesus, you start anything here and you're wondering if you'll get blown away by a couple of machine-guns. Makes you think twice. I wouldn't bet on it lasting, though. Odds-on someone'll lose the head. Unless something happens with Clarke to keep them entertained.'

nineteen

Nine-fifteen, someone threw a stone from the crowd.

The stone landed harmlessly between the outer cordon and the squad in riot gear, kicking off a footpath into a cluster of nettles and dock leaves in the grass margin. The next one, about a minute later, was aimed a little better, thudding off a perspex shield and bouncing from there to the ground, forcing a little evasive movement from the riot squad. A cheer went up from the crowd. A few in the front row did a little dance in mockery of the riot squad's movements. And another missile came across. This fell short. It was followed by a groan. And then by yet another missile. There was obviously a group in there, hidden by the crowd, making a competition out of it.

Tom Byrne, another politician and a few of the community leaders rushed across and addressed the crowd near the trouble spot. The stones kept flying over their heads. After a while, Byrne and the others consulted and disappeared into the crowd to plead their case. When they came out, everything was quiet again.

Swaggering a little, the group went back to join Chief Superintendent Cody and Inspector Boyce while they watched the house with the bright red door.

And two minutes later, someone threw a stone from the crowd . . .

It went on like that most of the night, never settling back to what it had been and never getting bad enough to force the riot squad into a charge. The pattern had as much excitement about it as clockwork. A couple of stones. The politicians' plea. A lull. A couple of stones. Twice, though, it was knocked out of the rhythm.

Nine forty-six. The rain finally came down. It came without a warning. A couple of light drops, hitting a squad-car windscreen, visible for a second in the floodlights, and then it was suddenly falling heavily. There was no wind to drive one way or the other. It came straight down, silent and heavy and persistent.

For a while, the whole crowd stood there quietly in the downpour, the water dripping from their flattened hair and sodden hoods, bouncing off their noses and shoulders, soaking into jackets, jeans and sneakers. Then a few started drifting miserably away. In ones. In twos. All silently. Behind them, though, even though the bonfire was no longer even smouldering and would never be re-lit, the rest doggedly held their places.

And ten minutes after the rain came down, someone threw a stone from the crowd . . .

Ten-eighteen, Peter Clarke finally picked up the telephone inside the house and asked to talk to the man in charge of all the cops.

McCadden, standing a little behind the command group, heard only Cody's half of the conversation. It wasn't hard to guess the other half.

Cody took the damp, unlit pipe from between his teeth and coughed to introduce himself. 'This is Chief Superintendent Daniel Cody speaking.' He listened a while and then said, 'Yes, he's here.' Then, 'Just a moment. I'll bring him to the phone.' He took the receiver from his ear and held it out to the man standing next to him.

Clarke wanted Alderman Tom Byrne.

Byrne looked frightened. His hand came up to accept the receiver, but it stopped in mid-air and hung there, trembling.

Cody said, 'He wants to talk to you, Tom. It might be helpful if you did.'

Byrne took the receiver, pressed it to his face and said warily, 'This is Tom Byrne speaking.'

He listened and then said, a bit more easily, a little relief in his voice, 'Hello. How are you, Peter? Yes, of course I remember you. I remember you both, you and your father. Very well.' He listened again, nodding this time, confident of something. 'I'll have to ask the chief superintendent about that. OK? OK, Peter? Good. Good.'

He took the receiver down, still clutching it tightly, and covered the mouthpiece with his hand as he said to Cody, 'He wants me inside. He wants to talk to me inside. He won't talk any more to anyone outside here. What do you think, Dan?'

Cody, Boyce and Byrne went into a huddle to whisper their thoughts. The squat, stocky figure of Boyce wedged between the two big men.

Of the three, McCadden watched the Alderman.

Byrne was pale and still looked anxious and frightened. He didn't look like a man who was going to end this siege. In his beige mackintosh and with his wet sandy hair dead on his skull, he looked like a shifty small-timer who made under-the-counter payments to his staff. Well, maybe that was unfair. Maybe most employers did that, some time or other. Most of them weren't politicians as well, though. They didn't have to preach about the national interest. They didn't have to preach at all.

No, McCadden decided then. What Tom Byrne really looked like, he looked like the weak character whose daughter had been sexually assaulted by Billy Power and who'd done nothing about it, who'd turned a blind eye because he was making illegal payments to the groper. He looked like someone who'd been easily compromised and easily broken.

The man just didn't have it in him.

But no one else seemed to agree with McCadden's opinion.

Five minutes later, stooping from the waist and with his hands raised high above his head, Tom Byrne was heading shakily towards the house.

Behind him, McCadden wondered aloud to de Burgh, 'Why is he ducking like that?'

'Television,' de Burgh said. 'Any time you see someone like that on the news, they're always crouched. He should have a white handkerchief too.'

119

The red door of the house opened slightly as Tom Byrne walked up the paved pathway through the neat front garden. As soon as he'd squeezed through, it closed again.

twenty

When it happened, McCadden was dozing.

He'd picked up a litre of milk and a couple of ham sandwiches from the food wagon they'd brought out to service the cops at the siege. The coffee, made with cheap powder, and served in polystyrene cups that left an odd sensation on your lips before scalding them, didn't even have the virtue of a high caffeine content. McCadden could only guess what it tasted like.

Wet and uncomfortable, he sat in the front passenger seat of the Sierra and turned the engine on to drive the heater, hoping to dry out and warm up a little. He drank the milk and chewed his sandwiches and tried to figure out Peter Clarke's movements over the past week.

Clarke had escaped from Mountjoy Prison in Dublin on Tuesday evening, exactly a week before. Right. Good start.

But then what?

Whatever road you took, it was a hundred miles from Dublin to Waterford. He couldn't have walked it. Had he hitched? Dressed in prison clothes? Admittedly not striped pyjamas with distinctive arrows, just jeans and a white T-shirt, maybe a blue denim shirt over that. But still. Hard to believe he'd take the chance, standing there hitching on the main roads with patrol cars passing back and forth, his photograph and description already out, everyone looking for him.

So, what? A stolen car or motorbike? Nothing reported stolen in Dublin had been found abandoned in Waterford during the past week. Or had someone . . .

McCadden pushed himself upwards a little in the seat, the way you move suddenly when a good idea hits you and you want to grab it before it slips away.

He thought. Had someone picked Clarke up in Dublin and driven him down to Waterford?

But then he relaxed again.

No, they would've brought a change of clothes. And Clarke had been wearing his prison clothes when he'd got back to his home town.

Say he got down to Waterford by some means or other, but reached it late Tuesday or any time Wednesday. He must've walked straight into that vacant house in Ballybeg, because he contacted Billy Power to arrange a meeting for Thursday and he obviously must've known in advance where they were going to meet.

Clever enough man, McCadden thought, out of the city like that for three years. How did he know about the vacant house in such an isolated corner? Did he scout around?

No, McCadden decided. Inside information. He had to be in touch with someone local. Someone who didn't collect him in Dublin, though. But who? Billy Power himself?

Anyway, contact or not, Billy Power is expecting trouble when he heads off to meet Clarke on Thursday night. He ropes in O'Shea and Barry as extra muscle, but goes alone when they back off.

Did he get killed on his way into the house before he had a chance to open his mouth? Or was it done on the way back out, after an argument?

Looking at it the first way, he was set up and you'd have to say Clarke escaped from prison just to kill Billy Power. Looking at it the second way, dead because of some dispute, you'd have to say Clarke had business with Power and thought Power had betrayed him. Looking at it either way, you'd have to say Billy Power himself was probably Clarke's contact, his eyes and ears in Waterford.

So what was the connection between the two that no one else knew about?

The trouble was, McCadden knew next to nothing about

Peter Clarke. He knew the man had slashed his lover, Theresa Cheasty, three years before. He knew there was a pattern to the couple's relationship. From the neighbours' point of view, anyway. Peaceful at first. Then the odd argument. Another period of quiet. And for the last two months of Theresa's life, more frequent rows, sometimes spilling on to the street. He knew the neighbours had called the police the day Theresa Cheasty had died during yet another row. He knew Clarke, caught in the act, had pleaded guilty at the trial. And he knew that no one really understood why any of these things had happened.

Certainly not Superintendent Cody, who'd closed the file on Peter Clarke three years ago with a lecture for McCadden that went, 'The law doesn't demand of us, Inspector, that we supply motives for every crime we prosecute. You may have a slightly different and perhaps less conventional approach, but when a man confesses to murder, I myself am not inclined to commit resources to imagining reasons he is uninterested in inventing himself.'

Well, Cody thought he'd closed the file. The last week, he'd had it open again on his desk. It couldn't have told him any more than the little he already knew. Whatever it was, though, he was keeping it between himself and Harry Boyce. McCadden's request to study and discuss the file that afternoon had been refused.

'The case is Harry Boyce's responsibility, Inspector.'

And trying to think it through now with such one-sided information, McCadden inevitably found himself going round in circles. Every question about Clarke seemed to lead only to Billy Power. Every problem with Power, like why his body had been moved the day after his murder, seemed to lead back to Clarke, who might have a network, an organization of people he needed to meet again in Waterford.

In the airless heat of the car, his mind circling the same unanswered questions, McCadden's eyes finally started closing. Twice his head fell forward on to his chest. Twice the snap of firecrackers and fireworks or stones on perspex shields jerked him awake again. The next time, his head went sideways, over his left shoulder, which was leaning against the side of the car. So when de Burgh suddenly pulled open the passenger door, McCadden almost toppled out on to the wet grass, shouting, 'Jesus, Liam!'

De Burgh pushed McCadden back up into a sitting position in the car and said excitedly, 'Something's happening in the house.'

'Like what?' McCadden demanded irritably.

De Burgh said, 'Like gunshots! Are you awake?'

'They weren't gunshots. I heard bangers just now. They were fireworks, something like that.'

'They were gunshots!'

'You sure?'

'Of course I'm sure. So is everyone else.'

'OK, OK. How many?'

'Two!'

Over the next thirty seconds, it looked as if McCadden and de Burgh, making their way back to the chief superintendent's position from the Sierra, were the only two moving on the entire estate. Everyone else seemed rigid. Everyone else seemed to be staring helplessly at the red doorway of the house Tom Byrne had gone into a quarter of an hour before. Some of the cops were still crouched behind the patrol cars, covering the house with guns. Some were standing in the open, frozen in odd, defenceless postures.

No one was saying anything. But you could hear the question anyway.

What are we going to do, sir?

Chief Superintendent Cody, trapped in the centre and at the head of all this, his mouth clenched around the stem of his dead pipe, was also standing still, also staring at the house. He was asking the question, too. *What are we going to do?* And he didn't know the answer. He'd just sent a friend in there. More than a friend, of course. An Alderman, a man with a local reputation, a man with a public profile. He'd just sent him in there to make two hostages. And now he'd heard two shots. Basic maths. Two hostages. Two shots. And Cody didn't know what to do.

If he moved in with an assault force and the hostages were still unharmed and got caught in the crossfire . . .

If he didn't move in and the hostages were only wounded, dying slowly in a room of the house or staring at Peter Clarke, waiting for him to finish them off . . .

What are we going to do?

Maybe a minute passed. Feeling much longer than that.

Cody did nothing. Didn't even take the pipe from his mouth.

Another minute passed.

And then the red door of the house opened.

All that came out first was an arm. A woman's long, slim arm, dressed in a light grey sweater. The hand unsteady, groping for support. For a second or two it looked as if she was wounded and staggering outwards.

But she wasn't alone.

Coming out beside her, holding her left arm up with his right and helping her along like that, was Alderman Tom Byrne.

There was something like a gasp from the crowd.

There was something like a cheer, everyone rooting for the two hostages, the man and the woman.

But the sounds died again. It was too early. No one knew what had happened, who'd been hurt, how badly.

As soon as they were in the open, Byrne raised his own left arm and gestured urgently. Calling the police in. Calling for assistance. Asking for medics. Encouraging the police past him and into the house.

Everybody moved then. Armed detectives filtered past the pair and in through the open doorway, their weapons ready, covering each other. Most of the rest ran to Byrne and the woman. McCadden. Boyce. De Burgh. Cody. Doctors and nurses to claim their patients. Stretchers came from ambulances.

The young woman was wide-eyed with fear and shock. Her red hair, shoulder length and nicely styled, had been pushed back untidily behind her ears. Her mouth was open and she was breathing fast. She looked like she wanted to cry, but couldn't.

Tom Byrne was pale and shaking. And still clinging to the woman's arm. A doctor had to gently prise his fingers off. Even though he was still offering help, it was obvious that Byrne's own legs were weak with shock, obvious they'd buckle if he wasn't supported himself.

'Are you all right?' the doctor asked.

What a question.

But Byrne muttered, 'Yes, yes.'

'Have you been shot? Have either of you been shot?'

'No, no, no, not us.'

'Have you been beaten? Have either of you been injured in any way?'

'No, no.'

And Cody stepped in and asked then, 'What happened, Tom?'

Everything stopped. Things fell quiet.

Byrne drew three long breaths. He said, 'We were talking, talking . . . myself and Clarke . . . I don't know, I . . . this lady here, she moved slightly, nothing . . . Clarke was extremely nervous, I mean, jumpy, very edgy . . . I think he thought, he thought she was going to attack him . . . he, ah, he turned suddenly and fired and missed. You see, he was going to shoot again, at her, again. I tried to stop him. The gun went off, while, in his hand, while we were struggling. I think, I think it killed him . . .'

'The bullet,' the woman sobbed. 'The bullet . . .'

She made motions, wild, almost uncontrolled, indicating that the bullet had passed close to her ear. And then she cried. She cried and her head dropped on to her chest and she kept repeating, 'The bullet, the bullet . . .'

And again, for a few seconds, no one knew what to do.

Until the woman finally fainted.

And Cody said to the medical people, 'You'd better take this lady out of here.'

'Ardkeen Hospital?'

Cody nodded and as they were leading her away to an ambulance he called, 'Sergeant!'

A uniformed sergeant stepped up. 'Yes, sir?'

'Take some men and escort that lady to Ardkeen.' He swivelled, addressing the doctor again. 'I suppose you'll need to keep her in overnight?'

The doctor nodded. He said quietly, 'We may have to sedate her, you know.'

'Yes. Well, we'll talk to her in the morning, please God. See that she's not disturbed during the night, Sergeant. Reporters and the like. You'll need at least two men outside her room. Organize the shifts yourself.'

'Yes, sir.'

Cody turned to Byrne, who was sitting in the back of an ambulance being examined by another doctor. 'You'd better do the same yourself, Tom. Get into hospital. And well done. In case I forget.'

'No, no,' Byrne protested. 'I'm all right, all right.'

The doctor shook his head at Cody, and spoke to Byrne himself. 'We'll need to bring you in for a check-up and observation, sir.'

McCadden left them there then and wandered into the house, gesturing at de Burgh to follow.

The front room, where Clarke had held the woman and talked to Byrne, still had the remnants of a recent kids' party. Two balloons were pinned to the wall under a framed religious print. One was pink. One was green. One was flat and shrivelled, and the other was still inflated. Coloured wrapping paper and empty toy boxes from the kids' presents had been crumpled and crushed and thrown into the fireplace.

Clarke had eaten in the room not so long before. Two open, emptied cans, one of Irish stew and the other of baked beans, each with a spoon in them, were standing on top of the television. The residue of sauce in both of them was still moist.

Didn't he know how to heat up food, McCadden wondered. Or was the electricity disconnected in the house?

Clarke himself lay on the floral carpet, bleeding into the green and brown pattern. McCadden was surprised. He had this image, didn't know from where, of a muscular, physical man. But Clarke was small. No more than five-five, probably. His cheeks had an unhealthy looking flush and a heavy stubble.

His lank black hair was thinning a lot, the scalp visible through the strands.

Unprepossessing. That was the word that came to McCadden's mind. Unprepossessing.

But it wasn't Clarke's physical appearance that really surprised McCadden. It was that Clarke wasn't wearing Billy Power's jacket and Opel T-shirt and blue jeans. Clarke was wearing navy slacks and cheap slip-on brown shoes and a grey sweatshirt with the word ANDIAMO across the chest.

Well, it had read ANDIAMO once. Right now, because the bullet had probably caught Clarke in the heart and because of the scorch marks from the close range shot, it was reading AND MO.

The gun, a Beretta 92SB semi-automatic, lay on the carpet in front of the body, near Clarke's open right hand.

And who'd given him that, McCadden wondered.

Who gave him the clothes? Who drove him from Dublin to Waterford? Who set him up in the vacant house in Ballybeg? Who knew the Donovans were away from this house? Who gave him a Beretta pistol?

Not Billy Power, certainly. Not the pistol, anyway.

Here, Peter, shoot me with that.

'There!' de Burgh said suddenly. His finger was pointing to the wall on the opposite side of the room. 'That's where the first bullet lodged. Lucky woman. If she gets over the trauma.'

Harry Boyce came in from the street. He had Frank Ryan and a couple of other detectives with him. They stopped inside the doorway of the room.

Boyce's eyes were neutral. His stance said nothing. His heavy black moustache kept hidden whatever expression was on his lips.

But he said in a slow, deadpan voice, 'Note the clothes worn by the casualty, lads, the escaped murderer Peter Clarke. Adidas runners. Light blue denim jeans. Opel Ireland T-shirt.'

McCadden shrugged. He wasn't bothered. Not about that, anyway. And the way his experience went, characters who couldn't live with their own mistakes always delighted in the mistakes of others.

McCadden asked, 'When do you intend interviewing Tom Byrne?'

Boyce said nothing. He chewed his thick moustache with his lower lip. The movement had the effect of dragging his eyebrows downwards and making him glower.

McCadden said patiently, 'I need his evidence to tidy up the Billy Power case. I thought if we did it together it might be better than putting him through two separate sessions.'

'Tomorrow morning,' Boyce said. 'He'll be in Ardkeen Hospital overnight. I'll see him and the woman tomorrow morning.'

McCadden nodded and headed for the front door.

'*Andiamo*,' he said to de Burgh.

twenty-one

Back in his flat, a little after midnight, McCadden had a long shower, staying in there until the hot water ran out and the cold stuff drove him backwards. He debated with himself then whether to change clothes and get dressed again or just slip into bed and read. In the end he compromised. He pulled on a T-shirt and tracksuit bottoms, made a jug of decent coffee and put an old Fairport Convention tape in the stereo deck, the one with Sandy Denny singing 'Crazy Man Michael' on it, and sat on the futon to read the day's *Irish Times*.

His mind was restless, though. He couldn't concentrate on the newspaper. Couldn't even keep the music in his head as background.

What he should do now, he told himself, he should take a few days' leave. Wednesday afternoon and all day Thursday and Friday. Run it into the weekend. Five days in all. Grab a holiday. Maybe go and call on Sarah in Dublin, see if there was anything still alive between them.

Because there was really no urgency with the Billy Power case any more.

By then, thinking about a holiday, McCadden was on his feet, pacing up and down the varnished floorboards in his living room, eight steps across, eight steps back again, the loose board on the turn creaking every time his weight came down on it, every time his weight came off it again. No urgency with the case. But he was still scurrying around. Still couldn't relax.

Once he stopped in front of the Russian poster that showed

the chain and the books. He read its slogan: *Knowledge Will Break the Fetters of Slavery*. What he had, he decided then, was a feeling of loss. Not personal loss. The loss of a contest. The loss of a vital game. He couldn't say exactly what game he'd lost. He couldn't even say who he'd lost *to*. All he was certain of was the emptiness of defeat. That, and the feeling there was a winner celebrating somewhere.

For a while then, for the sake of distraction, he let his mind pursue the theme of games. Games won and games lost. Games as a substitute for ordinary life. Games as superior to ordinary life. Games as immoral levity.

He pulled out books, checked references, accumulated connections. Stefan Zweig's *The Royal Game*. Vladimir Nabokov's *King, Queen, Knave* and *The Defence*. *The Natural* by Bernard Malamud. Herman Hesse's *The Glass Bead Game*. Peter Handke's *The Goalie's Anxiety at the Penalty Kick*.

He plucked quotations and opinions from his memory and strung them together to see how they lay. Bill Shankly, wasn't it, the manager of Liverpool, saying that football wasn't a matter of life and death, but much more important than that. Put him in the same camp as the lovers in W. B. Yeats' play *Deirdre*, who played chess while being executed, and the players in *The Glass Bead Game*, who knew nothing at all of ordinary life. Shankly probably hadn't any of those in mind. Might've been thinking of the puritans in the opposite camp, though, who'd reduce games to idle frivolity . . .

And finally, at twenty-two minutes after one in the morning, surrounded by open books, convinced that he understood at last why men were addicted to games, which were always more comforting and more manageable than the messiness of ordinary life, he had reached for the telephone and dialled all but the last digit of Liam de Burgh's number to ask the sergeant if he knew any books that used games as a theme, as a metaphor, as a method of structuring, when the sudden awareness of the time brought him back to the feeling of defeat.

He was too tired to struggle with it any more. Too tired to even evade it.

He was out of sync, that was the problem. Everyone else

asleep, content, relieved the siege hadn't thrown up a couple of innocent victims. He was out of sync.

He thought of another coffee, but knew it would keep him awake much longer, maybe through the rest of the night. So he climbed to his bedroom in the loft and undressed and tried to clear his mind.

Ten minutes before two, he finally fell asleep.

He was awake again, three minutes after the hour. Nothing outside himself. Just one last kick from his restless mind.

The next awakening was weird, though. A strange sensation creeping along the back of his neck, half felt, half dreamed, started it off. Coming slightly awake, he thought it was something crawling into or out of his hair. A spider. Head lice. An earwig. Something like that. He swatted at it with an open palm and scratched it with his nails, but the irritation stayed.

And then he heard. A sound that had been low and indistinct coming suddenly into clarity.

A lone drunk was passing under his open window on the street below, singing in a strong voice that was only slightly slurred:

We robbed and plundered many a ship down on the Spanish Main,
Caused many the poor widow and orphan child in sorrow to remain.
We made their crews to walk our planks and they hung . . .

The drunk passed out of range, leaving behind him in the dead silence only the memory of the words and the tune.

McCadden, fully awake now, the sensation at the back of his neck like small needles in the flesh, raised himself to a sitting position in the bed and said softly, but distinctly, 'Shit.'

He threw off the blankets and swung his feet out of the bed. He grabbed at the telephone, knocking the receiver off its hook. He tugged at the drawer of the small cabinet, looking for his personal telephone book to check a number. He felt along the surface of the cabinet, searching for the base of the bedside lamp, looking for the switch to hit.

132

The radio alarm clock came into his view as he was groping and fumbling about.

It was four-eleven. Neither night nor morning.

Five minutes it took him, five minutes before he was organized, before the phone was ringing at Frank Ryan's home. Four-sixteen in the morning. It took Ryan another minute to get out of sleep and pick up the receiver. Four-seventeen. McCadden, staring at the illuminated numbers on the alarm clock display, counting off the seconds as they passed.

Ryan said, 'Awwoaaah?'

'Frank?' McCadden said. 'Carl McCadden. Sorry about the time, about disturbing you, all the rest of the formalities. Are you awake, Frank?'

'Hah?'

'Are you awake?'

'Jesus, Carl, I am now.'

'Good! Listen carefully. This evening when you were in Ballybeg and the woman, the hostage, went to knock on the door of the house where Clarke was, and you called to her – are you with me?'

'Yeah, yeah, I'm with you.'

'Right. Frank, tell me exactly what happened after that.'

'Jesus!' Ryan took a breath, and let it out again. 'I called out to her. She rang the doorbell or knocked on the door. The door opened. She was pulled in. So Walsh and myself, we decided to ring the doorbell as well. But when Clarke opened it, he had one arm around her and he was holding a knife to her throat and — '

'That's what I thought you said,' McCadden interrupted. 'That's what I thought you said.'

'What's the problem, Carl?'

'A question,' McCadden said. 'Why, if he had a gun, was he subduing her with a knife?'

Ryan sighed again. But he took his time with it. Twenty-five seconds. A long silence. But he said then, 'Jesus, even at . . . what time is it? . . . even at *half-four in the morning*, Carl, if you have two weapons, you can choose either one at any particular time.'

133

'Yeah, yeah. But if you were trying to subdue one person and hold off two others, which one would you use?'

'I take your point, Carl, but — '

'Good! A few more small questions, Frank, and I'll let you get back to sleep.'

'No, I — '

'Twice you've said to me she rang the doorbell *or* knocked on the door. Why? Why the *or*? Did you see her knocking on the door?'

'It looked like it, yeah.'

'And it looked like she'd pressed the doorbell as well, just before that?'

'I suppose, yeah.'

'Before you called out?'

'Yeah, definitely.'

'And knocked *after* you called out?'

'Probably, probably. I mean, you don't usually do the two together.'

'You don't, do you?' McCadden agreed. 'Listen. Leaving aside the natural sympathy, all that, for the hostage, do you think she heard you when you called?'

There was another long silence. Longer this time.

Ryan thinking.

McCadden counting off the seconds while he waited.

Ryan said then, 'Yes.'

'And one more, Frank,' McCadden promised. 'Just one more. When Clarke opened the door, was she dragged in or did she push herself?'

Ryan exhaled. 'Jesus! Under oath?'

'Under oath.'

'Couldn't say for definite, one way or the other.'

'Thanks, Frank. I appreciate it.'

'Don't mention it,' Ryan said, the irony heavy. 'What the hell put all this in your mind, anyway?'

'Pirates making their captives walk the plank by prodding them on their way with the blade of a cutlass. No, I'm not joking. It's a song. *We robbed and plundered many a ship down on the Spanish Main, Caused many the poor widow and orphan*

134

child in sorrow to remain. We made their crews to walk our planks and they something something something. Do you know it?'

'Would you fuck off, Carl.'

'OK, OK. Go on, go back to sleep.'

'You must be joking. I'm not going to be able to get back to sleep after all this.'

'Wife awake beside you?'

'What do you think? Of course she is.'

'Try a bit of sex, then,' McCadden suggested.

And hung up. Quickly.

With the window open behind the bed and the fire dying in the room below, it was cold in the loft now, only two degrees above freezing. Sitting naked on the edge of the bed, McCadden became aware of it only after hanging up the phone. Shivering, he got up and hurried across to the wardrobe to dress. Something heavy and warm. Something for outdoors on a cold October dawn. Thick woollen socks, climbing boots, jeans, denim shirt, floppy sweater.

Pulling a heavy waxed jacket over that lot, he went back to the cabinet and flicked through his telephone book again.

There were two numbers opposite Vinnie Foley's name. One was his home number, the other the business number of the bookie Vinnie worked for. Which was which, McCadden didn't know. He hadn't given any indication in the book.

He took a guess and dialled the top one. It rang, fifteen times. So he disconnected and dialled the second one. And that rang, and rang, and rang.

A small thing, forgetting to list which number was which. But irritating.

He dialled the first again. This time the receiver was lifted almost immediately. Vinnie must've been woken by the first call. Maybe got out of bed, stumbled across the room or downstairs, got his hand on the receiver and lifted it to his ear, only to find it was dead.

'Vinnie?' McCadden said, writing an H after the first of Vinnie's numbers in the telephone book. 'This is Carl McCadden.'

135

Foley's voice was sleepy, but full of dread. 'Something the matter, is there?'

'No, nothing wrong. Look, I know it's early in the morning, but — '

'It's nearly quarter to five!'

'Very good, Vinnie,' McCadden said. 'At least you're awake. Now. In about a quarter of an hour, I'm going to call for you. You'll need to get dressed. For outdoors.'

'Wha?'

'You'll be doing me a favour. It won't take long.'

'Sure, we can do it in the morning, can't we?'

'The morning's too late. Now.'

'Ah, look, I'm feeling a bit shook, to be honest with you, and — '

'What's the comparative form of shook, Vinnie?'

'Wha?'

'You'll be feeling worse if you're not ready.'

Five minutes past five, a couple of minutes later than expected, McCadden was pressing the bell on Vinnie Foley's door. He'd never noticed this before, but the bell served up a pacy keyboard version of *Row, Row, Row Your Boat*. Every time you pressed it, it played *Row, Row, Row Your Boat*.

By seven minutes past five, McCadden had played *Row, Row, Row Your Boat* ten times. And the house was still in darkness. Vinnie had obviously flopped back to bed and turned over and fallen asleep again.

After that, McCadden kept his finger on the bell, kept churning out *Row, Row, Row Your Boat*, until a light came on in the hallway and Vinnie scurried out to open the door.

Vinnie was wearing light blue pyjamas with Pink Panthers spread all over them. Like everything else he wore, there wasn't quite enough of it to cover all of him at the same time.

'Come on,' McCadden said urgently. 'Let's go, let's go. Let's get dressed, Vinnie.'

'Yeah, all right, all right,' Vinnie mumbled, padding his way back through the hallway and into the sitting room, where he'd undressed the night before and where his clothes were still crumpled on an armchair. He pulled on jeans without taking off the pyjama bottoms, pulled on a sweatshirt without removing the top, and asked while he was sniffing at his socks, 'Where are we heading for, anyway?'

'Mystery tour,' McCadden said sharply. 'Come on. One of your shoes is in the fireplace, by the way, and the other is under that newspaper on the floor.'

twenty-two

McCadden cut across the south of the city, disregarding the traffic lights, meeting very little on the roads. A few travellers were already up, getting an early start on a long journey. A couple of revellers were trying to keep their car straight after an all-night session. Here and there a lone character on a bicycle was pedalling silently through the darkness. A factory shift-worker. Maybe a docker. McCadden heard the tinkle of milk bottles from a delivery round. It was somewhere in the distance, the sound carrying a lot in the stillness. He didn't get to see the lorry itself.

Vinnie Foley fell asleep in the front passenger seat within half a mile of leaving home. Thirty seconds later he was snoring loudly.

When McCadden reached his destination, turning through the main entrance to Ardkeen General Hospital and pulling into a parking space outside the reception area, he prodded the fat man in the ribs. Vinnie slept on. McCadden shook him by the shoulder and then yelled at him irritably. Vinnie just snored. Finally McCadden pinched the fat man's nose and clapped a palm tightly over his mouth, cutting off his air supply. Vinnie woke up fairly sharply then, gasping for breath.

Vinnie lumbered out of the car and looked around uncertainly while McCadden locked the doors, trying to figure out where he was, trying to work the night backwards so he could figure out why he'd been brought here. Like all men who were grossly overweight, he obviously dreaded hospitals, knowing he was going to end up in one sooner rather than later. When McCadden strode past him into the building, Vinnie turned and padded obediently after him like a giant, loyal, and slightly dim St Bernard dog.

The nurse at the reception desk looked up as McCadden approached. She smiled a little. Not showing her teeth, only promising she might if the problem wasn't too serious. She looked beyond McCadden to Vinnie. And then she said, 'Casualty?'

'What?' McCadden asked.

The nurse leaned to one side and aimed a biro at the slow-moving Vinnie. 'Your friend,' she said. 'Has he been in an accident?'

There were a lot of things you could answer to that. But McCadden wasn't in the mood. He shook his head.

'No,' he said, producing and showing his ID. 'I'm Detective Inspector McCadden. This is, ah ... a witness. The woman who was brought in here last night from the siege in Ballybeg Estate. Do you know where she is?'

'Yes. Just down the corridor. There's two guards there already.'

'Did they give you a name for her?'

The nurse checked her admissions. 'Vera Dunne.'

'Vera Dunne,' McCadden repeated. 'Maybe if the doctor who's treating her ... ?'

The nurse smiled again, showing her teeth this time. She flicked a switch on the PA system and paged the doctor.

McCadden paced while waiting. He would've preferred to pass the time chatting with the nurse, but he was too anxious, too preoccupied, to enjoy it. Behind him, Vinnie sidled towards one of the chairs in the corridor.

'Don't sit down, Vinnie,' McCadden warned him.

Vinnie looked appealingly at the nurse, his expression telling her that this was only one of the basic comforts he was denied.

The doctor, who came striding towards them without much delay, was young and affable and remarkably fresh for six in the morning.

'Michael Griffin,' he introduced himself, offering his hand. 'Would you like to follow me? This way.'

'Thanks. Carl McCadden and, ah . . .'

The doctor glanced back at Vinnie. Vinnie's Pink Panther pyjamas were visible underneath the sweatshirt around his paunch.

'Was she sedated?' McCadden asked quickly. 'Vera Dunne.'

'No. No need. Mild shock. Just a matter of keeping an eye on her. I expect she'll be perfectly all right in the morning. She's probably still asleep, though. And, ah, it's a little early for interviewing her, don't you think?'

'I won't wake her,' McCadden said. 'I just want to look. And ask Mr Foley here to look as well. Is that OK?'

'Yes, yes. As long as we don't disturb her.'

The two uniformed guards, both of them very young, certainly no more than twenty, were sitting with the ward nurse at her desk, sharing a quiet joke. They could obviously hear the voices and footsteps approaching, but must've assumed it was doctors. When the shadow fell over them and they looked up to see McCadden standing in the doorway of the little office, they jumped up and blushed and glanced at each other.

'Relax,' McCadden said. 'How long have you been here?'

'Since midnight, sir.'

'When are you being relieved?'

'At eight, sir.'

'Anything to report? Any visitors? Anyone ask to go in?'

'No, sir. There were some reporters here on the earlier shift, but they'd gone by the time we got here. They didn't come back.'

'Did the woman come out or wake up at any stage?'

'No, sir.'

The doctor had gently opened the door of the room and was holding it ajar for McCadden to pass. The room was in darkness. The light from the corridor fell through the open door, but didn't hit the bed, which was out of sight, over to the left.

McCadden, stopping Vinnie Foley from blundering into the blackness, said softly, 'We need some light.'

The doctor groped inwards, not wanting to switch on the overhead fluorescent strips. He found a low-watt desk lamp on the table and switched that on.

The dim light was enough to illuminate the bed. But not the woman. Because the woman was no longer there. The bed was empty.

McCadden stared at the empty bed for a few seconds, the pillows and bed covers neatly rearranged, nothing out of place. Going across, he lifted the covers and felt the sheets beneath. Cold. Stone cold. Long gone. His gaze shifted to the window, which had been unclasped and opened from inside the room and then pushed shut again from outside. The drop to the other side, into the hospital grounds, was less than six feet.

The young doctor, his right hand still resting on the table lamp, his forefinger still pressing on the switch, stared in bewilderment at McCadden.

In the silence, Vinnie Foley wandered over to the bed and sat on it sluggishly, too exhausted to ask what was going on.

And then McCadden sighed and said softly to himself, 'Shit.'

The two uniformed guards, attracted by the atmosphere, the lack of movement, the silence, impelled by their own vague feelings of guilt, were now standing just inside the doorway of the room. Both of them were awkward. Frightened.

McCadden heard one of them swallowing with difficulty and turned to face them. 'Switch on the lights,' he said.

And when the fluorescent strips flickered and jumped into life, he asked, 'What were your orders?'

'We were told not to let anyone pass, sir,' one said. 'For her not to be disturbed.'

'We had to stay in the corridor, sir,' the other added. 'Not go into the room.'

'Exactly,' McCadden said. 'All of which you did. Didn't you?'

Both of them nodded. 'Yes, sir.'

'So relax.'

'Yes, sir.'

'No, don't relax. You've got to report all this. Tell them I was here. Tell them they'll need a general alert. The woman is likely to leave the country tonight. You can give the description yourselves. Have you got all that?'

'We never saw her, sir.'

McCadden sighed. 'It doesn't matter. They'll know who you're talking about. Have you got it?'

'Yes, sir.'

'Good. When you're finished, go and search the grounds. Just in case.'

McCadden strode between and past them. He was already back at the reception desk, managing a polite nod to the nurse with the nice smile, when it suddenly hit him. With the nurse's curious eyes locked on to him, he wheeled sharply, strode back down the corridor, back past the two young guards, and back into the room.

'Vinnie,' he said wearily.

Foley had fallen asleep on the bed. He hadn't even stretched out. He was just sitting there, his head down on his chest, his feet still on the floor.

McCadden sighed and went across and woke him in the same style as before, nodding amiably at the look of horror on the young doctor's face.

He said, 'Come on, Vinnie. Let's go. We're not finished yet. And the night is young.'

twenty-three

Lennie Lombard scratched an adequate living as a freelance photographer.

A quiet, retiring character, a character who liked to hide behind his viewfinder, he had only one thing he was touchy about.

'My name isn't Lennie,' he'd say irritably. 'It's Richard. Richard Lombard.'

But everyone called him Lennie, although no one knew why any more. Probably because Lens had once sounded like a good nickname for a photographer; and then, because there was only one of him and he was small, it got turned into Lennie. But no one really knew. The city was notorious for weird nicknames that no one questioned the origins of. Stab the Rasher. Slip Me Fippence. Itchiewalla. Who Ate the Dog's Dinner. Bowl o' Cocoa. And a giant, six foot seven inch burglar known as Shorty Phelan.

Mostly, Lombard placed his snaps with the two local weeklies, *The Munster Express* and the *Waterford News and Star*. Very occasionally he struck a little gold and got something in one of the nationals. But he wasn't really a news photographer. Interiors were his forte, frozen poses more his style. Weddings, presentations, dinner dances, opening nights. He hadn't the newshound's nose or dedication.

Funnily enough, Lombard's studio was also in Lombard Street, in the east of the city. It was something he announced proudly right after telling you his first name was really Richard.

'Lombard of Lombard Street.'

It sounded much better than it was, the ground floor of an old Victorian building, half of which he used for living in.

When McCadden and Vinnie Foley reached there a little after seven o'clock that morning, Lombard was already up. Just finishing his breakfast, in fact.

He wasn't any more than five-two, slightly built, in his mid to late thirties and balding early. He also had a lousy dress sense. This morning he had on a greenish suit with wide lapels, a pink shirt, and a multi-coloured tie that exhausted the rest of the spectrum without touching either green or pink.

As he brought McCadden and Vinnie Foley in from the hallway to the kitchen, he kept snatching things from the furniture along the way, a magazine here, a discarded lemon tie there, a recent bank statement somewhere else, nervously apologizing for the state of the place. The only reason you noticed the things were there at all was because everything else was tidied away and everywhere spotless.

Lombard didn't sit to finish the remains of his egg and rasher. He stood anxiously at the head of the table, not knowing what to do with his hands.

'Would you like a cup of tea?' he asked finally.

McCadden shook his head.

Foley, wide awake by now and with a rumbling stomach, looked hungrily at the food on the plate. But Lombard wasn't watching him. Lombard was watching McCadden.

'I might as well have a cup, sure,' Foley sighed.

The teapot was under its cosy on the table. Lombard got another cup from the presses and poured.

McCadden said, 'You were at the siege in Ballybeg last night, weren't you?'

Lombard nodded. 'Yes.'

'How did the photos turn out?'

Lombard grew a little with pride. 'It should make the front page of the *Star* this morning. I haven't seen a copy yet. *The Evening Press* tonight. The locals, of course, at the weekend.'

'Let's have a look,' McCadden said.

The studio was across the hallway. A large room with bare floorboards, cameras, tripods, lights, backdrops, some chairs for portrait work. The place was as neat as the rest of the house, and with the same two or three items thrown thoughtlessly aside.

The photographs were already in his filing system. As you might expect from someone so organized, they were also in temporal sequence. The house. The police encircling it. The watching crowd. A closer shot of Chief Superintendent Cody and Tom Byrne and Harry Boyce and Patrick Kirwan. Tom Byrne going in under his raised arms, like a bandit surrendering. One for the Alderman's own files, that. Wouldn't do his political ambitions any harm at all. Then there was McCadden himself, sleeping in the front passenger seat of the car, chin on chest, mouth slightly open, looking a little dumb. Was that why Lombard was so nervous this morning? Or was he always like that?

The last batch of shots showed the hostage and Tom Byrne coming out of the house. There were a lot of them, some separated only by seconds.

McCadden took the best of the bunch: the woman and Byrne looking straight at the camera, both slightly blinded by the police floodlights, but both caught with fairly natural expressions.

He walked across the bare floorboards of the studio and offered it to Vinnie Foley.

Vinnie shifted the cup of tea from his right hand to his left. He wiped the palm of his right on the seat of his trousers. But he still didn't take the print.

'What's this?'

McCadden said patiently, 'It's a photograph, Vinnie.'

Vinnie accepted it then. He took a single glance at it, his face lighting up with recognition immediately.

'That's Tom Byrne!' he exclaimed. 'The Alderman.'

McCadden sighed, but said nothing. Vinnie read in his face that something else was expected of him, so he went back to studying the photograph.

It took him almost thirty seconds.

'Ah!' he said then. 'Now I got you. Now I know what you're on about.'

'Thank you, Vinnie.'

'That's the redheaded woman was out in Kilcohan at the dogs last Saturday night, the one with the fancy Italian laid the big money on Paul Hyland's dog, Dondory.' And then, sensing the hint of a local scandal, 'What's she doing with Tom Byrne?'

McCadden said, 'The Italian man, Vinnie. Describe him again, will you?'

'How do you mean, like?'

'How old he was, how tall, the colour of his hair and eyes, any distinguishing marks.'

'How old? I'd say he was, you know, maybe fifty-five, maybe a bit more. It's hard to tell with Italians sometimes. He wouldn't be as tall as you, now. A bit lower. What else did you say?'

'Hair colour.'

'Black. Jet black, boy. He had a beard, too.'

'Heavy? Light?'

'Fairly heavy, it was. There wasn't anything else. That I can remember, anyway. Except for the clobber. I told you he had money, didn't I?'

Afterwards, McCadden took the photograph back and turned to Lombard. 'Can I use a phone?'

The telephone was in the hallway. Lombard ushered Vinnie back to the kitchen, Vinnie asking along the way, 'You wouldn't have a slice of brown bread or something, would you?'

McCadden rang Liam de Burgh at his home on the Cork Road.

'Liam? It's Carl. Listen, you can get the details when you get in to work, but the woman hostage from Ballybeg last night, she's disappeared.'

'Abducted?'

'No. Voluntarily. Opened a window and into the hospital grounds. There's a general alert, but I wouldn't have much hope. This is what I want you to do. Have you got a pen handy?'

146

'Yeah. Go ahead.'

'She gave her name as Vera Dunne, obviously not her own. As far as I know, she wasn't carrying any personal identification. If she was, it's probably gone with her. I've got some photographs I'll leave inside for you. She was travelling with an Italian man, mid to late fifties, black hair, heavily bearded, very well dressed, obviously very rich. Do you know Vinnie Foley? I called into him Sunday morning when we were going out to see Billy Power's widow.'

'I don't *know* him, no.'

'I'm going to drop him off at the station. You can see him there. He'll give you a fuller description of the Italian. They must've stayed somewhere in town, maybe somewhere in the county. Find out as much as you can about them. Harry Boyce is going to be on the same trail sooner or later, but you've got a good start on him. Use it. Keep Vinnie Foley away from him. If I don't catch you at the station, I'm going to see Cody at his home now, then I'll probably go with Harry Boyce to interview Tom Byrne. After that I'm going home to get some sleep. I've been up all night. I'll get back in touch later.'

twenty-four

Chief Superintendent Cody lived in a three-storey, double-fronted detached house in Upper Newtown in the south-east suburbs, where District Commissioner Byrne of the Royal Irish Constabulary had also lived almost a hundred years before him. Formerly occupied by spirit merchants and corn merchants, clothiers, brewers, ironmongers and jewellers in the early years of the nineteenth century, it was still a prosperous area. Solid and respectable.

The first thing McCadden noticed when he was invited in was a strong smell of sour milk. He almost laughed. The way exhaustion sometimes took you when you met the unexpected. Your response was just as inappropriate.

The milk had been spilled in the living room, toppling from a coffee table into the fawn carpet and not properly mopped up afterwards. Two frail china cups were on the same mahogany table. A little tea was left in the bottom of each and a light grey scum had formed on the surface. The bases of the cups were staining the wood. Elsewhere, some old newspapers and discarded clothes were scattered on the armchairs, the settees, even on the floor.

It was all a weird contrast with the order in the chief superintendent's office at the station. And a weird contrast too with the neurotic tidiness of Lennie Lombard's flat.

'You'd better come in,' Cody invited uncertainly, nervously. 'Yes, come in. Has something happened?'

They sat in the living room, either side of the coffee table,

148

McCadden too indifferent and Cody too distracted to be embarrassed by the surroundings.

McCadden asked, 'Has no one contacted you yet?'

Cody stared at him fearfully. 'No, no one. What is it?'

With his wife still in hospital, every hour must be the same. Every knock bringing its own terrors. Every telephone call a summons. Sitting there, waiting for the dreaded words. *I'm afraid your wife, Chief Superintendent* . . .

'It's not your wife,' McCadden said quickly. 'The woman, the hostage from Ballybeg last night, has disappeared.'

Cody stared, struggled to understand. 'What?' he asked. 'What do you mean?'

And McCadden saw that he'd used the wrong word, given the impression of a magician's vanishing act.

'Run away,' he explained. 'Well, you'd have to say *escaped* from Ardkeen Hospital.'

'You mean she's gone?'

'Yes,' McCadden said patiently.

'What?' Cody asked. 'Concussion? Shock? Is she wandering around in some danger?'

McCadden shook his head. 'No. She was healthy. She just opened a window and ran away.'

Cody stood up suddenly then, his leg brushing against the coffee table and knocking it a little sideways. 'Who was responsible?' he demanded. 'Who was responsible for watching her?'

McCadden, expecting this irrational response, tried to keep his irritation hidden. 'No one,' he said. 'Everyone. If I remember, your own instructions last night were to see that she wasn't disturbed, to stay outside her room in the hospital.'

Cody wasn't listening. He'd moved away to pace. He said, 'There'll be an inquiry into this. A material witness like that. No one even knows who she is, where she came from. How are we going to find her again? There'll be an inquiry into this. You mark my words.'

'An inquiry,' McCadden said, 'will only show that your instructions last night were to see that she wasn't disturbed.'

Cody stopped and glared.

'It couldn't have entered anyone's head that she'd run away,' McCadden said. 'Anyway, that's not the important thing right now. The important thing is — '

'I'll decide what's important and what's not important, Inspector,' Cody snarled suddenly.

McCadden sighed. Maybe it was his own tiredness, the exhaustion making him less patient, but what respect he'd had for Cody, he was losing it rapidly. When you got to the stage of believing things were important because you decided they were, you weren't leading any more, you were out on your own. And the sympathy he'd had for Cody because of the man's sick wife, that was drifting away quickly too. He'd seen others lose their wives before. Never as rawly, as publicly as this, though.

They'd never been close, himself and Cody. Mutual tolerance was about as deep as they'd gone. And Cody had always placed his trust in the more conventional Harry Boyce, whose ambition made him more cautious, more predictable and much more amiable.

'The important thing is,' McCadden said again, 'that I don't think the woman was in Ballybeg by accident last night. I think she went there deliberately to meet Clarke and to help him escape, possibly out of the country. I also think it was she who brought the gun in, that Clarke didn't have a gun before that. Frank Ryan – Detective Sergeant Ryan – happened to be checking in the area at the same time. She went in to warn Clarke, possibly to get him out the back. But Ryan had seen her and rang the doorbell immediately. What happened then was a clever charade. The woman pretended to be a hostage.'

'Nonsense,' Cody snapped. 'They would simply have escaped through the back door and run away.'

'Ryan had a couple of uniforms blocking the back exit. Faking a hostage situation was the only chance they had of both escaping. The woman was safe from us anyway. We knew nothing about her. Whatever the outcome of the siege, she was free. The attempt was to free Clarke as well.'

Cody paced again, back and forth across the milk stain in the carpet this time. He tapped his pockets, searching for a pipe. When he couldn't find one, he rooted noisily along the mantelpiece above the fireplace.

He said irritably, but much more quietly than before, 'This sounds most unlikely. Most unlikely. No. Why in the name of God did Clarke ask Tom Byrne to come in and talk to him?'

'Because they needed a *real* hostage,' McCadden said. 'If you remember, Clarke insisted on Byrne coming *into* the house. I don't know how they were going to play it afterwards, but they were obviously in a stronger bargaining position with Byrne as a hostage. From our point of view, two hostages. Clarke obviously knew that Byrne would respond to his appeal. Didn't they know each other? Or Byrne knew Clarke's father?'

'But they ended up arguing,' Cody insisted. 'Clarke and the woman. They ended up arguing. Was that part of the charade too, Inspector? And Clarke's death? Also a charade?'

McCadden had to admit, to himself anyway, the more you repeated the word *charade*, the more unlikely it seemed.

But confidently, he said, 'Well, something went wrong. No doubt about that. What exactly, I don't know. Tom Byrne might help to clarify that. You see, I now believe that Clarke came to Waterford to meet Billy Power. He ended up killing him. There's some connection between Clarke, Billy Power and the redheaded woman, and probably others too, that we're missing.'

'Others?'

'Yes,' McCadden said, thinking about the bearded Italian. 'Billy Power's body was moved by someone on Friday morning. I'm almost certain it wasn't by Clarke himself, and certainly not by the woman alone.'

'I see.'

'What I'd like to do now,' McCadden said, 'is to follow Clarke's trail back *before* he murdered his lover, Theresa Cheasty, and —'

Cody was shaking his head.

151

McCadden broke off.

'No,' Cody said, still shaking his head. 'Peter Clarke is Inspector Boyce's case.'

'Yes, but since Clarke almost certainly murdered Billy Power, and since the Power case is somehow — '

'Do you understand what I've said? Peter Clarke is Inspector Boyce's case. If you have any suggestions that might help clarify the situation, you can pass them on to him.'

'I don't want to harp on this,' McCadden said, 'but if we knew why Clarke murdered Theresa Cheasty three years ago we'd probably also know why he killed Billy Power.'

'We know why he killed that poor woman.'

'Why?'

'Clarke was an unstable man, Inspector. Intense about everything, including his relationship with that unfortunate woman. It only takes something small, insignificant to us, to snap the mind of a character like that.'

'My contention is,' McCadden insisted, 'that if she betrayed him — '

'With what?' Cody interrupted. 'What could she have betrayed him with? I've already discussed this with Harry Boyce. There was no other man. There was no money they could have fought over. There were no secrets between them that we know of, no ideals they were devoted to, no political or religious causes they served, no — '

The telephone rang in the next room. Cody started and broke off, and headed towards the sound. It was only when he was at the connecting door that he turned and said, 'I won't be a moment. Wait here.'

Then he was gone, closing the door behind him.

McCadden took the chance to get up and escape the stench of soured milk for a while. He wandered around without intruding. It cost him an effort because there were doors hanging sloppily open all over the place. The glass-fronted bookcase. The sideboard. The drinks cabinet. Maybe with his wife dying, Cody couldn't see the point of closing doors just to open them again. Why bother? Why go on? Not the best attitude, the way things were just then.

Cody had opened the connecting door to the next room and was just going to say something, had got as far as 'Nothing important', when the telephone rang again and he went back in.

This time he took longer, almost ten minutes. When he came back he left the door open and said, 'That's Inspector Boyce reporting now. He wants a word with you.'

McCadden went through and picked up the receiver from a heavy rolltop writing desk. Cody had found his pipe, filled it from a pouch, stuck it in his mouth and searched for matches, all while hanging around the other side of the open door.

McCadden asked, 'Any news?'

There was a silence.

'Of what?' Boyce asked coldly.

McCadden took it there was no news. No good news, anyway. They hadn't found the woman yet. And they still had no idea who she really was. They hadn't even a lead in that direction. If things were any different, Cody would've been smiling coming back from the call and Harry Boyce would've been crowing now.

McCadden asked, 'Have you interviewed Tom Byrne yet?'

'No.'

'When are you going to?'

Squeezing blood from stones.

'I'm leaving the station now for the hospital,' Boyce conceded.

'Wait for me. I'll go with you. As we agreed. I'll take about ten minutes from here. One more thing. Has anyone told Byrne that the woman has disappeared?'

Boyce said impatiently, 'He's asleep. I called and checked on him ten minutes ago.'

'Well, we won't tell him until the end of the interview.'

'Why?'

'Because it will only distort the way he remembers things if he knows, that's why.'

153

Not bad, McCadden decided. Not bad at all for an instant invention.

Harry Boyce seemed taken by it, too. He grunted. He said, 'I'll see you in ten minutes.'

And then he hung up the phone.

twenty-five

Tom Byrne's room in Ardkeen Hospital was on the same level as the one Vera Dunne had vanished from, but it was in a different wing.

And Byrne looked genuinely ill. He looked dull and ashen, slow with his hands and unsteady on his feet. He was sitting outside the covers on the side of his bed, wrapped in a heavy dressing gown. His wife was sitting beside him. A tall, physically imposing woman, but not occupying the space with the same confidence or authority as her husband. More balanced on the edge. Happy to be allowed the privilege, but ready to leave the moment it was withdrawn. Probably a posture she'd perfected during her marriage. Byrne's two daughters, Catherine and Tina, were sitting in chairs either side of the bed.

When Harry Boyce appeared and greeted them, they had nothing but smiles for him. When McCadden came in behind him, they all looked for a moment or two as if they wanted to be somewhere else.

McCadden was puzzled. He could understand the embarrassment of the two daughters. They'd said some things to him their old man wouldn't like to hear and they'd given him impressions that were exposed as lies or half-truths now. He could even account for their mother's anxiety. Except when she was in her own home, she was probably dogged with the suspicion that she should be somewhere else. But Byrne himself? Why was he so apprehensive?

Just as McCadden was asking himself the question, they all

suddenly settled back to the comfort of knowing that the civilized world, including its police, always approves of caring families.

And then McCadden discovered something about the Alderman's relationships with his women. When Byrne got up to shake Harry Boyce's hand and nod at McCadden, he just ignored the three women. And he obviously expected the two detectives to ignore them as well. They didn't figure in what was going to happen, no more than the grapes and the portable phone on the locker could've figured. So the women were left with a choice. They could either hang around there like spare ribs or go somewhere else and feel useless in private. Either way they were nothing, and made to feel nothing, without the Alderman's approving eye on them.

The three reverted quickly to form and left. The wife went first, showing the good example to the kids and thinking she was covering the indecency with a shrill, 'I see you men have nothing on your minds except business. Come on, girls!'

Catherine and Tina at least kept their eyes turned away on the way out.

Byrne sat on the bed again as the women were leaving and gestured Boyce and McCadden into the emptied chairs. As soon as they were alone he said, 'So the woman, the hostage, vanished, did she? She wasn't all she said she was, then?'

'Who told you that?' McCadden asked sharply.

Byrne faltered. 'Well.' He took a breath. 'Well, it's more or less common knowledge around the hospital by now and, ah, my wife, my wife brought me the news.'

'Well, not to worry,' Harry Boyce started saying soothingly. 'I'm sure — '

'What did Peter Clarke want to talk to you about last night, Mr Byrne?' McCadden interrupted.

Boyce flashed an irritated glance across Byrne and right into McCadden's eyes. But Byrne was looking at McCadden, who was on his feet again now. And McCadden, even though he started pacing slowly, kept staring at Byrne.

There was something odd going on between McCadden and Byrne. Had been since McCadden had come into the room. A contest? A game? Even McCadden himself didn't know how serious it was.

Byrne said, 'He never got round to saying, to tell you the truth.'

'What do you *think* he wanted?' McCadden persisted.

'I couldn't say for certain. But I'll tell you this. He didn't want to harm me, Inspector. He was genuinely glad to have someone to lean on in there, someone who wasn't judging him at that particular point in time and who – '

'Yeah, right,' McCadden said impatiently. 'Did Clarke mention Billy Power, at all?'

Byrne bowed his head. You had to imagine the sorrow in his eyes.

He said, 'He told me he killed Billy, yes. He seemed to know that Billy worked for me. He seemed contrite about it, seemed to regret it.'

'Did he tell you *why* he killed him?'

'To settle an old score. Those were his words.'

'What do you think he meant by that? What old score?'

Byrne's head came up again then. So you could see the honesty clearly. 'I don't really know. He didn't say.'

'As you are no doubt aware,' McCadden said, 'Billy Power had a history of sexual assaults on women, including the attack on your own daughter, Tina, which you told me about yourself – '

'I never told you of any attack on Tina.'

'Didn't you?' McCadden seemed flabbergasted.

A pause.

Byrne wasn't going to pursue it.

McCadden said, 'Do you think that might've been the old score? An attack on Peter Clarke's girlfriend or sister? Clarke had a sister, didn't he?'

'I wouldn't know that, Inspector. I mean, what the old score really was. Peter has a sister, of course. Mary. Mary Butler, as she is now.'

'Hmm,' McCadden said. 'Tell me. When you got inside the house last night, what *exactly* happened?'

Harry Boyce, who'd been restless the last few minutes, stood

157

up suddenly and noisily. He walked across the room, breathing furiously, over to the doorway and back again. Byrne glanced at him once, but saw nothing of any significance in the movement. McCadden didn't take his eyes away from Byrne.

'The front door was open,' Byrne began, 'Peter was standing in the doorway between the hall and the front room.'

'Where was the woman?' McCadden asked.

'She was in the room behind him.'

'*Behind* him? Didn't you think that was odd?'

'Why?'

'Think about it. Where was he holding the knife, by the way?'

'Knife?' Byrne repeated. He frowned. 'I don't remember a knife. He had the gun. That was in his right hand. Not pointing at anything, though. Held limply, at his leg. Like this.'

'OK, he was standing in the doorway, holding the gun. Then what?'

'He gestured me into the front room with his free hand. He told me to sit on the settee. The woman was already sitting in one armchair. Peter sat down in the other one.'

'Was the woman frightened?'

Byrne frowned again. 'Well, no,' he said. 'No, she wasn't, now that you mention it.'

'Didn't *that* strike you as odd at the time?'

'I didn't really think about it,' Byrne admitted. 'I hardly thought about her at all, except to check that she was healthy, not in any immediate danger, obviously. I was thinking about Peter, really.'

'OK, you were on the settee, they were in the armchairs. Then what?'

'Well, we — '

'Which armchair was she in? Your left or your right?'

'My right. Why?'

'Nothing. Go on. Then what?'

'We talked about old times,' Byrne said, his head dropping a little again, the touch of a sad smile around his lips. 'I did most of the talking. You see, I had to work on the assumption that he'd got himself into a jam and didn't know how he was going to get out of it. So I kept talking to ease the pressure down a bit. I knew his father very well. I've known Peter a long time now, since he was a child.'

'Did you know the woman he sliced and murdered, Theresa Cheasty?'

The sad, wistful look went away from Byrne's face. Otherwise he didn't react much to McCadden's language.

He said, 'I met her once or twice in Peter's company, that's all. Peter's father had died a year before that, after a long illness. I visited him a lot at the time, of course. I always thought his father's death had some bearing on Peter's actions afterwards. It seemed to change him from an outgoing lad. He became withdrawn, unpredictable.'

Harry Boyce, not trying any more to keep the bad humour out of his voice, now asked abruptly, 'How did the shooting come about, Mr Byrne?'

Byrne turned towards him. 'I was trying to convince him at that stage to give himself up, Inspector Boyce. I think I was winning, too. Well, I suppose that's what he really wanted himself. To give himself up. He was holding the gun very slackly, as if he was getting ready to pass it across to me, but then the woman stood up suddenly. I don't know why. Maybe to stop him surrendering, because she said, "Don't, Peter!"'

It was Boyce who came up with the inevitable question. 'Do you mean they already knew each other?'

Byrne said, 'Well, I thought ... It puzzled me, yes.'

'Go on, Mr Byrne.'

Byrne continued. 'She said, "Don't, Peter!" Before I could even think of anything else to say or do, Peter just as suddenly shouted, "No!" He swung towards her and fired. He missed, of course, as you know. I was almost on top of him by then. I was shouting, "No, Peter! No, Peter!" Peter swung the gun back. I'll never know until the day I die whether at me or at himself. I'll never know whether I had nothing at all to do with the direction it ended up in or whether I pushed it away from myself and into him. The fact is anyway, that when he squeezed the trigger the barrel was pointing at his own chest.

159

Of course his hand went limp and I was able to pull the gun away then. Too late. It dropped to the floor. The gun. The woman was screaming. I left poor Peter there where he'd fallen and led the woman out of the house. That's it. The rest of it you know.'

After a short, a very short silence, Harry Boyce said, 'Thank you very much, Mr Byrne.'

And then Boyce stroked his heavy moustache and said, 'I'm sorry to have disturbed you so soon after your ordeal. We'll need to speak to you again, for a formal statement, but not for a while.'

And then Boyce turned and strode from the room.

And McCadden, even if he didn't follow the other's example with the gratitude, still had to follow his figure through the door.

Outside, Tom Byrne's wife was still sitting in the corridor. Harry Boyce had already nodded and passed on. McCadden sat beside her and said, 'Your husband is a very brave man, Mrs Byrne.'

'Thank you, Inspector.' A little glow on the cheeks as she said it, because it reflected well on her too.

McCadden placed a hand sympathetically on her forearm. 'And that poor woman who was with him in the house last night. Have you visited her yet?'

Byrne's wife suddenly put her hand up to cover her gasping mouth, one of those gestures that asked, *What will you think of me?* She said, 'No, no, I completely — '

'Maybe you'd like to visit her now, as you're here,' McCadden suggested helpfully.

Mrs Byrne's eyes brightened. 'Oh, yes!'

'Ask the nurse where she is,' McCadden said. 'And when the nurse tells you, don't forget to mention to your husband that I suggested the visit. Inspector McCadden.'

'Oh. Why?'

'Your husband thinks I have no heart. Don't forget. Inspector McCadden.'

McCadden got up, smiling. Feeling anything but amused, though. If Tom Byrne hadn't been told by his wife that the

160

woman had vanished, who *had* told him? There were no other visitors to Byrne that morning. McCadden had already checked it out at reception. Useless to ask if he'd made any phone calls. Byrne had a mobile phone by the bedside. And of course, Chief Superintendent Cody had taken two calls earlier that morning. And of course, if you wanted information on a case and you were a personal friend of the chief superintendent's . . .

Harry Boyce, in foul humour, was sitting at the wheel of the Ford Sierra, the engine ticking over. As soon as McCadden sat in, Boyce hit the accelerator and sprung the clutch out. The front wheels spun and screeched away, turning the heads of spectators.

McCadden made the effort.

Fairly reasonably, he said, 'You can go back to question him any time you like. I was always only to get one official shot.'

Boyce, burning the rubber on the way out the main gates as he turned back towards the city, said nothing.

McCadden asked, 'What did you think of his story?'

'You can ask the chief superintendent for a copy of my report,' Boyce snapped.

'Right,' McCadden said.

They drove the rest of the way to the station in silence and parted there, McCadden to key in a preliminary report on the computer, Boyce to report in person to Cody's office.

So when the summons came, less than ten minutes later, McCadden thought he was ready for it.

He wasn't.

Because something radical had changed in the meantime. McCadden sensed it immediately. Harry Boyce seemed to be *visibly* smiling, something that was hard for him to manage, given the cover his moustache offered the mouth. As for the chief superintendent, Cody wasn't tense or anxious or jumpy any more. He was leaning well back in his chair, comfortably stretched out, well on top of things.

Cody said, 'Sit down, Inspector.'

McCadden took a seat and said, forcing the play, 'I'm going

home to get some sleep, if that's all right. I've been up all night.'

'Yes,' Cody agreed. 'Yes, you do that. But before you go, would you please ensure that the Billy Power file and all related material are safely passed over to Inspector Boyce here. And you could make yourself available to him for consultation, say . . . tomorrow morning?'

McCadden wasn't ready for having his only excuse for butting in on the Peter Clarke case whipped away from him like that.

'The Power file?' he repeated. 'Why?'

Cody sighed. He said with exaggerated patience, 'As we're all satisfied that Peter Clarke killed Billy Power, and as Inspector Boyce's responsibility is Clarke, there is little point in both of you covering the same ground. The same holds for Sergeant Hyland, incidentally.'

'Hyland?' McCadden repeated. 'Paul Hyland isn't working with me on this case.'

'I'm quite aware of who's detailed to work with you — '

'In fact, he's not working at all. He's on sick leave.'

'I'm quite aware,' Cody said again, 'of who's detailed to work with you on this case. I'm also quite aware of who *isn't* detailed to work with you. Is that clear?'

'Yeah, sure.'

'Good. Any further questions?'

'Yes,' McCadden said. 'Did Tom Byrne telephone you from hospital this morning?'

The silence that followed, all fifteen seconds of it, a long silence, was finally broken when Cody rose slowly from behind the desk and said, 'Let's get a few things straight, Inspector. One, the events surrounding the death of Peter Clarke are Harry Boyce's responsibility. No one else's. Two, Tom Byrne's courageous involvement in that episode is not therefore your concern. And three, outside the times I summon you to this office, my own movements are not a matter I wish to make a topic of conversation among my subordinates. Is that understood?'

What could McCadden say, and mean it? Nothing. So he said, 'Yeah.' And meant the opposite.

162

'Good,' Cody said crisply. 'Thank you. That is all.'

But it wasn't.

As McCadden was rising, the chief superintendent started into it again.

'I will remind you,' he said, 'that above all, I will not have confusion in my district as to who is responsible for what and who is answerable to whom. We must have recognizable structures, a chain of command . . .'

Five minutes later, McCadden left the chief superintendent's office, everything gone from under him, all his potential targets snatched away from in front of him, and with hardly the energy any more to get in the car and drive home. He got in the car all right, but he didn't go back to the flat. He drove past it and onwards, out to Ballybeg Estate.

Ian Wilkins was sitting alone behind his desk in the Young Salamanders' house.

'I'm looking for Tina Byrne,' McCadden said.

'She's not here,' Wilkins told him sourly.

'When do you expect her back?'

'I don't.'

'Has she gone home?'

'Yes.'

'For good?'

Wilkins looked upwards, the hurt and anger in his eyes giving the answer.

'This is important,' McCadden said. 'Important for her. So I need the truth. When she told you about Billy Power accosting her, did she tell you that he had physically assaulted her or did she say that he had made verbal suggestions only?'

'Pestering her only.'

'Right. Thanks.'

McCadden got back in the car again, drove to the flat, undressed and crawled into bed, too exhausted to think, but not too exhausted to worry.

No one is ever too exhausted to worry.

twenty-six

Twelve-thirty the next day, McCadden was sitting at his desk, trying to process the evidence from a spate of burglaries in the prosperous South Parade, trying to motivate himself with the invention that the break-ins were interesting to anyone other than the thieves and the victims.

Over on the left of the desk the daily newspapers from the previous day were stacked in a neat pile. Over on the right were yesterday's evening newspapers. All the papers he'd missed out on buying and reading. More than ten of them in all. And Lennie Lombard's photos of Tom Byrne and the redhead hadn't made it into one of them. The siege and the death of Peter Clarke were reported, but not on the front pages. The front pages had the massacre of ten civilians in Northern Ireland and a shoot out at a bank robbery in Dublin. The good things they said about Alderman Tom Byrne, they said them on page four, or page five, or page six. They didn't name and didn't even feature the woman, saying only that she'd been held for a few hours and had made a full recovery.

A local story, really. And small beer.

If the siege had dragged on, of course, the story would've clawed its way into the national consciousness, advancing about a page a day, until it ended up on the front. That's what sold, the slow increase of tension, the constant threat of explosion, the human interest serial with the recognizable types. The Unstable Gunman. The Trapped Mediator. The Frightened Young Woman. Quick resolutions didn't sell, though. No investment for the editor putting it on the front page, because its legs weren't strong enough to carry it over to the next day. It was finished. Dead.

Now, if only McCadden himself could believe that, reconcile himself to that.

In between the two piles of newspapers on the desk, he had notes on the burglaries spread out in front of him. But he wasn't thinking of them. He was thinking of the redhead named Vera Dunne. He was thinking she wasn't Italian, she was Irish or English, maybe Dutch. And he was thinking it was a mistake to assume she was just a messenger, just an appendage, simply because she was a woman.

English, he decided then. English born. Maybe Irish parents.

The complexion, the colour of her hair, the structure of her face. Definitely English or Irish.

He'd only heard her speak two words. *The bullet.* And those while she'd been crying. Well, probably only pretending to cry. And if she was faking that, she was probably disguising the voice as well.

He tried to remember her accent, her pronunciation, her diction. Two words. Only three syllables. But he was certain of one thing at least. Even though she was meant to be hysterical, the tongue was properly between her teeth when she was saying *the*.

Twenty to one, Liam de Burgh came into the office. De Burgh was no longer assigned to McCadden. Neither were Jerry Tobin, Andy Laffan and John Widger. Or anyone else, for that matter.

De Burgh asked, 'You free for lunch?'

They didn't eat in any of the usual haunts. They drove to McCadden's flat in Manor Street. McCadden had only cheese in the fridge and they picked up a couple of French sticks on the way, but they'd come to get away from prying eyes and ears, not for the food.

McCadden said, 'Put on the water, will you. You'll find some teabags somewhere. I've got to make a call first.'

He went upstairs. In the loft, sitting on the bed, he flicked through his telephone book to find a number for Jeremy Grayson. Grayson, a policeman too, had the same rank as

165

himself, Detective Inspector, but in the Greater Manchester Police Force in England.

McCadden didn't cultivate official contacts in other police forces – official contacts, he reckoned, bought you official information – but he had friends here and there, England, elsewhere in Europe, two or three Americans, characters he'd met at conventions and training junkets and enjoyed their company.

The trouble was that McCadden was lazy about keeping up connections.

And it told.

'Inspector Grayson is no longer at this number, sir. You'll find him at the following number now. Are you ready?'

McCadden wrote the new number in his book and dialled it afterwards. Twice he got an engaged tone. Twice he was wrongly connected and had to abort the dialling and start again. The fifth time, with de Burgh calling from below that the water was boiling, he got through. Only to be told Grayson wasn't there, either. He was out to lunch.

McCadden left a message asking Grayson to ring him at the station. Then he went downstairs, a little irritated, and made some coffee and sat at the kitchen table with de Burgh.

And what de Burgh had to say didn't much improve his humour.

'That Italian character you asked me to check out.'

'Uh-huh. What about him?'

'He's not Italian.'

'He has to be Italian,' McCadden said.

De Burgh shook his head. 'Well, he's not.'

'Has to be,' McCadden insisted. 'As soon as I realized the woman must've brought the gun into the house, I also realized the make of the gun was important. It's Italian. A Beretta. It brought me back, back to ANDIAMO on Clarke's sweatshirt, which was just coincidence, back to the Italian watercolours in Billy Power's house, which might or might not be coincidence, and back to a rich Italian seen around town with a redhead. Has to be Italian.'

'He's not Italian,' de Burgh said again. 'He's an Iraqi.'

'Iraqi?'

'His name is Sayed Salman,' de Burgh said. 'Who told you he was Italian?'

McCadden thought of Vinnie Foley, the man with a brother-in-law who imported fruit from Italy. 'An expert on racial characteristics,' he said.

'I thought you didn't believe in experts.'

'And I was right,' McCadden said ruefully.

'He's Iraqi,' de Burgh said again.

'All right, all right. Iraqi, then. What've you got?'

'Sayed Salman is a trade official with the Iraqi government. We're not dealing with them at the moment, because of the UN embargo, so he can't be here officially. He arrived in Dublin, from London, on Monday 23 October, in a travelling party of four Iraqis, all male. Which sounds suspiciously like a trade delegation to me. However. He travelled from Dublin to Waterford last Friday 27 October, and stayed in Jurys Hotel from then until he booked out the day before yesterday, Tuesday 31 October. They asked about the things tourists usually ask about. Christ Church Cathedral, Art Gallery, the Glass Factory, Reginald's Tower. What they actually did when they went out, though, nobody knows. Possibly business meetings, but maybe not. You see, Sayed Salman is no stranger to Ireland, or to Waterford. Before the Gulf War and the UN embargo, he was in the country fairly often. He's been in Waterford a number of times before.'

McCadden looked glum. Another of the drawbacks of being a detective. Finding out people were decent sometimes only made you miserable.

'What about the woman?' he asked.

'I think you've got something wrong there,' de Burgh said. 'For a start, no one knows anything about Vera Dunne independently, no one knows a thing about her. And apart from what you say yourself, there's nothing to connect Sayed Salman with her. She didn't arrive with him. She didn't leave with him. She was never seen around the hotel in the meantime. You've got something wrong, but I think I know how you might check it out.'

167

'How?'

'This chap called Robbie Knox, he works as a reception clerk in Jurys. Do you know him?'

'No.'

'I know him from a group,' de Burgh said. 'Well, widowers and separated husbands, you know. He was on duty Sunday evening when someone rang the hotel and said they were from the Garda station and asked if there was a foreigner registered answering to a description which fitted Salman to a tee.'

McCadden sighed. He said, 'Yeah, and I know who it was made that phone call.'

'You couldn't.'

'It was Paul Hyland.'

De Burgh stared.

McCadden said, 'Paul saw the Iraqi at the greyhound track last Saturday night. But he didn't tell me about him at the briefing on Sunday. Afterwards he was pissed off because I left him off the team, so he obviously decided to follow the lead independently. He wanted to make an impression, to put two fingers in my face. We were talking about foreigners at the briefing; French container company, Italian watercolours. Anyway. What did your friend Knox do about the phone call?'

'He said he couldn't discuss guests over the phone, which was as much as admitting that the character was staying there. Paul told him to ring the station switchboard and ask to be put through to Detective Sergeant Hyland. Which he did. Except that Hyland wasn't in any longer when he called back. He'd just stepped out. What do you think?'

McCadden considered it and said, 'Paul won't have come up with anything major. He wouldn't have kept it to himself.'

'He's out sick,' de Burgh cut in.

'Well, that's the official line, isn't it? You can't follow a lead while you're stuck at a desk doing something else all day. Paul would've freed himself. That's his style.'

'So I've heard.'

McCadden paused. Something about Hyland niggling at his mind here. Something odd. Worrying. He couldn't pin it down. He said, 'I reckon he'll have *something* to offer. Maybe the redhead. Maybe the Iraqi doing a little private business. So it's good. It's good.'

But the way the afternoon wore on it was hard to keep hold of the feeling that anything was good.

Paul Hyland still wasn't in work. Hadn't been now for four days, Monday to Thursday. Good or bad? Was he really off chasing down the Iraqi in maverick style, or just sitting on his arse at home, still moping about being slighted?

McCadden wasn't able to find out too quickly, because Hyland's home phone kept ringing engaged all afternoon.

Three-thirty, Jeremy Grayson finally got through to McCadden's desk from Manchester. By then, McCadden was out himself, chasing down suspects in the South Parade burglaries. When he got back and found the message, he returned the call immediately. But he couldn't talk in comfort. Harry Boyce came into the office just then and stood by McCadden's desk, chewing on his heavy moustache.

'Listen,' McCadden said to Grayson, 'will you be there for another hour or so? I'll ring you back.'

When he replaced the receiver, he heard Boyce droning away above him.

'We still haven't had that consultation about the Billy Power case.'

'Yeah,' McCadden said. 'Hang on. I'm just going to the jacks.'

He did, too. But from the toilets he went to the car park, and from the car park drove back to his flat.

'I need a favour, Jeremy,' he said to Grayson. 'I've got a woman I think is English. I've got a name, Vera Dunne, which is probably false, but which she might have used before. She had papers in that name. I've got a good description, and I've got some photographs I can send you. She may have Iraqi associations. What can you do for me?'

'I take it that this is not an official request, Carl?'

'It may have gone through official channels already. I don't know. I can't use them, though.'

Grayson's tone was amused. 'Are you in trouble, Carl?'

'Not yet,' McCadden told him. 'It depends how far I push it. And what gives.'

'Delighted to help you push yourself into the shit, Carl. Send the stuff on as soon as you can.'

And finally, a little after quarter to six that evening, it wasn't looking anywhere near good any more.

McCadden was sitting in the front living room of Paul Hyland's three-bedroom estate house in Lisduggan with Hyland's wife. And Tracy Hyland was crying. She was crying the way women cry when they've sworn to themselves that they won't do it, more with rage and frustration than grief, fighting it all the way with long breaths and long silences.

On the glass-topped coffee table between them there was a small mountain of scattered envelopes and letters. All the letters were bills or final demands, all of them threats of one kind or another. A notification of impending legal action to repossess from a building society. Disconnection notices from the Electricity Supply Board and a cable company. Demands from financial institutions about various loans. Totting it all up, even roughly, you could see Hyland had been in for fifteen, twenty thousand. It came as a shock to McCadden. He'd thought Hyland had come back to gambling only recently, and that just a temporary fall after a long struggle.

All the letters were addressed to Hyland himself. But all the recent ones had been opened by his wife. And the reason Tracy Hyland was opening her husband's mail was that he hadn't been around to do it himself the past week.

'He's gone, Carl,' she said to McCadden. 'After you rang him last Sunday when we were having dinner, he said you asked him to go into the station.'

'I did, yes,' McCadden said.

Tracy Hyland raised her eyebrows. 'Did you? He said you did, but I didn't believe him. It was getting like that. I didn't believe him any more. He didn't come back all Sunday night. Was he working with you, then?'

McCadden shook his head. 'No, no, I just needed to see him for a few minutes, that was all.'

'He rang me early Monday morning,' Tracy Hyland said.

170

'He was in Liverpool, in England. He has a brother there. He said he needed time to himself, to sort himself out. He had a medical certificate sent in to the chief superintendent. Didn't you miss him at the station? Didn't you know he was gone?'

'No,' McCadden said, feeling awkward about it. 'I've been busy, you see, and, well, with the medical certificate, we assumed he was sick, on leave.'

'I thought he'd been working on a case with you.'

'No,' McCadden said again. 'No.'

He paused. He didn't know if Tracy Hyland was aware of it too, but there was another of those silences between them, the silences loaded with memories of their old friendship, with everything left unsaid, with questions about where they were going from here.

She was sitting on the floral settee, her head bowed, staring at her fingernails. He was opposite her in an armchair. He wished she'd raise her head, look at him again with her deep brown eyes, let him see what the options were.

But maybe she was uncertain, too. Even if she was, all he had to do was sit beside her. Put his arm around her shoulder. She'd rest her head on his chest. He'd stroke her long black hair . . .

Easy, then. Easiest thing in the world.

You couldn't even call it lust. Not even desire, really. Tracy's eyes and cheeks were red from crying. She looked exhausted. And she'd dressed carelessly, throwing on an old sweatshirt and the faded bottoms of a baggy tracksuit. But she was a friend. He liked her. More than that. Just looking at her, he felt the same hurt as she herself was feeling. And he hadn't been like that with a woman since his marriage had broken up.

Easy, then. All he had to do was get up and walk across and touch her. Touch her anywhere. Just once. Just one clear, unambiguous message between the two of them. And they'd both know where to go from there.

But instead he cleared his throat and asked, 'What time did Paul ring Monday morning?'

Fear. Too afraid to commit herself. His scepticism, his rejection of absolutes, having its down side too.

'What time did Paul ring Monday morning?'

Tracy Hyland raised her head and looked at him then. Now that the danger was past. And the opportunity, too. Her brown eyes seemed even duller than before.

She said, 'Six o'clock. That early.'

So McCadden put aside his shock and his sympathy and his regret. He thought.

If Hyland had reached Liverpool by early Monday morning, he must've sailed Sunday night. He must've packed it all in right after phoning Robbie Knox at Jurys Hotel. Which explained why Knox couldn't raise him when he rang the station back. In any case, Hyland hadn't been following an Iraqi in Waterford the past week, he'd been in Liverpool running away from things.

A dead end. Just another dead end.

And still. Still. Something about Paul Hyland still niggling at his mind. Something odd. Something out of place. And it wouldn't clarify. Wouldn't come back into focus.

He asked Tracy Hyland, 'Did you contact him in Liverpool? Did you ring him there?'

She shook her head. 'I rang once and his brother answered. He said Paul was fine. Imagine. Fine.'

'Did Paul ring you again?'

'He's to ring at the weekend.'

'Would you ask him to contact me?'

'If I remember, Carl. If he rings at all. If we're not shouting at each other. Why don't I give you his brother's number and you can ring yourself?'

'Yeah,' McCadden said. 'Yeah, OK.'

She scribbled on a newspaper and tore off a long section to offer him, too long for their hands to touch while it passed between them.

twenty-seven

Friday morning, they buried Peter Clarke in Ballygunner Cemetery. The graveyard was on top of a windswept hill in the south county, overlooking the city. By the time you got there, after a steep climb in second gear behind the hearse from the main road to the entrance, and then an even steeper climb on foot to the new graves, you were aching and breathless enough to be reminded of your own mortality.

McCadden, who took the morning off – to attend a funeral, as he told the chief superintendent over the phone – made the first climb, but not the second. There were no mourners to hide among. There was Clarke's sister, Mary Butler, a small, plump woman whose face was obscured by a black veil. There was another group of four, what looked like an aunt and uncle of Clarke's, with two children in their late teens. And that was it. The undertaker and the driver of the hearse, a couple of gravediggers, and a thin, self-conscious priest. A grim, depressing sending-off on a miserable day, with a freezing November wind driving the intermittent rain into your face.

McCadden stayed in his car at the main entrance to the cemetery. When the others came back down after a hurried ceremony, Mary Butler squeezed into the back seat of her relatives' Austin Metro, in beside the two pouting teenagers. McCadden followed them back to her home in Military Road. The relatives didn't stay, probably pleading a tiring journey somewhere or other. They drove away after dropping her outside the house.

McCadden parked on the opposite side of the street and

173

watched her unlock her door and go in, leaving the door open behind her to receive the sympathizers. The wind swept the rain into her hallway, wetting the mat and gathering in pools on the linoleum. At times, when it gusted, you could see it forcing the door itself back, knocking it against the wall.

McCadden waited almost ten minutes. In all that time, no one else approached the house. So he left the car then and went across and knocked himself, using the brass knocker over the black-edged funeral card that gave the times of the various ceremonies.

From inside, even though she couldn't have seen who it was, Mary Butler called out loudly, 'Come in! You're welcome!'

The interior was gloomy, almost black. The old-fashioned roller blinds had been pulled down over the windows and the one bulb that was lighting in the narrow hallway was weak, no more than thirty watt.

Mary Butler was in the front room on the left. Even in modern estate houses owned by relatively young couples, McCadden had noticed that these front rooms tended to be kept like museums, available only for christenings and foreign visitors and wakes.

Today's was a wake without mourners, though. Along two sides of the room, tables covered with old lace cloths held plates of home-cooked food. Sliced baked ham. Salads. Cold roast chicken. Soda bread. Brack.

McCadden stood in the doorway, thinking to himself that the woman must've worked to prepare all this since early that morning.

'Come in, boy!' Mary Butler called to him. 'Sit down. I'll make you a cup of tea.'

McCadden, his aloofness slipping a little, opened his mouth to tell her that he never drank tea, but then changed his mind and nodded agreeably.

It was only when Mary Butler came back from the kitchen with a fresh pot of tea, when McCadden's eyes had become used to the gloom, that he could see her properly. She looked matronly. She looked almost any age between thirty and fifty, although he knew that she was forty-three. Her face was as

174

plump and fleshy as her body. Her brown eyes gave no impression of sadness, only of a quiet acceptance, almost of fatalism.

She poured tea for both of them while McCadden took a plate, and then a knife and fork wrapped in a napkin, and helped himself to the buffet.

'I buried my husband two years ago this December,' she said, putting down a cup and saucer to bless herself. 'Lord have mercy on him. The house was crowded then. There was hardly enough to go round.'

'I don't suppose they mean to insult you,' McCadden said. 'I imagine they're uncomfortable. They wouldn't know what to say about your brother or what to talk about. They wouldn't even know whether it's right to talk about him at all.'

'Maybe you're right,' she agreed. 'But even if you are, 'tis only their own comfort they're concerned about, isn't it? Were you a friend of Peter's?'

She'd placed the cups of tea on a low table near two fireside armchairs and sat down on one side of the open fire. McCadden, putting his plate beside his cup, sat in the other armchair. Even here, you were aware of the bitter November wind, fighting to get down the chimney.

He said, 'No. Not a friend. I'm a Garda detective inspector. I knew your brother from another case. But I'm not here officially.'

He offered her his ID. She took it and produced her glasses to study it closely, with the kind of interest only someone totally indifferent to the police could've had.

'McCadden,' she said. 'Do you know what that means? You're not from Waterford, anyway.'

'No. I think we came from Ulster originally. Armagh.'

Mary Butler handed back the ID. 'It's good to know where you come from, anyway. It was Peter got me interested in the names, you know. He collected all the ones in Waterford once. First all the ones on the street, then everywhere else. He was always collecting something, Peter was. Always something. He had that list of names from the library.'

'The electoral register?'

'That's it. He had that to check out all the names.'

'He was never interested in politics, though, was he?'

'You'd think he would be, wouldn't you? All the figures. The results of things going back years. He was interested in everything else like that. It was the father put him off the politics. It was I reared Peter, you know. My poor mother, God rest her, died when he was born. I was nine years old at the time. That's all. Nineteen fifty-nine. The father had been fighting fifteen years or more for trade unions in Waterford. He lost three or four jobs all because of it, till they took him on as a union official himself. We saw even less of him then than before. That's why Peter was never bothered with the politics. He blamed the father for never being at home. And that's how I came to rear him. Not that you'd say I made much of a fist of that.'

'Well, I don't know,' McCadden said.

'But I'd better shut up,' Mary Butler apologized. 'Putting talk on you you don't want to hear, wasting your time like that.'

'No, no,' McCadden said quickly. 'Just the opposite. You see, I don't really understand your brother.'

'You wouldn't be the first one, Inspector. And you won't be the last.'

'Did he write to you from prison?' McCadden asked.

'No. Not once in all the three years. We didn't keep up after I was married. Peter was eighteen then, after doing his leaving examination in school and getting the office job for himself. We didn't keep up. We hardly knew one another the last sixteen years. The last time I saw him before they put him away was when the father died, four years ago. He brought the poor woman he killed, Theresa Cheasty, in to live with him after we buried the father.'

'What was she like?'

'I never met her. Not once. From what I heard, she was a decent soul. I never heard bad of her.'

'Do you know why he killed her?'

'I couldn't tell you, boy, no more than the man in the moon could. It came completely out of the blue, as far as I could see.'

176

Everything seemed to come out of the blue with Peter Clarke, McCadden thought. The murder of his lover. The escape from prison. Even his own death.

Mary Butler was saying, 'I never saw Peter raising a hand to anyone. He wasn't that type of man. All he ever cared about was collections. Coins, stamps, cigarette cards, the lot. The only thing I could ever think of was that she crossed him some way or other there. When he was a young lad he used to lock himself away in a room and the father'd be shouting at him to come out for one reason or another, or no reason at all most of the time, but he wouldn't budge, wouldn't even let on he heard. The only way you could ever get at him was to mess up his stamps or coins, although he wouldn't do anything even then except tidy them up again.'

'What about Tom Byrne?' McCadden asked. 'Did he know Peter at that stage?'

Mary Butler smiled. 'Ah,' he said, 'there's a story there.'

'I'm sure there is.'

'You'd want a long time to get through that story.'

'Well,' McCadden said, 'I don't have much of an inclination to go back out in this weather.'

Mary Butler leaned forward in her armchair and picked up the poker from the fireplace. She prodded carefully at the fire, rearranging the coals. Then she placed a couple of logs and a sod of turf on top of the pile. She kept the poker in her hands and kept staring at the flames.

'You see,' she said, 'the father was forty-nine years old when they took him on at Connolly Hall as a full-time trade union official in nineteen sixty-three. He was a Labour Party man all his life, of course. And that was when Tom Byrne came into the Labour Party as well, nineteen sixty-three, when he must've been, what, let me think, twenty-three, because he was born in April nineteen forty, exactly ten years older than myself, and I was thirteen at the time.

'I remember the two of them well. Like father and son they were, holding meetings together, drinking together. That was a great time for the Labour Party in the city. A lot of young people were coming into it then.

177

'That went on anyway for a good few years. Tom was always around our house. I thought the world of him, too, although he didn't look at me much except to say hello. I was a dumpy young one, sixteen at the time. Peter wouldn't give him the time of day at all, though. But that was the same as he always did with the father's friends.

'It went on, anyway, until nineteen sixty-eight or sixty-nine, I forget which, when the Labour Party was talking about going into a coalition with Fine Gael to make a government. The father wouldn't hear of it. Tom was all for it. They argued something bitter, the two of them, some nights in the house. Something bitter. Calling one another every name they could think of under the sun. And when the party went against the father, Tom never came back to the house.

'Peter would've been ten or eleven at the time, and that's when he started taking up with Tom Byrne himself. I suppose just to spite the father. And I suppose Tom encouraged it just to turn the knife as well.

'Of course, Tom didn't only vote for coalition. He left the party and joined the other crowd about a year later, and then he started setting himself up in business as well. Himself and Peter stayed friends all the years, though God knows what they ever found to talk about, because Peter wasn't interested in politics and Tom Byrne was never interested in anything else.'

There was silence for a while.

'I was at the graveyard earlier, you know,' McCadden said. 'I didn't notice Tom Byrne there.'

'Tom?' Mary Butler repeated, as if she was saying the name for the first time. She shook herself from the reverie and put the poker away and sat back in the armchair. 'Sure, they kept him in Ardkeen Hospital, didn't they?'

McCadden was taken aback. 'Did they?'

'They say it's the heart. It's not the best. I wouldn't blame the man, after all he's been through.'

McCadden had a flash of inspiration. He asked, 'Was Peter ever involved with or interested in either of Tom Byrne's two daughters? That you know of.'

178

Mary Butler shook her head. 'I wouldn't know, now. Sure, I hardly saw him these last sixteen years. I saw him when we buried the father and it came as a shock to me then that he was going steady with a woman. I saw him again after they put him in jail for murder and he asked me to sell the house. I didn't want to, but that's what I did. What money was left over after everything was waiting there for him until he came out. It's still waiting there now. He asked me to take out his own stuff and keep it all safe, and that was waiting for him too, up above in the attic, gathering dust. Myself and Seanie, my poor husband, God rest him, we nearly broke our backs putting it up there. Seanie was a lot older than me, nearly seventeen years. His old heart gave out in the end.'

'Would you mind,' McCadden asked, 'if I took a quick look at the stuff in the attic? Would that be possible?'

'You're welcome, boy.'

'I don't want to put you out.'

'It's no trouble. I don't know what you're looking for —'

'I don't know myself.'

'You're welcome to it, anyway, if you find it. There's one of those folding ladders, and I don't know if I have a torch or not —'

'It's all right. I've got one in the car.'

There were thick layers of dust-filled cobwebs around the attic door, and heaps of dead and desiccated spiders in the webs.

Inside, the space was neatly organized. Over to the left, under the lowest part of the sloping roof, there was a dusty but unused panda toy and the various parts of an infant's cot. Bought for who, McCadden wondered.

On the opposite side, five large cardboard boxes held Peter Clarke's material. Again there was the same neatness. Well, the same *mysterious* neatness, McCadden decided, as he climbed in and crouched and started unpacking and examining the material in the torchlight. Everything was either held in a folder or written or pasted in a notebook, but, apart from the albums of stamps, coins and cigarette cards, the folders and notebooks were all impenetrably titled. *AAB001OWA. CWC5060. BROC088. LHOR20.*

The range of material was bewildering, the reasons for keeping a lot of it not particularly obvious.

There was, for instance, an undated newspaper clipping of the sinking of the SS *Iowa* off the French coast:

> Everything possible was done to save the noble ship, but her fate was sealed. The sea claims its own, and the once proud and stately ship that was launched at Waterford found her grave on the rocky coast of Cherbourg.

There were short histories of Irish surnames and Irish families:

> *The Celtic family of CLARKE bears as arms three nettles leaves vert, symbols of antiquity and strength. In Irish the name is 'O Cleirigh', literally 'the descendants of Cleireach', a 9th century descendant of the King of Connacht, whose personal name meant 'a cleric' or 'a clerk'. Famous as poets and chroniclers, the family were also compilers of The Annals of the Four Masters . . .*

There was a list of books in stock at The Dublin Book Shop. *The History of Armagh by Stuart*, 15/-.

There were historical notes on local amenities and buildings:

> *Waterford owes its pretty public park to John A. Blake, one of the most useful and popular mayors who ever ruled in the city. The ground was cleared in 1855 and Lord Carlisle, the Lord Lieutenant of Ireland, opened the park in 1857.*

There was an index of song titles, cross-referenced with some other volumes where the words were recorded. 'Mary Arnold the Female Monster.' 'Mary Hamilton.' 'Mary of Dunloe.'

There were obscure lists of jumbled letters and numbers. *STA2310SOP. 056JHCRAIG. FU102OWDEWGODWIN. WE17PISHIGHCROTTY.*

There was a diary entry that caught McCadden's eye because of a reference to the greyhound track:

> *Went from the Old Tramore Road to the New Tramore Road. I was informed by an old man I met that a new Borough Boundary was marked out here in 1947. The old Borough Boundary mark is on the Ursuline Wall, so that the dog course at Kilcohan is outside the old Boundary mark.*

And more press cuttings, more local jottings, more local history, and more and more lists.

After an hour McCadden had a headache. Not from the poor light. Not even from the effort of reading Clarke's fairly convoluted handwriting. Just from knowing that if the key to the murders of Theresa Cheasty and Billy Power and to the death of Clarke himself was buried somewhere in this lot, it would take a team of trained detectives a week to sift through the stuff, and even then with no guarantee of recognizing the clue if they came across it.

McCadden felt beaten. Overwhelmed. He put the folders and notebooks back in the boxes, put out the torch, climbed out, and put back the door and the ladder.

When he went to thank Mary Butler, she was at the sink in the kitchen.

'Will you have another cup of tea?' she asked.

McCadden sighed.

He said wearily, 'Yeah. Thanks.'

181

twenty-eight

When McCadden came from Mary Butler's kitchen, he stood in the wet hallway outside, looking out at the slanting rain through the open doorway, and he thought there was something too neat about Tom Byrne's absences the past week.

The Thursday Billy Power was killed, Byrne threw a rare dinner party for one wife, one estranged daughter, one married daughter who saw him in secret, and one son-in-law who hated the sight of him. Why did he do that? A family council, maybe? Discuss Billy Power's attack on Tina? Explain to the others why he couldn't sack or prosecute the man, but assure them he'd taken steps to prevent anything like it happening again?

And now, the Friday Peter Clarke is buried, Byrne is still in hospital. Three nights. Still genuinely ill? Or faking it to avoid meeting Peter Clarke's sister? Lots of awkward things they might get round to talking about if he was there.

McCadden pulled up his collar and sprinted back to the car and took a few deep breaths before using the mobile to phone Ardkeen Hospital. Tom Byrne was still there, all right, but due to be discharged in forty minutes at two o'clock.

'Two o'clock?' McCadden repeated. 'I thought you always threw them out in the morning?'

'Mr Byrne requested further tests.'

'Hmm. Right.'

Just in case the tests were finished sooner, or Byrne changed his mind, or they got tired giving him the same clean bill of health, McCadden drove to the hospital immediately. Planning nothing, really. He couldn't afford to, not being on the case any more. But maybe he'd make a meeting look coincidental. Maybe he'd mention the Iraqi, Sayed Salman, and then the woman, Vera Dunne. Maybe he'd throw in Peter Clarke's notebooks and scrapbooks. Anything. Everything. Just to get a reaction that'd point him the way to go, tell him if his antipathy towards the man was only prejudice or not.

And that's how McCadden came to see, at two o'clock that afternoon, the look of terror in Tom Byrne's eyes.

The rain had eased by then. The wind had dropped. There was a light drizzle drifting straight down. The temperature had fallen too, getting cold enough to start you thinking of winter and snow.

McCadden was outside the car, standing with his elbows resting on its roof and looking over from the car park towards the hospital's reception area, wondering if he should stay put or go in and flush out Byrne himself. He'd been like that for twenty-five minutes, and asking himself the same question for twenty-five minutes. And he was still undecided.

Two o'clock on the button, Tom Byrne came out alone through the main doors, carrying an overnight bag. He stopped at the top of the steps and stood there to search around, looking for someone who'd arranged to pick him up. And he saw McCadden immediately.

Byrne's eyes widened with dread. He stared helplessly for a few seconds, not knowing what to do, like a rabbit caught in torchlight. Then, a little shakily, he came down the steps staring at his own feet and slunk away left to a waiting taxi.

McCadden got in the car and swung round to follow the taxi. Thinking, it had to be. Had to be that Byrne assumed he was following him, watching his movements, waiting for a slip. Had to be, too, that Byrne had something tucked away in his life, all ready to slip on.

The taxi brought Byrne to his home three miles south of the city, an ugly, sprawling residence on the main road to the sea at Dunmore East, mock Georgian in the centre, with what looked like two wings of imitation Victorian flapping out from it. There was a short driveway to the front door. Its grounds were all behind the house itself.

McCadden drove past, took a right down a lane and pulled the Sierra out of sight. He got out and climbed to the brow of the hill overlooking the house. He'd been settled there for fifteen minutes when the patrol car finally rolled into the driveway and two uniforms got out to chat with Byrne at his front door. Afterwards they searched the grounds. Then they got back in the patrol car and drove up and down the main road a couple of times. And finally they went back to Byrne to report that no, there were no intruders in the grounds, no one staking out the house, no burglars, no reporters, and no protesters.

Once they'd left, McCadden came down off his perch and got the Sierra into a better position for pulling out again quickly. He didn't have to wait long. Byrne's gold Mercedes eased past him almost immediately.

At the next fork, the Mercedes swung left, heading for the small fishing village of Passage East. An impossible place to follow a car in or through without being seen. The village was a labyrinth of narrow streets and tall houses packed into a pocket of land between the sea and an overhanging cliff.

Coming down the steep hill that ended in the village itself, McCadden was hoping the Mercedes had passed through and he'd be able to pick it up on the other side. He was out of luck. As soon as he turned the corner at the bottom of the hill he saw its distinctive gold sandwiched between two red Toyotas in the middle of a five-car queue for the ferry across Waterford Harbour and into County Wexford. He swung sharply right into the tiny square, screeching the tyres a little, but not so much that anyone sitting inside their car on a wet November afternoon with all the windows closed would notice. Glancing across the harbour, he saw that the ferry had just reached the other side on its outward journey. So it would take a while to unload and pack them in over there and then make the trip back to Passage East.

McCadden parked the Sierra around the corner. He took a small pair of binoculars from the glove compartment and got out and walked back to the little square, keeping out of sight as much as possible, hogging the Mercedes' blind spots. From there he climbed the overgrown, winding pathway up the lower part of the cliff that dominated the village. About half-way up, concealed by blackberry bushes and commanding perfect views of the harbour, the pier and the entrances to the square below, he settled down to watch.

That was his gamble. The small ferry held ten or twelve cars. Probably no more than that. Once on it, you couldn't possibly conceal yourself from other passengers. Byrne would see him, give him that look of terror again, and not go through with what he was up to. And above all, McCadden wanted to find out where Byrne was heading, whom he was meeting. So he'd let him go. Watch him through the glasses. If he drove off on the other side, McCadden could always radio someone to pick him up over there. It would mean showing his hand to the superintendent. But what the hell. That was the gamble.

The light was starting to go. As the ferry pulled away from the opposite pier on one of its last backward journeys of the day, Tom Byrne suddenly got out of his car. He looked across the harbour at the approaching ferry. He looked closely, *peered*, as if he was trying to distinguish the cars and the travellers. He closed the door of his own Mercedes and walked away from it a bit. He glanced at his watch. He stared at the ferry again. Turning, frowning, he marched back along the line of cars behind his own, furtively searching through the windscreens, wondering if he'd missed someone earlier. He hadn't, obviously, because he turned back with the same worry on his face. After that he paced. And then, as the ferry docked and lowered its ramp and the cars either side of him coughed into life, he finally panicked. He tore open the Mercedes' door. He sat in. With the Toyota behind him blasting its horn, he reversed a small distance, crunched into first to jerk forward while locking right, then moved back and forth like that, repeatedly, the sweat matting his sparse sandy hair over his pale face, until he had enough space to swing out and park again to one side.

McCadden understood. Byrne had planned to meet someone on the ferry itself. They'd get through a little business.

Byrne would come back to Passage East on the ferry. The other would roll off the opposite side and drive into County Wexford. Something like that.

Only the other hadn't shown. And why? You don't make elaborate arrangements like that and then not bother even to show. So why?

McCadden spent another hour and a half on the hill, chewing over that question, because Byrne spent an hour and a half chewing it over below him. Since McCadden was the only one of the pair who knew that Byrne was under surveillance, he had a better crack at the answer. Someone had seen McCadden himself and backed off.

The ferry came back on its final journey and threw out a red Mini driven by a white-haired old lady. The Mini rolled on to the quay and then crunched and roared up the steep hill, out of the village and off towards Waterford. Nothing else entered or left the village in the ninety minutes.

The hour and a half brought them into darkness and almost up to five in the evening. And then Byrne finally turned the key in the ignition, hit the headlights and swung the nose of the Mercedes towards Waterford and headed home to his mock mansion. Stiff and cold and hungry, McCadden went back down the winding pathway to follow him.

He didn't expect Byrne to leave home again that evening. He thought the Alderman would make a few phone calls, have someone tell him what the story was, warn him to keep his head down for a few days or quickly clear up the problem. But the man was anxious now. He was confused and edgy, disappointed, in the mood for getting something done. So if he was going to make some more mistakes, he'd probably make them now.

Still hungry, but warmer and looser than before, McCadden decided to stay with it a while longer.

And eight o'clock, with a church bell pealing somewhere and the rain coming down heavily again, the front door of the mansion opened under the semicircular fanlight, and Tom Byrne came out between the stone pilasters and stepped down towards the Mercedes in the driveway. This time, though, his wife and Tina came out behind him and joined him in the car.

They drove back towards the city, a slow, uncomfortable journey in torrential rain, turning towards Parade Quay and then swinging into a parking space outside the Munster pub, a rambling, fashionable old place behind the famous Reginald's Tower that the invading Danes had built in 1003, the oldest tower in Ireland guarding the river entrance to the oldest city.

McCadden had trouble finding another parking space and got wet sprinting back from Parade Quay to the Munster. Then he had trouble finding the Byrnes in the pub, a place of numerous bars and lounges, and all of them crowded. He was getting to the point of worrying about it, wondering if they'd slipped him, going in one entrance and out another, when he finally caught up with them.

They were sitting in a small back lounge, behind a white-haired old man who was on his feet in the centre of the room, belting out something from *HMS Pinafore*. The trouble was, they were sitting between Chief Superintendent Daniel Cody on their right and Cody's wife, Anna, on their left.

McCadden stopped dead in the doorway, momentarily closed his eyes and muttered, 'Shit!'

Someone next to him hissed angrily: 'Ssshh!'

And the hiss jumped from drinker to drinker in the rapt audience, like an electrical spark, until everyone was staring angrily at the sodden newcomer in the doorway.

'Ssshh! Ssshh! Ssshh!'

Cody. And Cody's wife. She must've been discharged from hospital too, also with a clean bill of health. She had that glowing look about her. And Cody himself must have taken the welcome phone call on Wednesday, when he'd changed in a few hours from nervy to relaxed, from dour to sunny, and kicked McCadden off the Billy Power case as a present to himself.

Cody wasn't sunny looking now, though. A few words from Tom Byrne into his ear, enquiring about McCadden's current workload, and a few words from Cody back to the Alderman confirming McCadden shouldn't be following him, and Cody's cold eyes were staring hard, while a little of the colour had come back to Byrne's cheeks.

And then, as the white-haired old singer finished to loud applause and the session's MC called a short break, McCadden had an inspiration. He needed to muddy the waters, that was all. Just make a case for coincidence. He crossed the room to greet Anna Cody and enquire about her health. Byrne's wife was smiling inanely at him. Tina Byrne was considering him curiously, but without apprehension now. Byrne himself was looking to Cody.

Still talking, not leaving any gaps to be exploited, McCadden sat on a vacant stool at the table, and flourished his inspiration, saying, 'It was Sergeant Ryan who recommended here. You see, as I told Ryan, there's a song's been bothering me. All I heard one night was part of a verse and it stuck in my mind for one reason or another. But nobody seems to know what the song is.'

'Sing it,' Anna Cody said.

McCadden laughed. 'I can't sing.'

'Nonsense,' she insisted. 'Everyone can sing.'

'No, honestly. I can't sing.'

'Say the words, then.'

McCadden said, 'Well, OK. It actually goes, *We robbed and plundered many a ship down on the Spanish Main, Caused many the poor widow and orphan child in sorrow to remain. We made their crews to walk our planks and they hung* something something something. And that's it, really.'

Anna Cody was frowning. She said, 'I don't think I've ever heard that. Do you know what it is, Dan?'

Cody was glaring furiously at McCadden, but the wife that had just been restored to him had first call on his emotions. He said gently, 'No, dear. I don't.'

'Tom might know,' Anna Cody said. And turned to her right. 'Tom? Tom? Are you all right, Tom?'

Tom Byrne had gone deathly pale again. His mouth was slack and hanging open a little. And he was staring at McCadden with haunted eyes that were also full of hatred.

McCadden looked back at him with astonishment. Until

188

something clicked in his mind and he thought, No, don't show surprise. Make it look deliberate. Whatever it is.

Things came together then.

Byrne's wife and daughter were anxiously about him, holding his hand, feeling his forehead.

Byrne himself, the tough years on the hustings coming good for him, was pushing them away, saying, 'No, no, I'm all right, I'm all right. It must be the air in here. I just felt a little faint for a moment.'

'Try and remember you're only out of hospital today, dear.'

Superintendent Cody was leaning across the table, presumably to invite McCadden to somewhere quiet for a grilling, when the MC started calling for order again, tinkling a little bell and saying, 'Thank you, ladies and gentlemen. Thank you. Quiet now. Thank you. The very best of order now for "Happy Moments" from *Maritana* by Waterford's very own William Vincent Wallace, with . . . Chief Superintendent Daniel Cody.'

Cody was suddenly on his feet, far away from McCadden. And Anna Cody, the Byrnes and even McCadden himself were all applauding. And all the others in the lounge were applauding too.

The MC had both his arms outstretched, one an invitation to Cody, the other a request for quiet from the audience.

Cody took a deep breath and sang in a powerful, but sensitive voice:

In happy moments day by day,
The sands of life must pass,
In swift and tranquil thoughts away,
From time's unerring glass.

And everyone in the room was mouthing the words along with him. Everyone except McCadden, who had the words of another song on his mind as he got up from the stool and quietly slipped away.

twenty-nine

Saturday morning, early, McCadden rang de Burgh.

He said, 'I know I'm close to something, Liam, but I don't know what. Tom Byrne left hospital yesterday and tried to make a meeting, or a drop, or a collection, on the Passage East car ferry. His contact didn't show. Probably because I was spotted following Byrne. Two things. Byrne knows from Cody I'm not supposed to be tailing him. And I need to do something else right now. Would you be able to keep a discreet eye on him for the day? Whoever is trying to meet him has to make another attempt soon. Ring me at home, say, five this afternoon?'

De Burgh said, 'Yeah, sure.' Without thinking too much about it.

As soon as McCadden broke the connection, he started dialling again, scratching around, looking for a reason for Tom Byrne's weird reaction to half a verse of an obscure ballad. He bothered everyone he knew that morning with the two and a half lines he already had. The response was always the same.

'You know who might be able to help you with that, now? You should try . . .'

So he tried. He tried musicians. He tried local historians. He tried arts organizers. He tried poets. He tried visiting folk singers in their hotel rooms.

Michael Drohan, a bus driver, amateur historian, editor of a booklet of local love songs, chewed over McCadden's request a long time, but said finally, 'You know who might be able to help you with that, now?'

190

McCadden groaned. 'I've already been there,' he muttered. 'Whoever it is, I've already been there.'

Drohan said, 'No, I'm pretty sure of this. That's a sea song, right? Pirates and that. Three old brothers. All of them went to sea and all of them good singers. I'm pretty sure they'll help you out.' He paused and said without irony, 'If they're not all dead by now.'

McCadden took up the pencil. 'All right. Who are they?'

'That's the funny thing, their names are gone right out of my head.'

'Where can I find them, then?'

'You can't miss the place. It's a whitewashed cottage on the road between Woodstown and Passage East, just at the turn off there to the old Geneva Barracks.'

'Passage?' McCadden repeated. 'I was out there yesterday.'

'Well, you should've asked me yesterday morning, then.'

'I didn't know yesterday morning, Michael.'

'Where did you hear it, anyway?'

'Somebody singing it passing by the flat in the middle of the night last . . . Wednesday.'

'But, sure, you must've known it yesterday, then.'

McCadden started to say something, but muttered instead, 'It doesn't matter. Listen, Michael, as I have you here. You'd know most of the people involved in local history, wouldn't you?'

'I would, I suppose, yeah.'

'Ever come across Peter Clarke in that line?'

'Clarke?' Drohan repeated. 'You mean the chap escaped — '

'Yeah. Ever come across him?'

'Not at all. No one else ever did, either. That's the sort of thing fellas would talk about.'

'OK. Thanks for the tip, anyway.'

It was twelve o'clock, the city's churches pealing out the Angelus in the background, when McCadden hung up on Michael Drohan. It would take him twenty-five minutes to get to Passage East, maybe an hour for the round trip. Not long, but no guarantee the journey wouldn't be wasted. And there was another thing he had to do first.

191

So, still in the dark about the song, he went back to Mary Butler and drank another cup of her tea and went back up the ladder to her attic.

He found the notebook with the index of song titles without too much bother, remembering where he'd left it the day before. The cross references in the margins all listed other notebooks containing the lyrics. *BALYSE001/082. BALYL0179/234. BALYREBO71/149.* And so on. And on. And on.

McCadden found them all, eventually. He read or flicked through them all, eventually. Lots of bold, undaunted heroes riding out. Lots of mornings in the merry month of May. Lots of emigrants dreaming of home from the shores of Amerikay. But not the words he was looking for.

In one of the notebooks, though, he found a sheet of notepaper with the lyrics of a ballad set out in someone else's handwriting. A note above the song was signed *Theresa*. The sheet had been stapled to the page where Clarke himself had transcribed the words of the ballad:

> *This is the one my Aunt Sarah sang for me. She says her own mother had it, but she doesn't know where it came from before that.*
>
> *Theresa*

DUNGARVAN!

Dungarvan, no great Muse has spoken for thee:
Thou must have some laurel, fair child of the sea:
My pen (being a quill one) can't give thee thy due,
But such as it is I bestow it on you.

Gay champions of fashion may sneer at thy name,
And give poor Dungarvan a very bad fame:
'The town is so dull! there is no one to see!
'The streets are so poky! the shops are so wee!'

The whole notebook was devoted to songs about places in County Waterford. Dungarvan. Woodstown. Passage East. Cappoquin.

McCadden lifted the staple and took out the loose sheet

and folded it carefully along its original creases before putting it in the inside pocket of his jacket.

The batteries were dying in the torch and its light fading, but McCadden stayed on a while longer. He picked up notebooks at random, let them fall open, skimmed over the contents of pages. Everything was fascinating, everything potentially significant, and yet nothing was clear enough to be exciting. All tantalizing. Opaque. Frustrating. In one notebook, transcribing reports of crimes and court cases, McCadden kept turning the pages, enjoying the familiarity for a change, until he suddenly struck a slightly richer seam:

'You have heard the defendant claim,' said Mr Justice Owlett, 'that he was driven mad by the unfortunate woman's attentions. Her obsessive behaviour, her jealousy, her constant weeping and her spying are all advanced as mitigating factors. While neither premeditation nor motive is essential for a conviction of murder, you are asked by the prosecution to believe that the defendant, in inflicting the fatal head injuries with the hammer he had purchased the day before . . .'

The torch failed. In the darkness, still holding the open notebook, McCadden sat on the old wooden fruit box he'd been using as a chair and thought that the notebooks were like curtained windows on to Clarke's mind. Mostly they gave back only your own puzzled reflection. Now and then you got a glimpse through parted material.

He closed the notebook and put it in his pocket and brought it back downstairs with him.

Mary Butler was in her kitchen. She took a glance at him and said, 'Well?'

McCadden shook his head. 'Would it be all right if I took this one home with me over the weekend, to have a closer look at it?'

'You know you don't have to ask.'

'Thanks.'

'I'll make you another cup of tea,' Mary Butler offered. 'Sit down there.'

McCadden shook his head again. 'Do you know where Theresa Cheasty's family is living?'

'She was from Hennessy's Road herself. Any more than that I don't know.'

It was two in the afternoon when McCadden reached Hennessy's Road, a long, densely populated street running from the external walls of the old Viking Town almost to the outskirts of the present city. But he didn't have to ask much before being directed to the Cheastys' house. When you had a murder victim in the family, everyone knew where you lived.

A teenage girl opened the door.

'Is your mother or father in?' McCadden asked.

She showed him into the front room. After a while a woman in her mid-twenties came in and sat in one armchair and gestured McCadden into the other. Obviously a sister of the teenager, who came back to lean in the open doorway, anxiously biting a fingernail.

McCadden said, 'My name is Carl McCadden. I'm a Garda inspector.'

'Do you have identification?' the woman asked.

When she took it from him she studied it closely, as if she suspected it was a forgery. She checked McCadden's face against the photograph a couple of times. Handing it back, she asked, 'What do you want, Inspector?'

The girl in the doorway took her fingernail from her mouth and said bitterly, 'He wants to ask questions about Theresa. What else would he want?'

'Is that true?' the woman asked.

'Yes,' McCadden said. 'But can I explain?'

The woman said coldly, 'Theresa is dead, Inspector. My mother died less than a year after her. Nothing is going to bring either of them back. And now with Peter Clarke escaped from prison and dead himself, there are reporters out here every day looking for stories to sell their newspapers. Isn't it time you all let Theresa and mother rest in peace?'

'Can I explain?' McCadden asked again. 'Or better, can I ask you just one question?'

'What question?'

194

'Do you know *why* Peter Clarke killed your sister?'

The woman hesitated. The anger in her eyes softened to let through a dart of interest as she glanced at McCadden again. Finally she said, 'No, I don't. Why *did* he kill her?'

'I don't know,' McCadden said. 'But I'd like to. Wouldn't you?'

The woman was silent for a while. McCadden could hear a clock ticking in the room and his gaze found it after a quick search. It was on top of the glass cabinet, trapped in a monstrous wooden case that was shaped like a sitting dog.

The woman, sharing a look with her sister in the doorway, said, 'I'm Margaret Cheasty. This is Caroline.'

McCadden took out the sheet of paper with the note and the lyrics of the song on it. 'Was that written by Theresa?'

'Yes, that's her writing. Aunt Sarah died nearly four years ago, though. Before Theresa herself.'

'Did Theresa do a lot of that sort of thing for Clarke?' McCadden asked. 'Research. Gathering information. Recording material.'

'I don't really know anything about what they did together, Inspector. I know what Theresa was like before she met Peter Clarke and I know what she was like afterwards.'

'A change for the worse, was it?'

'I thought so.'

'In what way?'

She hesitated again. Not from hostility this time, but from surprise. She wasn't used to finding a questioner in sympathy with her.

She said, 'Theresa was outgoing. She had plenty of friends. She read a lot, but she also went out a lot. Sport. Discos. Drinks. After meeting Peter Clarke she became quieter, more a loner, much more serious. Another of our aunts had a caravan by the seaside and she took to spending a lot of her time alone down there, even in winter.'

'Even after moving in to live with Clarke?'

'No. That's one of the things I *do* know about their life together. When Clarke's father died and she went to live with him in Poleberry, she didn't stay in the caravan any more. In

195

fact, she cut off contact with all of us, not only Aunt Margaret.'

'Was that bad?'

'I thought so, yes. You see, she neglected all her own interests and all her own friends and devoted all her time to what he wanted to do. He had no friends, really. I thought something as one-sided as that was unhealthy.'

'How much older than you was she?'

'Three years.'

'So you would have been quite close, in terms of experiences.'

'We were very close, yes.'

'Did she talk to you about Clarke?'

'Never, no.'

'About other boyfriends?'

'She had few enough. She tended to develop serious rather than casual relationships. But those she had, we discussed.'

'Why not Clarke?'

Margaret Cheasty shrugged. 'She could probably anticipate my objections, although that never bothered her before. I don't know. There was an element of secrecy about their relationship, furtiveness, you know, right from the very beginning. It was almost like guilt.'

'What did Theresa work at before she died?'

'In the year or so before she was killed, she didn't work. That was another thing. She gave up her job when she went to live with Clarke. Before that she was a secretary with an import company here in town.'

'Do you know how they met, herself and Clarke?'

'No. I don't think it was any of the usual ways. Clarke didn't go to dances or discos or pubs. It might have been through work. She didn't tell me.'

'So,' McCadden said, 'to go back to my original question, in the light of what you've said, do you think she did a lot of research work for him?'

'I couldn't be sure, but I suppose so, yes.'

'Was she unhappy?'

'I wouldn't say she was unhappy, no. But I wouldn't call her happy, either. She was obsessive. Like Clarke himself.'

'You knew Clarke, obviously.'

'I met him a number of times, always by accident. He never came to the house. I didn't like him. He didn't like us. He tried to keep Theresa to himself and was jealous of anyone else having time with her. I think he encouraged her to lose contact with us. I thought he was like a dog with a bone, quiet until he imagined you threatened him. We kept away from him as much as we could. Like I said, we didn't see much of Theresa after she went to live with him.'

'Do you know Alderman Tom Byrne?'

'I know of him, yes.'

'Do you know if Theresa ever had any dealings with him?'

'With Tom Byrne? No, I don't think so. He's not in our constituency.'

'Do you know if she ever met a character called Billy Power?'

'You mean the chap who was murdered here, whose body was found last weekend?'

'Yes.'

'No. The first I heard of him was in the newspapers.'

'Before her death, did Theresa ever give any indication that she was in danger?'

'As I said, we'd largely lost touch by then.'

'Before that. Before she went to live with him. While she was at home and developing the relationship. Did she ever indicate that Clarke had threatened her?'

'No, there was never any question of that. His influence over her was psychological.'

'Do you have any of her papers? Any possessions? Any stuff that might've been taken from Clarke's house after her death?'

'Mother had, yes. Well . . . she had Theresa's photo, some of her jewellery, other bits and pieces, on the dressing table in her bedroom. My father hasn't lived here for a long time. We left it there after mother died. Nobody uses the room.'

'Would you mind if I had a look?' McCadden asked. 'I won't disturb anything.'

'No, it's OK. It probably wouldn't do any harm to, you know, finish with it. This way.'

197

The coloured photograph on the dressing table in the musty bedroom showed Theresa Cheasty in her mid-twenties, two or three years before her death, the same age as her sister Margaret was now. She had the same coal-black hair as her sisters, the same deep brown eyes and the same dark skin, but she'd been unluckier than they were. Her face was rounder, plainer, more studious. It didn't help that she was wearing a fairly ugly pair of glasses with broad rims.

There was more than the photograph and a few trinkets involved in the memorial. In the three drawers of the dressing table, Theresa Cheasty's mother had collected and stored everything that could be found relating to her daughter's life. School copy books. Bracelets. Valentine cards. Medals and certificates. Items of clothing. A colouring book from early childhood.

McCadden removed them one by one and laid them carefully on the bed. Two paperbacks. A diary from Theresa's fourteenth year. A folder of notes and exercises from a French language course. A small parcel of letters tied with a pink ribbon.

'Would you mind?' McCadden asked.

Margaret Cheasty shook her head.

The letters were mostly predictable. Early ones from pen pals in Malta and America. Later ones from a boyfriend in Dublin, from girlfriends on holidays. A couple of official notices. And then, in the middle of the bunch, a blue Belvedere Bond envelope with no stamp, with only her name and no address written on the front in a shaking hand. No address, but still sealed. And inside the envelope, a sheet of matching blue notepaper and two lines of text in the same handwriting:

My dear Theresa,
Do keep in mind, dear child, that I am not dead, yet.

G.B.

McCadden handed the note to Margaret Cheasty. 'Who's G.B.?'

'I've no idea,' she said finally. 'No idea at all. I don't think I know any G.B. It looks like a joke, though.'

'No,' McCadden said. 'It's no joke. If it was a joke the stationery would be cheaper and the form of address would be different, lighter, more humorous.'

My dear Theresa, on the other hand, was serious, familiar, slightly condescending. It had to be from someone older, probably much older than Theresa Cheasty. The same familiarity, the same condescension, the same slightly dated touch in the phrasing, were all evident in the note itself as well. And the placing of that comma between *dead* and *yet* intrigued McCadden. Someone condemned to death? Someone awaiting death from illness? Someone threatened with death? Someone whose death would have rough consequences for Theresa Cheasty?

'Would you mind if I kept that?' McCadden asked Margaret Cheasty. 'For a while, anyway.'

'If it helps.'

'Well,' McCadden said. 'It might. It might.'

Back in the flat at four o'clock, McCadden tried another few people with the verse of that obscure ballad that had ruffled Tom Byrne. He kept at it, without success, for thirty minutes, then rang a Chinese take-away for a delivery and left the phone free afterwards. Five minutes to five, he started into a special fried rice. Five o'clock, on the button, de Burgh rang.

McCadden snatched at the phone. 'Yeah?'

De Burgh said, 'I've had an easy time so far. Byrne's been sitting in the house all day. The daughter, Tina, went out at two o'clock in the afternoon, came back about an hour ago. The wife went out shopping this morning. I couldn't follow either of them, so they could've got away with something. What do you think?'

McCadden said, 'Even if they knew what he was in to, I don't think he'd trust them. He's got a pretty low opinion of women. No, he's got something else lined up, maybe this evening, maybe tomorrow.'

'I think I know what it might be.'

'Hang on,' McCadden interrupted. 'What's the wife's first name, do you know?'

'Georgina,' de Burgh said. 'Georgina Byrne. Why?'

McCadden felt a tingling in the back of his neck and down his spine. 'Just curious. What were you going to say?'

'There's a fund-raising dinner in the Tower Hotel tonight,' de Burgh said. 'Tom Byrne will be there. The thing about it is, it's all-ticket. You won't be able to get in.'

'Shit!' McCadden said. 'Look, hang on for me there, will you? Say about an hour, an hour and a half.'

McCadden got up to pace after hanging up, leaving the rest of the Chinese dinner going cold in the kitchen. Eight steps across the floorboards, eight steps back, the loose board creaking on the turn.

Fund-raising dinner. Who'd mentioned a fund-raising dinner to him recently? Fund-raising dinner. Tower Hotel. Saturday night. He flicked backwards, back through the days, separating them by events, back through the funeral of Peter Clarke, through Lennie Lombard's studio, through the siege in Ballybeg, until he finally hit it.

He went up to the loft then to check the telephone book he kept in the locker there. He sat on the bed to dial a number. The phone at the other end rang seven times.

'Good evening to you,' the voice said. 'Michael Terry speaking.'

McCadden sighed with relief. He said urgently, 'Michael. Carl McCadden.'

'Carl,' Terry said richly.

If he'd had time, the suggestiveness Terry got out of his name would've worried McCadden as much as usual. But he was in a hurry, didn't even notice it on this occasion.

'Last Monday,' he said. 'You remember, Michael? At the station you were selling tickets for a fund-raising dinner in the Tower Hotel tonight . . .'

thirty

McCadden had forgotten to ask what the Friends of the Brockenshaw Collection wore to their annual fund-raising dinner. He didn't own a dress suit. And by the time the problem hit him, seven-thirty that evening, it was too late to hire or borrow one.

He put on the lightweight, cream linen suit he'd bought a few months earlier, with a cream waistcoat and black vest and brown loafers, and when he reached the Tower Hotel drank in the bar for ten minutes to gauge the effect. He didn't see any monkey suits. And no one paid much attention to him. So he finished his vodka and white and strolled back to the reception desk out front.

'Hi. I've got to collect a ticket for tonight's dinner that's been left for me.'

The clerk was scribbling and didn't raise his head. 'And the name, sir?'

'McCadden. Carl McCadden.'

The clerk stopped writing and looked up then. He said, 'Ah, yes,' in an odd, timid kind of voice. He moistened his lips and added, 'I believe the, ah, Secretary of the Brockenshaw Collection has your, ah, ticket himself. Would you wait here, please?'

McCadden turned and leaned against the desk while waiting. Most of the passing faces he didn't recognize. One he did belonged to the photographer, Lennie Lombard. Lombard, his slight figure lost in a baggy lime suit, was weighed down with cameras and equipment.

'Lennie!' McCadden called out.

Lombard started and looked about and then shuffled across.

'It's Richard, Inspector,' he said inevitably. 'Richard.'

'Tell me,' McCadden said. 'I didn't see the local provincials that came out yesterday. Did your photographs make the front pages?'

Lombard looked up at him with sad, wistful eyes. 'I thought it was you who blocked them, Inspector.'

'Blocked? Me?'

'I was given to understand that they were being used. But they never appeared.'

'It wasn't me, Lennie.'

'It's Richard, Inspector. Richard.'

McCadden felt a hand on his left shoulder and saw the expression in Lombard's eyes change to anxiety at the same time. Expecting the Secretary of the Brockenshaw Collection with his ticket, he turned and found himself staring at the bald, furrowing brow of Chief Superintendent Daniel Cody. And behind Cody, relaxed and smiling, stood Alderman Tom Byrne. And behind Byrne, slinking back to his work place, was the reception clerk who'd put the finger on McCadden.

Cody's mouth twitched and he said, 'Your sudden interest in local heritage we'll take as a healthy sign, Inspector.'

'Well, I don't know,' McCadden offered agreeably. 'Given the rapid advances in technology which keep changing our environment and the desperately slow rate at which human consciousness changes from generation to generation, maybe the preservation order is an unnecessary complication of that gap.'

Cody took a deep breath and let it go again and said quietly, 'Now, while I never like discussing business on social occasions, you've become so elusive lately that I'm willing to take any opportunity. You will report to my office at nine o'clock on Monday morning and in the meantime consider yourself not assigned to any particular case. Is that clear, Inspector?' He said it so quietly, only one other person overheard him.

Tom Byrne, still relaxed and smiling, was still standing behind him.

'Is that clear, Inspector?'

For the next twenty minutes, as the dinner guests drank and chatted in the hotel's bars and lobbies, McCadden discreetly followed Byrne, keeping him in sight, noting whom he talked to.

But Byrne seemed unconcerned tonight. He seemed to be back in the groove, back to freely offering that hand of his to all comers. That hand that told you you were remembered and appreciated, the hand that sympathized and congratulated and encouraged, all in one, the hand that boasted it was strong enough to change the world. A politician's hand. Clean on the outside. And it didn't seem as if it was going to dirty itself tonight.

Well, you never knew. The man felt cocky now. The man felt safe and might be careless. You never knew.

But when it happened, it was McCadden who made the mistake, McCadden who was careless.

Eight-thirty, a gong sounded somewhere and everyone instantly converged on the narrow entrance to the dining room. McCadden was too far adrift of Byrne, who made the head of the queue, obviously anticipating the summons to dinner, obviously judging things from previous years. Byrne was among the first through to the dining area. Not to meet someone there, McCadden thought, but to slip out another side, make a rendezvous elsewhere.

McCadden broke away and walked briskly back, through corridors, into bars, checking everywhere, seeing nothing, neither Byrne nor anyone vaguely suspicious, until he reached the reception area again and saw ahead of him, sitting with his back to him in the lobby just inside the main entrance, a black-haired, dark-skinned foreigner, Middle East, Indian, it was difficult to tell from such a distance, at such an angle. Turning his head a little, revealing a heavy black beard, the man seemed to notice McCadden advancing. And suddenly he was out of the chair and through the entrance and into the night.

McCadden ran. Coming out on to the front steps, he saw the other opening the passenger door of a Volvo on the street below and he shouted a warning to stop. The man turned warily and waited while McCadden descended and showed his ID and stooped to look inside the Volvo and saw a young Indian woman in the driver's seat and a sleeping infant strapped into a baby seat in the rear.

'Sorry,' McCadden said. 'My mistake. Looking for someone else.'

Back in the dining room, everyone was polishing off the hors-d'oeuvre and there was only one vacant place at the crowded tables. They'd put a little card with INSP. C. McCADDEN on it, right beside another little card with INSP. H. BOYCE on it. Difficult to tell exactly why, whether as a precaution or a punishment.

'You haven't resigned, have you?' Boyce asked coldly as McCadden sat. 'Or are you into suicide these days?'

'Re-evaluation,' McCadden said. 'I'm into re-evaluation.'

'I thought you already tried that. Don't you remember? With Peter Clarke.'

'No,' McCadden said. 'Wordsworth. He once wrote to a painter pal of his, *High is our calling, friend, Creative Art*. Self-elevation. Self-importance. Mystic vocations. Capital letters. And cosiness. I hate cosy professional friendships.'

Boyce snorted and hacked irritably at the remains of his hors-d'oeuvre. But he didn't pursue the point.

McCadden picked at the food. He drank a glass of mediocre red and waited for the coffee while the others cut and chewed and swallowed and reminisced about mythical meals. But even the coffee wasn't much to his taste.

So when the Chairman of the Friends of the Brockenshaw Collection at the top table finally got to his feet and tapped his glass with his spoon for silence, McCadden was relieved. A couple of dull speeches to get through, he thought, and he could get out of there.

The chairman was saying, still tapping his glass, 'Ladies and gentlemen! Thank you! Thank you!'

The crowd fell silent.

The chairman said, 'Ladies and gentlemen, two collections of artefacts and memorabilia recalling Waterford's past are already housed in this city, one in Reginald's Tower and one in the Arts Centre. Impressive as both of them are, neither can at all compare with the Brockenshaw Collection, in terms of both artistic and monetary value, if not historical importance.

'And yet, the entire Brockenshaw Collection lies under wraps, securely it must be said, in a storeroom in Reginald's Tower, not accessible to the public, or indeed to anyone. The funds are not available, and are not being made available, to purchase and maintain a suitable gallery. Which is why we're all here tonight, of course.

'When Lord Clonea – whose family name was Brockenshaw, as you all know – when Lord Clonea died some years ago, no one expected that his extensive private collection would be bequeathed to the city of Waterford. No one, that is, except the man who has made the public ownership of the Brockenshaw Collection possible and who has yet to have his unique vision of having that collection made accessible to all realized. Alderman Tom Byrne, ladies and gentlemen.'

A round of applause. Loud, generous applause.

From across the dining room, Chief Superintendent Cody looked sharply at McCadden's hands resting on the surface of the table.

Timing it nicely, giving the applause a boost just as it was dying, Byrne stood up to take his bow.

When he sat again, the chairman said, 'I'll now ask Alderman Byrne himself to say a few words.'

And when Byrne stood up again, he got another round of applause.

Byrne said his few words. And after him, Canon Whaley said *his* few words. The Treasurer of the fund-raising committee said *his* words, and Michael Terry, the auctioneer and valuer who'd organized McCadden's ticket, said *his* few words, and the applause rippled along the top table until it came back again to the chairman.

And the chairman said, 'In conclusion, as is usual on these

205

occasions, we have brought along a couple of items from the collection for your enjoyment.

'This here – it doesn't matter if you can't see it properly now, you'll have all the time you like to study it afterwards – is a dagger owned by the eighteenth-century Waterford highwayman, William Crotty. We also have a pistol of Crotty's in the collection.

'Crotty's hideout was in the Comeragh Mountains in the north of the county. When he was finally betrayed by his accomplice David Norris, he was hung and quartered and his head was cut off and fixed outside the county jail as a warning to other highwaymen.

'The policemen at the dinner tonight will probably be green with envy, considering the number of times they have to put the same characters back in jail.'

A little laughter. Cody had his pipe in his mouth and laughed around the stem.

The Chairman continued, 'This second item is older. In fact, it's five hundred years old. It's an animal skin and it's endorsed with the words, "The charter of Henry VII, for building a goale, for the remittance 30 pounds yearly for ever, and for the remitting of the poundage, anno regni 3rd year. Dated at Westminster, 12th May, 3rd year of reign." We do seem to be harping on a criminal theme tonight, don't we?

'Both items, ladies and gentlemen, will be on display later on and I'm told if we all retire to the bar while they're clearing the tables and the band is setting up . . .'

Afterwards, an old man at one of the tables was rising unsteadily with the help of his walking stick as McCadden was passing by on his way to the exit. McCadden put an arm under the old man's other hand.

The old man said, 'I haven't seen you before.'

'McCadden. Carl McCadden.'

'Pat Crotty,' the old man said, cackling loudly. 'No relation to the highwayman. Will we head for the bar or what?'

McCadden looked reluctantly at the throng pressing through the narrow entrance back to the bars.

'Bloody silly things, these dinners,' the old man grumbled. 'I'll have a Scotch and water, by the way.'

'I'd better get you a seat first.'

'Still,' the old man sighed, 'it's a good old cause. Put the water in a separate glass. Don't pour it on, whatever you do. Did you know George, yourself?'

'No,' McCadden said absently. 'No, not at all.'

'Queer fellow. He showed me that dagger of Crotty's once, must be thirty years ago now, and said to me, he said . . .'

End of story, McCadden was thinking to himself as he walked with the old man. End of the road. Monday morning, nine o'clock, he'd put his case against Tom Byrne in front of Cody. Two and a half lines of a little-known ballad. An attic full of impenetrable notebooks written by a dead murderer. And a jokey note by some person or persons unknown. End of story. Definitely the end of the road.

'. . . that he ever added anything much to it himself,' the old man was rambling on. 'All inherited. Didn't have the money any more, you know. Beyond me why he didn't sell a few things. Here, we might as well sit down here, sure. Won't get anything better further on. Scotch, now. Remember.'

'Right,' McCadden muttered.

'And keep the water separate, mind.'

The crowd had thinned when McCadden reached the bar. He ordered a double Scotch, water in a separate jug, and a vodka and white lemonade for himself. Leaning against the counter while waiting, thinking about Tom Byrne's relaxed humour, trying to find hope even in that, he felt again a hand settling on his left shoulder. The night coming to an end the way it had begun.

Expecting Cody's return, half-expecting to be ticked off for boorishness at the meal, he turned lazily, practising indifference. And even though he was surprised, even though he imagined, for an instant, a new opening in the case, he still held that careless attitude when he found himself looking into Paul Hyland's wholesome face.

Hyland was laughing. Hyland was always laughing, of course. That was the way the world struck him.

He had a full pint of Guinness with a thick head in his left hand. His right arm, coming back from tapping McCadden, was draping itself possessively across the shoulders of a red-headed woman beside him. She was young, no more than twenty-one, almost a generation away from Hyland. She looked a little embarrassed, kept on a pouting, aggressive expression, and sipped constantly from her drink to give herself something to do while on parade.

She wore a low-cut, strapless dress. Every time she inhaled, the top of her right breast came into contact with Hyland's dangling fingers. And the fingers responded, every time, offering a quick caress. And as her breathing quickened, so did the stroking.

Hyland didn't introduce his prize. But it was obvious he'd brought her here for display.

He said, 'We didn't make the dinner. We got held up.'

And the redhead giggled. Just in case anyone was missing the point.

'Didn't really make it myself,' McCadden said.

'What? Late?'

'No. Wrong course.'

Best way to kill off a smiler was to feed him jokes he couldn't understand. As Hyland raised his eyebrows and struggled for something to say, McCadden came back with, 'You recovered, by the way?'

Hyland frowned. 'Eh?'

'You were out sick,' McCadden said. 'Are you well again? You *look* better.'

Hyland laughed, catching the drift. He squeezed the red-head towards him. 'Oh, yeah, sure. Back in harness Monday morning, you know.'

'Good,' McCadden said. 'I'll see you then. Right?'

He turned to pay the barman for his drinks. After pocketing his change he slipped his fingers round the stem of his vodka glass, held the neck of the lemonade bottle in the same hand, and then grasped the handle of the water jug and the glass of Scotch in the other hand. Didn't want to make the journey back.

As he was leaving he stopped by the redhead, looked her up and down, and said chattily, 'You must be the brother from Liverpool, are you?'

Nicely pointed, he thought. Give Hyland something to chew on over the weekend.

The sort of cut that gives a sour pleasure when you're beaten. The sort of pleasure that won't let you see you're missing something much more important.

And McCadden couldn't see what he was missing just then. Couldn't even see he was missing anything at all.

thirty-one

Towards the end of the night, around five forty-five, McCadden turned sharply in his sleep and extended his arm to shake someone's hand and said, 'George. Did you know George, yourself?'

Then he opened his eyes, lowered his arm and looked at the shadows gliding along the bedroom walls as the headlights of a passing car hit the window behind him, and he felt again the strange tingling sensation creeping around the back of his neck, spreading down and outwards over his shoulders. He sat upright in the bed, worried for a second about his health.

Then he said again, 'Did you know George, yourself?' This time using the voice of the old man he'd bought the Scotch and water for in the hotel.

Rubbing the back of his neck, he got out of bed to pace the small area of floor left free in the loft. The temperature was low, no more than two or three centigrade. He hadn't been in to light the fire the night before. But even though he was naked, he wasn't aware of the cold yet.

In his own voice, he said, 'No.'

No, he hadn't known George Brockenshaw. He'd never even heard of George Brockenshaw until last night. But he reckoned that George Brockenshaw had been an old man when he'd died. Old, not so mobile any more, possibly incapacitated, but definitely suffering from an illness he had to take particular care of. Given his age, it probably implied a heart condition. Something to do with the circulation, anyway. And he reckoned also that George Brockenshaw had that old-fashioned, chivalrous attitude to women. Slightly condescending. Saw them as gentle creatures to be protected. Fond of young women, old George Brockenshaw had been. Very fond. No, not that. Not *particularly* that, anyway. But you know the affectionate, sort of *understated*, *gently* sexual way some old men have with young women. What else? Well, old George had been a bit of a traditionalist in the way he talked. *Old girl. Dear child. Splendid.* And something of a traditionalist in the way he wrote, too. All round, something Edwardian about him. Not that he went that far back himself. But that was the pedigree, the style. He was never colloquial, for instance. Always graceful. Anglo-Irish, of course. Probably served in the British army. Yes . . .

'George Brockenshaw,' McCadden said to himself. 'G.B. George Brockenshaw.'

Amazing what you could guess about a man you'd never met, never even heard of before.

And if the guess was right, it might not be the end of the road any more.

'George Brockenshaw.'

Still talking to himself, McCadden got dressed and went down to the kitchen to make some breakfast. His mind was unsettled, racing through a theme and then suddenly jumping sideways to something else and chasing that for a while.

He wondered what to eat with coffee at six in the morning. Especially as he'd only really had half a Chinese fried rice the day before. In Waterford, most of the bakeries did a distinctive round bread roll that the locals called blaas, a French-style bread that had been introduced to the city by the Huguenots. Great with coffee.

Then he suddenly forgot about bread rolls for a while and thought about the Huguenots instead. They'd come to Waterford in . . . When? 1692, was it? Exactly fifty years before the highwayman William Crotty was hanged and beheaded.

He poured a mug of coffee from the pot he'd made and since there was no French-style bread, settled for brown soda bread to go with some bacon and black pudding.

While he was grilling he thought about William Crotty's

211

dagger. Then he tried to remember where else he'd seen Crotty's name recently. In a folk song? Possibly. He'd been reading the titles and lyrics of hundreds of folk songs the past few days, hearing hundreds more suggested or recited to him, and there *was* a ballad called 'Lament for William Crotty', supposedly written by the highwayman's wife.

He finished the first mug of coffee and turned the bacon and pudding on the grill, and decided that, no, it wasn't the ballad itself or the title – although he'd read both in one of Peter Clarke's notebooks – but something different, more complicated, more concealed than that; something that wasn't detailed, that wasn't in its own shape . . .

It was six-thirty when he rang Liam de Burgh. De Burgh was fairly sharp answering the phone and fairly alert when he spoke. Must've been awake already.

'Liam? Carl. Can you do something for me again today? I can't myself, I've got to go somewhere else.'

'What?' de Burgh asked. 'Right now?'

'Yes, I've got to go now.'

'I mean, what I'm supposed to do.'

'You? No, later on will do. You won't be able to now.'

'What is it?'

'The character's name is George Brockenshaw,' McCadden said. 'Lord Clonea. You ever hear of him?'

'No,' de Burgh said.

'The dinner last night – '

'That's right,' de Burgh cut in. 'Brockenshaw. It was the Friends of the Brockenshaw Collection. How did it go, by the way?'

'It led to this. Where this is leading to I don't know.'

'Go on. You were saying. George Brockenshaw.'

'Well, he seems to have been fairly reclusive. He died four years ago. Before that he lived in what was left of the family estate in Woodstown. You should probably start there, Liam. You know the place. Small community. The beach, a pub, a few houses. He would've employed some of the locals. Cleaning lady. Gardener. That sort of thing. You should talk to them first.'

212

'What do you want to know?'

'Everything you can find out. But I'd be particularly interested in what visitors came to the house over the last year or so of his life. Find out also how he died, the exact circumstances. And check on his will.'

De Burgh drew a breath between his teeth. 'It's Sunday, Carl,' he said.

'What?'

'Today is Sunday. I can't check on the will.'

'Oh, right, I forgot. The rest of it, then. Can you manage?'

'It's going to take the best part of the day.'

'I know, I know.'

'Is this Peter Clarke again?'

'Yes.'

'Well,' de Burgh said, 'I don't know. I suppose I could always get a job in security. You know Cody's ready to shoot you down, don't you? Have you got a case?'

'Depends on this.'

'Where are *you* going at half-six in the morning, anyway?'

'I'm going to visit our old friends in John's Park, Henry Barry and Martin O'Shea. I want to get to them before they leave for work.'

De Burgh sighed. 'Carl, it's Sunday. Sunday. They don't have any work on Sunday.'

'Right,' McCadden said. 'I forgot. Again. To hell with it. I'm going early, anyway. Maybe I'll leave it for an hour or so.'

At quarter past eight, Henry Barry's household was just starting to come alive. Barry himself, his feet bare and his pyjamas half open, was in the kitchen organizing a bowl of cereal for himself and waiting on the rest of his breakfast. His wife had their youngest child resting sleepily on one hip and was working the grill pan and the electric kettle with her free hand. There was a warm, sleepy air around the place. Not the kind of warmth McCadden enjoyed himself. Too many bodies in too small a space. But it was relaxed, more relaxed than most houses that time of the morning.

Barry's wife had opened the front door and called back

down the hallway, without a hint of surprise in her voice, 'It's the Garda Inspector again, Harry.'

When McCadden was shown to the kitchen, Barry yawned and scratched his stomach and said, 'You're up early, Inspector.'

What could you say? Nothing in the crowded kitchen, anyway.

Without waiting for the invitation, McCadden turned and walked back down the corridor and into the empty front room. Barry followed reluctantly, not wanting to leave the food behind. When he'd sat on the settee, a look of friendly curiosity on his face, McCadden took the Italian watercolour from the wall and placed it gently in his lap.

McCadden said, 'I know what you were up to, Henry. I know *exactly* what you were up to. What I don't know is whether *you* knew what you were up to. Do you understand what I mean?'

'No.'

'Stay quiet, Henry.'

'I only thought you wanted me — '

'Shut up, Henry.'

'All right, all right.'

McCadden said, 'I mean, I don't know whether you were doing a mate a favour, you know, turning a blind eye, no questions asked, and taking your nice little backhander for keeping your eyes closed and your mouth shut. Or whether you were part of it all, whether you were in on the deal from the start. One way, you're clean enough. Not the brightest, but safe enough. The other, you're not going to be seeing your family or your mates for a few years. Now, I'm reasonable enough, Henry.'

'Sure, I know that, Inspector.'

'I'm inclined to think you were used,' McCadden said. 'The trouble is, if you don't *confirm* that you were used, I'll have to accept that you and O'Shea are crooks. Are you following me?'

'Well, to tell you nothing but the truth — '

'Good,' McCadden said. 'So tell me. All I want to know is

whether you knew what you were doing or not, whether you know even *now* what you were really doing.'

Henry Barry smiled a little then and looked puzzled and shrugged. 'You've lost me, Inspector, to tell you nothing but the truth.'

McCadden sighed. 'Henry,' he said, 'I don't want to squeeze you, but you'd better believe that I will if you don't co-operate.'

'But you haven't even told me what I'm supposed to have done. Is it Billy Power's death again, or what?'

Quarter of an hour later, a *barren* quarter of an hour later, things were different across the road.

Evelyn O'Shea was still in bed and O'Shea himself, in rough humour, was trying to find something edible in the cold kitchen, probably the same as he did every morning of the week. If it *was* Sunday, McCadden thought, and he only had de Burgh's word for it, then O'Shea's house must have weird bedrooms to make a cold kitchen a more inviting place before nine in the morning.

McCadden talked to O'Shea in his kitchen. 'You can forget about breakfast for a start,' he barked. 'In fact, you can forget about breakfast for the next few years unless you have the right answers for me. You see, I *know* what you and Power and Barry were up to. So we'll cut the shit. Straight through the shit. I haven't got the time.'

And it was O'Shea who sweated, of course. O'Shea who had trouble swallowing and who had to sit down, even before McCadden got to the details.

'One question,' McCadden said. 'Just one. Was it your idea? Because then you're talking about doing a lot of time. You're talking about accessory to murder. Or was it someone else's idea and you were doing a favour? One question. One minute. Then I settle on the belief that it was your idea.'

O'Shea considered it a while. Not long, though. Much less than the minute. Then, having always known the world would screw him anyway, he raised his head and asked, 'Who told you, hah? Who told you?'

'Never mind that,' McCadden said. 'Let's get the hell on

215

with it. You've wasted enough of my time already. You handed the stuff over on your continental holidays. Right?'

O'Shea nodded.

'Where, exactly?'

'I thought you already knew all that,' O'Shea whined.

McCadden said quietly, 'Look. What I know and what I don't know, you needn't worry about. What you *have* to worry about is what *you* know and what you don't know. *That's* what's going to decide whether you do time or not. Have you got that? And I'm not going to sit here repeating my questions. I can get two uniformed bruisers to do that for me at the station.'

Evelyn O'Shea, in bare feet and a vivid red dressing gown, came half-way down the stairs, just enough to bend and peer sleepily through the open doorway at whoever was arguing in her kitchen so early in the morning. O'Shea, harried now from both sides, glared at her furiously. His hatred nearly brought her down to join them. But she was probably just a little too tired to enjoy the spectacle.

When she'd turned and disappeared again, O'Shea said, 'Majorca, Ibiza, Tenerife. You know. The resorts.'

'Who gave you the items to bring across?' McCadden asked.

'It was Billy Power.'

'Always Power?'

'Yeah, it was always Billy.'

'Did he tell you where to go as well?'

'It didn't work like that, at all. You just told Billy where you were going that holiday, and he gave you the thing the day before you left.'

'Ever open any of the parcels?'

'I didn't.'

'Ever ask what was inside?'

'No.'

'Come on.'

O'Shea was violently shaking his head. 'I didn't, no, never. I didn't want to. Billy said they were all right, there was nothing in them like drugs or anything like that, nothing you'd get in trouble for. That was good enough for me. It was just, you know, trade barriers, like.'

216

'How big were the parcels?'

'Well, they weren't all the same size.'

'What was the biggest? Big enough to hold a large book? Something like that?'

'They weren't like that at all. Some were just in envelopes. Most of the time they were, you know, a business envelope, like, that size. Sometimes you'd get a box the size of a ring box. Nothing bigger than that.'

'Envelopes?' McCadden repeated. He thought for a while. And then he asked, 'What were the instructions if you were questioned by customs or the police?'

'You wouldn't be seen with an envelope, would you?'

'The other things!'

'They were still too small. And sure, you were only bringing a present for someone wherever you were going, weren't you? That's all.'

'Did you expect customs officials to accept that, without asking you where you bought the stuff?'

'That's what Billy said, anyway.'

'Hmm. Right,' McCadden said. 'How were they passed on, then?'

O'Shea rubbed his chin, as if he had to think about it. 'The arrangement was,' he said, 'the second day of your holiday, between eleven o'clock and twelve, you left the gear under a towel in your apartment and the apartment open. We had these towels printed with the Waterford colours on them, the coat of arms. Anything went wrong, we'd do the same the next day, and the next. It never did, though.'

'Don't tell me you never saw any of them picking the stuff up.'

'Well, I might've got a glimpse once or twice, I suppose.'

'What nationality?' McCadden asked.

'Jesus, I don't know, do I? I wouldn't know one from the other.'

'Black?' McCadden said impatiently. 'White? Brown? Yellow?'

'Kind of Arab, I suppose. Henry said once he thought they were kind of Arab.'

217

'All men?'

'The ones I saw, anyway.'

'And the little presents you got sometimes. How did you come by them?'

'How do you mean, like?' O'Shea was asking. 'You mean the money, is it?'

McCadden pointed to a watercolour. 'That,' he said. 'There's another in Power's home and one in Barry's.'

'It was Billy himself gave us those.'

'Billy Power?'

'That's right.'

Yes. Yes. Come to think of it, it had Power's mark, all right. *Anyone ever ask you, say we picked them up at Italia 90.* Power's mark. No one else would've given watercolours from the same series of Italian universities to three separate couriers from the same city. Wouldn't have given *anything* to couriers.

But how had Power got his hands on them?

McCadden got up, slowly zipped up his leather jacket. He stood there, then. He didn't move. After a while, O'Shea looked up at him stupidly, a bit of contrition and a bit of shame mixed in with the resentment.

No, McCadden decided, neither Barry nor O'Shea knew what they were carrying. Billy Power did, though. Power knew it all. He knew the origin of the parcels, he knew the contents, and he knew the contacts on the other side. McCadden thought suddenly of Power sexually assaulting Tina Byrne, and realized now why the Alderman had never done anything about that episode.

O'Shea stood up as McCadden was turning to leave. He asked desperately, 'What do I do?'

'Let us know if you're planning a continental holiday,' McCadden advised.

thirty-two

Ten o'clock, Sunday morning. This time McCadden took the cardboard boxes down from Mary Butler's dark attic and laid out Peter Clarke's notebooks on her dining-room table.

'Now I know what I'm looking for,' he told her. 'You ever hear of William Crotty?'

'The highwayman?'

'That's right.'

'Sure, the father used to bring me out to the Comeragh Mountains to show me Crotty's cave when I was small. They say he robbed the rich to help the poor.'

'They also say he murdered people just for amusement.'

'They'd be redcoats, though, wouldn't they, that he killed?'

History was treacherous ground in Ireland, no matter who you were talking to. A place for deep commitments or strong nerves. One or the other. Another time, McCadden might've played out the ironies in the situation. A modern policeman discussing a nineteenth-century criminal with a local woman who'd inherited the attitude that if the law was English and you broke it, you had to be a hero. But this Sunday morning he had a more contemporary villain, an even more dubious hero.

'I suppose they would,' he agreed. 'Listen, I could take this stuff home to work on, if you like, not be in your way all morning.'

'Not at all. I'd be glad of the company.'

So he lifted the notebooks from the cardboard boxes and stacked them in random order on the dining-room table and sat down to examine them as they came to him.

Two hours, it took him. Two hours in which Mary Butler finished her breakfast and went out and attended Mass and came back again and put on the Sunday dinner of roast chicken and roast potatoes and vegetables. Shut away in the dining room, surrounded by books and boxes, McCadden caught the whiff of boiled turnip at precisely the moment he located the notebook with the line of coded entries containing Crotty's name.

The line read: *STA2310SOP, 056JHCRAIG, F102OW-DEWGODWIN, WE17PISHIGHCROTTY.*

It was a small A6 booklet with a soft black cover and the words *UNIVERSITY EXERCISE BOOK* embossed on the front. The cover also held a dirty adhesive label with *BROC088* on it in felt marker.

McCadden wrote the Crotty entry – *WE17PISHIGH-CROTTY* – on a separate sheet and tried to separate its elements. *CROTTY.* Obviously. Now he could immediately see the surnames CRAIG and GODWIN in two of the other entries on the same line. Just as obvious, the number 17 was separating *WE* from *PISHIGH. PISHIGH? PI SHIGH? PISH IGH? PIS HIGH? HIGH?* Highwayman? Crotty the highwayman? *PIS?* A pistol? A pistol belonging to the highwayman William Crotty?

McCadden laughed. With relief. With the realization of how blind he'd been.

It wasn't a code at all, he could see now. Not properly, anyway. It was just a series of basic abbreviations.

So the title of the notebook itself, for instance, *BROC088*, had to be the Brockenshaw Collection, catalogue number or list number 88 . . .

No. Eighty-eight was a date. Catalogued in 88. The complete Brockenshaw Collection, as it was catalogued in 1988.

But that was the year before George Brockenshaw had died. And presumably the year before his collection became the property of Waterford city.

McCadden went back to the entry he'd been working on, *WE17PISHIGHCROTTY*.

A dagger owned by the highwayman, Crotty, the Chairman of the Friends of the Brockenshaw Collection had said the night before. Something like that. *Also a pistol in the collection.*

So, if 17 was just a number in a series and identified Crotty's pistol, then the dagger should be listed in Peter Clarke's home-made catalogue in exactly the same way, except as 16 or 18.

After a long search, McCadden found it, tucked away towards the end of the entries in the notebook. Predictable in everything but one element. It wasn't numbered 16 or 18. It was 74. *WE74DAGHIGHCROTTY*. WE number 74, a dagger owned by the highwayman, William Crotty. But why such a huge numerical difference between two such similar items?

And WE? It grouped a dagger and a pistol together.

Weapons?

Yes, weapons. The prefix WE- identified and classed all the weapons in the Brockenshaw Collection. He searched for others. He found *WE39REVWW1CAPBRO*, guessed a revolver from World War I owned by a Captain Brockenshaw, and *WE49PIK1798*, a pike supposedly used in the 1798 Rebellion.

Although the little black notebook was half empty, it obviously wasn't Clarke's only or last list of the Brockenshaw Collection. Similar entries were scattered elsewhere. Crotty's pistol and dagger. The revolver and the pike. And the entire contents of the notebook were completely out of numerical sequence: the items were listed as they stood or hung in a house, not a museum. A large and disordered house. A weapon here, then a painting, then some pieces of cutlery, then another weapon. You finished a room like that. And then you went on to another room. This soft-covered book was one you carried in your hand, recording as you walked.

Where the proper index, the finished catalogue, had got to was anybody's guess. It wasn't in any of the cardboard boxes from the attic.

McCadden intended taking a break to ask Mary Butler if he could boil some water to make a jug of coffee, her tea having finally got to him, but he kept pacing and thinking instead.

If the prefix WE- always signalled weapons, he thought, what categories did the other prefixes indicate? STA, for instance. Stage? Stained glass? Statue? He didn't know, couldn't make sense of that entry. FU, then. Fur? No, no. Furniture. Had to be furniture. And O? O? Oils? Yes. *O56JHCRAIG.* J.H. Craig, an Irish landscape painter, lived around . . . McCadden couldn't remember. And there, too: *O16WORPENSELPOR.* And *O17WORPENPOR.*

Early in the afternoon, after putting away Mary Butler's Sunday lunch, McCadden made a call from the telephone in the hall of her house, a place that was beginning to feel like a private office in his exile from the Garda station. Mary Butler herself had gone out again, to visit a friend across the city.

McCadden's call was to the auctioneer and valuer, Michael Terry. They chatted for a while about the dinner the previous night.

Then McCadden said, 'An oil painting by J.H. Craig, Michael. How much would that set me back?'

'James Humbert Craig,' Terry mused. And instructed, 'What is it, dear? A landscape, one fears?'

'Well, ah, I don't really know. I haven't seen it yet.'

'You're not pulling my leg, Carl, are you?'

'No, no. Bear with me for a while, eh? Give me a range of prices on a kind of average J.H. Craig.'

'One simply cannot *get* anything, Carl, except an *average* J.H. Craig. But I imagine two-and-a-half to five thousand.'

'How about a self-portrait by William Orpen?'

'Depends on the period. Depends on the quality.'

'But we could be talking about what?'

'Shall we say, forty thousand?'

'And a portrait by Orpen?'

'Very, very variable. Sotheby's did one recently for seventy thousand, but it was very well known. Depending on the sitter and the quality again, perhaps up to twenty thousand. Have these works been stolen, Carl?'

'I don't know, Michael. Is there a furniture maker called E.W. Godwin?'

'Designer, my dear. Edward William Godwin. He was British. Latter part of the nineteenth century and now very, very expensive. Might one ask what sort of piece you've got?'

'An OWD.'

'You must come again.'

'An OWD. It's an abbrev — Hang on. It's just come to me. O has to stand for oak, doesn't it?'

'Writing desk,' Terry supplied. 'An oak writing desk.'

'Very good, Michael.'

'I hope you're keeping it out of the rain, Carl. It's worth over one hundred thousand pounds. In excellent condition, of course.'

McCadden drew a breath and said, 'Now I'm going to ask a few questions you won't remember between the time you put the phone down and I get back to you. OK?'

'How could I refuse, Carl? You have me enthralled.'

'You've seen the full Brockenshaw Collection, haven't you? The one stored in Reginald's Tower.'

'Actually, I did my civic duty cataloguing it. With the assistance of others, of course.'

'I know it has a dagger supposedly used by the highwayman, William Crotty. I saw it last night. Does it also have the pistol that was mentioned?'

'It does, yes. Both rather ugly objects, and quite impossible to authenticate, as you can imagine.'

'Does it have a World War I service revolver owned by one of the Brockenshaw ancestors and a seventeen ninety-eight pike?'

'Numerous pikes and the Captain's revolver, belt and holster, yes.'

'How about an Orpen portrait and self-portrait?'

'I thought you'd never get to it, Carl. There's nothing by Orpen, no. Or by J.H. Craig.'

'How about a Godwin oak writing desk?'

'Certainly not. And now, Carl, if I can regress from my evidence to your theory, you are suggesting, aren't you, that these items were part of the Brockenshaw Collection when it was bequeathed and subsequently disappeared?'

'That's what I have to get back to you on, Michael.'

'I'll be holding my breath, Carl.'

thirty-three

Too impatient to wait for de Burgh to come and report to him, McCadden himself drove from Mary Butler's house on Military Road across the city and out along the eight miles of narrowing roads to the sea at Woodstown.

It wasn't really a village, Woodstown. The few houses were too scattered for that. It was really only a strand. But a strand that was four miles long and half a mile deep, its sand covered with dried shells from its crowded cockle beds.

De Burgh's car was parked outside the only pub, the Saratoga. De Burgh himself was about the half-mile out at the edge of the turning tide, his feet bare, his black chinos folded and pulled up over his knees, picking cockles from the soft wet sand with a man so fat he could hardly stoop to gather the shellfish.

McCadden got out of the car and walked to the beach. On the dry sand he took off his own shoes and socks and rolled the jeans above his ankles.

The water was freezing when he hit it first, but he got used to it quickly enough. He could hear a couple of seagulls squawking every so often and then, when the wind gusted a bit, the laughter of the pair at the edge of the sea. Otherwise there was just peaceful silence. It was one of those calm, untouched places that made you wonder what you were chasing in life.

When de Burgh turned and saw him, McCadden pointed a finger to his own left, down the coast towards Passage East, indicating a walk along the beach. De Burgh had a last joke with the fat man, dropped a final few cockles in the other's bag, and set off. He took a notebook from the back pocket of his chinos when he joined McCadden and talked as they strolled.

He said, 'George Brockenshaw died on the fifteenth of September, 1989, aged eighty-five years. He was a Peer of the Kingdom of Ireland, which doesn't exist any more. There were no surviving relatives. No individual inherited anything and there were no claimants on the estate. Did you pass the cricket ground on the way in? Weird place for a cricket pitch.'

'Just down the coast,' McCadden said, pointing straight ahead as they walked, 'at Passage East, Henry II, King of England, landed in eleven seventy-one with his army and nobles and courtiers to claim Ireland as his own, the first of the English kings to do that.'

'Yeah,' de Burgh said, 'but he didn't bring any cricketers with him, did he?'

There were times, very few times, when it was hard to tell if de Burgh was still being serious. His expression didn't change. His delivery stayed the same. And yet the words had skidded off into absurdity.

Generally it was safer to ignore the aberrations.

McCadden said, 'There have been military garrisons around here ever since. All the garrison towns, you get strong cricket and soccer traditions.'

'Anyway,' de Burgh said, 'the estate was just before you come to the cricket ground. The house and lands are sold now. The locals thought he was odd. He wouldn't let anyone into the grounds or near the house. Not even children. They said when he died that September, the chestnuts on his land were collected by children for the first time in thirty, forty years. He had no cleaning ladies. No gardeners. No one in or around the house. But whenever you met him outside, he was fairly friendly and chatty. Sort of a split personality.'

'He didn't want anyone to see the extent of the art collection in the house, that's all,' McCadden said.

'Yeah,' de Burgh said, 'but the story locally was that they

were all just family mementoes, maybe fetch a few quid in an antiques shop, but nothing much, and he'd given everything to a museum thirty years ago, anyway, in the sixties.'

'All the more reason not to let anyone in the house. The story wasn't true. Did the doctor make house calls, by the way?'

'Doctor Raymond Kearns,' de Burgh supplied. 'Brockenshaw insisted on seeing him in the surgery, except in the last year, nineteen eighty-nine, when he was sometimes too weak to make it. This is the interesting bit. Whenever the doctor called that year, he was let in by a black-haired young woman. She wasn't qualified, but she seemed to be nursing Brockenshaw. Kearns recognized her. You notice the caravan park by the Saratoga pub?'

'Uh-huh.'

'Most of the caravans are parked there permanently. The young woman's relatives owned one of them, so Brockenshaw must've met her like that. You'll never guess her name.'

McCadden stooped to pick up a tangle of fishing line with three flies and a lead sinker attached that had been snared and snapped on the rocks at full tide. He wound the line carefully around his left hand and said, 'Theresa Cheasty.'

De Burgh sighed and kicked a razor shell. 'Why do I bother?'

'What was wrong with Brockenshaw?' McCadden asked. 'Medically.'

'Old age,' de Burgh said. 'The heart. He was on medication.'

'What was the cause of death?'

'Heart attack. Certified by Doctor Kearns. Long expected. Something else interesting, but you probably know it already. When Kearns came to the death bed, there were two people in the house. Neither of them was Theresa Cheasty. She was away somewhere. She only barely made it back for the funeral. One of them was Tom Byrne. Kearns knew him and he'd seen him with Brockenshaw before, once or twice over the previous few months. Byrne was the executor of the will, by the way. The other, from the description, I took to be Peter Clarke.'

'No,' McCadden said slowly. 'I didn't know that, Liam. Why did Brockenshaw invite Theresa Cheasty into his house?'

'The locals say Brockenshaw lost a daughter about Theresa Cheasty's age in an air raid in London during the Second World War.'

'Bit long to wait though, isn't it, forty-six years, before you start compensating?'

'I suppose it is, but when you're that age, you know, eighty-five, you get some odd notions, too.'

'What did the locals think of Theresa Cheasty?'

'They liked her. By and large. But the first thing crops into your mind, an old man with money and a young woman, is the obvious thing, and I got a lot of that too. Do you think they were lovers? Might make more sense of Clarke killing her.'

'Not impossible, I suppose, but I don't think so. What about the will? Oh, I forgot. Sunday.'

'No, the doctor knew the details. Everyone else did as well, really. The house and lands were put up for sale and the proceeds donated equally, after costs, between two charities, Saint Vincent de Paul and the Rehabilitation Institute. The contents of the house went to the city and people of Waterford. There was three and a half thousand in a savings account and that went to a third charity, the Samaritans. I haven't checked the charities yet.'

'Nothing for Theresa Cheasty?'

'She wasn't mentioned.'

'Were the house contents listed?'

'Not that I know of, no.'

McCadden was still holding the fishing line with the hooks and sinker. 'Get back and hunt up those charities, will you? Give Shorty Phelan a ring. Tell him not to go out tonight, I want to see him. He's not inside, is he?'

De Burgh shook his head. 'Not right now. Nothing pending, either.'

'I'll ring you when I get back,' McCadden said. 'I've got someone else I want to see up the road. And here, take this stuff and throw it in a bin.'

When de Burgh left, McCadden found a rock to sit on.

228

There was no one else now on the four miles of strand that he could see. The cockle picker de Burgh had been talking to had left.

McCadden looked out at the slowly advancing tide and tried to think it through, the sequence of events from the time Theresa Cheasty had first come to Woodstown.

A young independent woman, outwardly happy and lively, but concealing a sadness: the desertion of her father, who'd run away from the family home. As the eldest of three daughters, she would've been closest to him, would've felt the loss more sharply than her sisters. Certainly her sister, Margaret, had been cold, a little bitter, when talking about the old man.

So what Theresa liked about Woodstown, about coming to stay in her aunt's caravan here, was exactly what McCadden himself had felt a while ago. The place made you inclined to forget your ordinary life.

And then, met by accident one day, a quaint, interesting old man she'd never seen before.

In the beginning, all their meetings were accidental. Soon, though, the accidents found a pattern. Walking along the beach in the afternoon. Drinking in the pub at night.

And then, one day, one evening, one night, the old man didn't make it. Didn't make it the next day, either. Or the next. Until Theresa, knowing where he lived, went to check on him.

And after that, they didn't have to rely on accidents any more.

Something like that. Something like that.

Were they lovers?

No. Not that kind of relationship.

'Don't you have a young man, my dear? You should, you know. Bring him to see me.'

They probably got along fine, Peter Clarke and George Brockenshaw. The two of them a little reclusive, a little bookish, interested in local history and local artefacts. The two of them enjoying the attentions of Theresa Cheasty. Probably got along fine, Clarke and Brockenshaw.

So there was nothing sinister about Clarke listing the contents of the house. Nothing even unique about it. Clarke, as

McCadden knew now, always dealt with life by making lists of its materials.

And after that, the months passed happily enough.

Theresa no longer needed to stay in her aunt's caravan. She felt she no longer needed her family, felt she had another family here with the two men. Clarke was absorbed. Brockenshaw, after years of reclusiveness, had lively and reliable company.

Everyone happy.

Until Clarke's mentor, Tom Byrne, was also invited to the house.

Why was the outsider invited in?

Well, at first, Byrne, of the open hand, the honest face, the public servant, looked like a blessing to everyone. Brockenshaw had a city, the city his ancestors had helped to build, worthy of his collection and an executor worthy of his trust. Clarke had the pleasure of becoming part of the fascinating history he recorded.

Everyone happy. Still.

But something changed. No doubt after the will was drawn up.

Did Clarke start wondering what it would be like to own some of those precious things himself? Did Byrne's business hit a rough patch just then?

Something changed, all right.

And Theresa Cheasty got wind of it.

And when one thing changed, everything else changed with it.

Everything became darker. Ambivalent. Uncertain. The politician's promises. The old man's rambling complaints about his treatment when Theresa wasn't there. Clarke's attentiveness. Everything encrusted with suspicion.

And Theresa's mind a dark chamber where all the conflicts raged.

At some stage, apart from idle conversation, Theresa and Brockenshaw started communicating by notes only, using an agreed drop somewhere in the house. They couldn't talk freely any more. Clarke or Byrne was always about.

230

But Theresa was caught between the two men. Between her lover, Clarke, who pleaded with her not to overwork or worry herself, who said the old man was becoming senile, slightly paranoid, possessive, too demanding, too hot-tempered. And Brockenshaw himself, close to death and fearing it, getting agitated when Theresa had to leave him.

Theresa must have stood back, weighed it up for herself.

Because one day, shortly before she had to leave Waterford and Woodstown for some reason, she wrote Brockenshaw a note, sharing her own suspicions with him.

And the note Theresa got back in response to her warning read, *Do keep in mind, dear child, that I am not dead, yet.* In other words, nothing is finalized, I can change the will.

A reassurance to send Theresa away with an easier mind.

Two, three days later, Brockenshaw *was* dead. And the will was unchanged. And with the old man's corpse lying somewhere in the house, the Brockenshaw Collection was divided in two, the lesser part for the city of Waterford, the greater for Tom Byrne and Peter Clarke. How long had they taken to transport the antiques from the house to Byrne's warehouse, McCadden wondered. Had they already started before Brockenshaw died?

Theresa Cheasty suffered from depression for months afterwards. Her friends thought it was caused by living with Clarke. It wasn't. It was guilt. She blamed herself for the old man's death, for going away when he needed her.

But the one thing she did not suspect was murder.

Because she blamed herself.

McCadden thought of the old man bedridden in the isolated old house, harried and tormented by the two worthies, the local historian, Peter Clarke, and the local politician, Tom Byrne, until he gave up the warning note Theresa had sent him.

There must be rooms in that house still echoing with his fear.

For more than six months, Theresa Cheasty locked herself away in Clarke's house in Poleberry. Impossible to know what darkness she'd lived through.

But then, in March 1990, something changed again. Something snapped Theresa out of her depression. Did Clarke bring an item from the Brockenshaw Collection home with him, to touch, to hold, to know it was his? Did himself and Byrne have a careless conversation in Theresa's presence. Whatever. Theresa discovered, or rediscovered, the plot against George Brockenshaw; and Peter Clarke, after a violent row, a series of violent rows, faced with the threat of exposure and the loss of his treasure, finally silenced her with a cut-throat razor.

Why did he use that weapon? What was he doing with the razor?

'Shaving himself, McCadden,' Harry Boyce had said.

Had he really shaved with one of those? Fancied himself as an old-fashioned working man? Or had he been using it as a tool, scraping or cutting with it?

Whatever.

While he was using it, from behind him and for the umpteenth time that month, Theresa Cheasty said, 'You killed old George, didn't you? You and Byrne between you. Admit it.'

Clarke saying nothing. He'd been here before.

Or else saying, 'You should go and see a doctor, Theresa.'

'I'm going, all right. It's not a doctor I'll be seeing, though.'

Clarke rising, facing her.

Theresa pushing past him. And Clarke striking out. Once. Twice. Three times. Maybe even forgetting he had the razor in his hand. Driven mad by the threat to his obsession.

And Harry Boyce, of course, with a half-assed motive – domestic quarrels, end of tether man and clinically depressed woman – put Peter Clarke away for a life sentence.

In the summer of 1990, shortly after Clarke's trial, the Iraqi trade delegate, Sayed Salman, came to Waterford on official business. And Sayed Salman met the local Alderman, Tom Byrne.

You could imagine the exchanges between them; the wealthy Iraqi businessman with a passion for Irish artefacts, and the local man with a private collection he was willing to trade. The pair of them making plans for the future, discussing prices, arranging the deal, sorting out the options for shipment.

A couple of weeks later, however, Saddam Hussein invaded Kuwait. The United Nations slapped a trade embargo on Iraq. And Sayed Salman was not seen again in Waterford.

So Tom Byrne ingeniously improvised at his end, using Billy Power, Martin O'Shea and Henry Barry as couriers for the smaller items. Small and light, but extremely valuable. Antique jewellery, probably. Miniatures of any kind . . .

And then it suddenly occurred to McCadden.

What could you fit in the envelopes Martin O'Shea had said they'd carried? Not oil paintings. Not oak writing desks. Manuscripts. Hand-written sacred texts. The Koran. Letters, diaries, workbooks of the famous. Things like that.

McCadden remembered *STA2310SOP*. One of the coded entries in Peter Clarke's notebooks he hadn't understood earlier. Not statues. Not stained glass. You couldn't fit either in an envelope. STA was an abbreviation for *stamps*.

STA2310SOP. Stamp number 2310 . . . No. Stamp number 23. 10S was the symbol for the old currency. Ten shillings. And OP? Easy, now. Overprinted. Probably an Irish stamp. For years after gaining independence in the nineteen twenties, the Irish Free State had continued using English stamps, over-printing them with . . . *Saorstat na hEireann*, was it? Or *Saorstat Eireann*? One or the other.

Rare stamps. Pages from sacred texts. Antique jewellery.

The Iraqi so pleased with the hoard that he'd given little gifts, little tokens of appreciation, to his Irish friend. A set of Italian watercolours. A set of Italian figures. Had he an Italian brother-in-law with some talent? All via Billy Power, of course. Had Tom Byrne laughed at the gifts and waved them away? Or had Power just kept them to himself?

Whatever.

The fact was Tom Byrne had ingeniously improvised on this side, using Power and O'Shea and Barry as couriers. And Sayed Salman had improvised at his end, using whomever he could to collect from the holiday resorts of southern Europe.

Fine.

So far, so good.

But what exactly happened when Sayed Salman came back to Waterford more than three years later, in October 1993? What?

When McCadden got back to his car in drizzling rain a little later and drove along the coast road towards Passage East and pulled in outside the old whitewashed cottage at the turn off to Geneva Barracks and knocked on its front door, he found part of the answer to that question.

The door swung open from his knock, straight on to the main room of the cottage. Inside, three old men sat around a smoky turf fire, puffing on pipes. They looked expectantly at McCadden, saying nothing.

McCadden said, 'Who told me to drop in was Michael Drohan from Waterford.'

'Drohan,' one of the old men repeated.

The sound was so dull, it was impossible to tell if he meant it to convey recognition or enthusiasm, disgust or derision.

McCadden, knowing how long these rural rituals of introduction could take, said desperately, 'He thought you'd give me the title of a song if I recited the words of one of the verses.'

After a while, a long while, one of the old men pushed a dodgy-looking three-legged stool towards McCadden, who sat and recited the fragment.

There was a long silence afterwards.

Until finally the nearest old man eased back the peak of his cap to scratch his forehead, then pulled the cap down again and said, 'What is it, Ned?'

Ned, closest to the fire and clearly the eldest of the three, took the pipe from his mouth and spat into the burning turf and sang:

My name is Edward Holland as you might understand.
I was born, brought up in Waterford's town in Erin's
happy land.
When I was young and in my prime, kind fortune on me
smiled,
My parents doted on me, I being their only child.

The old man stopped singing and said, 'The name of that song is "The Flying Cloud",' and paused to take a teasing puff on the pipe, 'because that was the name of the clipper Edward Holland sailed in after running away to sea. Her captain was a man be the name of Moore and they took the black men from Africa and sold them as slaves in the West Indies until Moore up and said, "There is gold and silver to be had if with me you'll remain, We'll hoist aloft the pirate flag and scour the Spanish Main".'

'Right,' McCadden said. 'Right. What about the end of the verse I already had?'

The old man spat again. And sang again:

*We robbed and plundered many a ship down on the
Spanish Main,
Caused many the poor widow and orphan child in sorrow
to remain.
We made their crews to walk our planks and they hung
from out our sails,
For the saying of our skipper was that a dead man
tells no tales.*

And McCadden, whose neck had been prone to tingling the last few days, now felt something cold along his spine.

thirty-four

Early next morning, after a night of rain and into another wet Monday, one of the last pieces of the problem slotted nicely into place.

As McCadden left his flat to collect the car, crouching under the driving rain as he ran across the road to Railway Square, he almost stopped dead when the thought hit him. But he was risking it with the heavy morning traffic, and a blast from a car horn kept him moving. Wet and slightly out of breath, he sat in the car and thought it through.

On the night of the siege in Ballybeg Estate, Tom Byrne had crouched under the rain as he was heading towards the house where Peter Clarke was holding the woman. But he also had his hands high in the air. The position you adopt when you're surrendering and frightened of being shot. Funny really, when everyone from Chief Superintendent Cody down to the youngest uniformed guard was certain that Peter Clarke was armed only with a knife.

Coming into the station about thirty minutes later, a quarter of an hour before the appointed nine o'clock, McCadden spotted Boyce heading casually for the chief superintendent's office. McCadden called out, moved across the room, winked and then deftly slipped past Boyce and in through the door, saying, 'I won't be long, Harry.'

McCadden was two and a half hours.

Cody looked up slowly from the papers he was working on, not thinking a great deal of subordinates who burst into his office without knocking. When he saw it was McCadden, he took the pipe out of his mouth and put it away.

'Wait outside,' he said coldly. 'I'll call you.'

'Morning,' McCadden said. 'Peter Clarke wasn't killed by his own gun in a scuffle with Alderman Tom Byrne.'

Cody put down his Parker pen and closed his eyes, rubbed them and sighed wearily.

'Don't you think,' he said, 'it might be better if you let me know why you haven't reported for duty since last Thursday? Don't you think it might be better if you offered some explanation for your extraordinary behaviour over the weekend? For your own sake.'

'Peter Clarke,' McCadden said again, 'wasn't killed by his own gun in a scuffle with Alderman Tom Byrne. He was murdered by the woman called Vera Dunne. I'll keep the reason simple for now. For years, Tom Byrne has been selling parts of the Brockenshaw Collection to Vera Dunne's boss, the Iraqi Sayed Salman. Clarke objected and was killed.'

Cody took up the pen again and tapped its end on the surface of the desk for twenty long seconds. There was a ritual to these meetings between men of different ranks. And McCadden wasn't sticking to it.

Cody said then, 'It is now my unpleasant duty, Inspector, to inform you that you are — '

McCadden was too tired for silly games. He put his palms on the desk to support himself and leaned forward to stare into Cody's eyes.

'Look,' he said, 'Tom Byrne spun a tale in his statement about getting the impression that Peter Clarke and Vera Dunne already knew each other. Since we know it wasn't true and only existed in my head as a theory, and since you were the only person I shared the theory with, it must be obvious that Tom Byrne can read either my mind or your mind. And I'm damn sure he can't read mine.'

Cody stood up.

'Last night,' McCadden said, straightening as well, 'someone who knew the code to close off the alarm system broke into Byrne Plastics and found furniture and silver and

237

paintings once owned by George Brockenshaw in a locked basement-room. Naturally, he came straight to me with the story.'

It was twelve-fifteen when McCadden left the Chief Superintendent's office. By then he had two search warrants, one for Tom Byrne's home and another for Tom Byrne's factory. He rounded up de Burgh and six of the uniforms, sending a uniformed sergeant with two others on to the house and keeping the rest with him to search Byrne Plastics. He plonked de Burgh in the passenger seat of the lead car and drove it himself. And he talked.

'Sayed Salman came back to Waterford because he'd figured out how to smuggle some of the larger stuff back home.'

'How?' de Burgh asked.

'I don't know,' McCadden admitted. 'Not yet. We'll ask him when we catch him. Until we see what's left in Byrne's bargain basement, I don't even know if he got away with anything this trip. I doubt it. When Tom Byrne came out of hospital Friday, I think he was going across the harbour to meet Salman on the ferry and finalize the deal. I screwed that one up.'

McCadden suddenly fell silent. And then he punched the steering wheel and said angrily, 'Shit!'

'What?' de Burgh asked.

'Paul Hyland,' McCadden said.

'What?'

'Paul,' McCadden said again. 'Something's been bugging me all week about Hyland and I couldn't figure out what it was. Paul was at the Brockenshaw dinner Friday night. Did I tell you?'

'No.'

'Michael Terry came into the station last Monday morning looking for him. You remember? Hyland. Cody. Boyce. With tickets for the dinner. It's not that, though. It's something Cody said to me about Paul. The morning I saw Byrne in hospital. Wednesday. Cody took me off the Billy Power case and told me to tell Hyland as well. Thought Hyland was working with me. I reckoned he was just confused. You know, his wife and that. But he wasn't.'

238

McCadden fell silent again.

'So,' de Burgh said uncertainly. 'What? You think he's still here?'

'Who? Paul?'

'No,' de Burgh said. 'The Iraqi. Sayed Salman. You think he's still around?'

'Still in Ireland?' McCadden said. 'Probably, yeah. Maybe not in Waterford. They're waiting for things to quieten down. Which is why Byrne has been inactive the last few days. A bit of nifty footwork and we'll catch them all. He's been unlucky, Salman has. When he came to Waterford more than a week ago to open negotiations with Byrne, it was Peter Clarke who screwed it up. Considering the timing of the prison break and the way he acted afterwards, Clarke must've known what was happening long before it happened. Which means he must've had eyes in the city.'

'Who?' de Burgh asked.

'I don't know, Liam,' McCadden said again, a little irritably. Didn't like that phrase. 'Someone who knew what Byrne was up to, and the only people I can think of are Power, O'Shea and Barry.'

'Not any of them,' de Burgh said helpfully.

'No,' McCadden muttered.

He took a breath, worked himself back round to the brighter side of things, the feeling of victory he'd woken with this morning. There were times when de Burgh's stolid temperament tested the patience.

McCadden continued, 'Anyway, this is how it went. As soon as Clarke hit Waterford, he got fixed up in the vacant house in Ballybeg and rang Tom Byrne. His idea was to stop the sale of the Brockenshaw Collection, by threatening to expose Byrne, by actually exposing him if threats didn't work, even by killing Byrne or Salman. The man was obsessed. Knowing he owned all those treasures, even while he was sitting in prison, was enough to keep him happy. He was also naïve, though. He rang Tom Byrne and arranged to meet him in the vacant house. You can imagine the instructions.'

De Burgh nodded. 'Come alone. If you're not alone, the deal's off.'

'Byrne sent in big Billy Power instead,' McCadden said. 'The mistake I was making all along was thinking Power and Clarke already knew each other. They didn't. Power roped in his two mates, O'Shea and Barry, as extra muscle, but they balked. So Power went in alone. Blundered in alone, more likely, right into Clarke's knife in the dark hallway of the vacant house. I've been wondering if Clarke thought it was Byrne himself in the darkness. Or did he know it wasn't? Did he cut that X into Power's face afterwards, out of bitterness and disappointment, when he found out it wasn't Byrne?'

'You'll never know that,' de Burgh said.

'No,' McCadden admitted. 'Clarke split after the killing, anyway, to find a new hideout, to keep the war going from a new base.

'And Byrne is really sweating at this point. Not only hasn't he got rid of Clarke, but he has a dead Power on his hands as well. And the deal with the Iraqis can't go through until he gets rid of both of them. He can't have Clarke captured. Clarke will only squeal. He can't afford to have Billy Power's body found. It will only lead us to Clarke and from Clarke to him.

'Byrne is way out of his depth. This isn't something he'll be able to handle alone. So, when the Iraqis arrive in Waterford that Friday, he lays the problem on them.

'Sayed Salman has a travelling party and no doubt a couple of heavies among them. The Iraqis move Power's body, which explains why the people who moved it didn't know that Power had been killed in the hallway. They only cleaned the front room.

'The Iraqis have the muscle, then, and Tom Byrne has the local knowledge. Combine the two and Billy Power's body ends up in a container due to sail for France the next day. We mightn't have found it for two weeks, maybe more than that, if the strike hadn't happened. By then, the Iraqis would've been gone and Clarke would've been dead, covered in stuff that linked him to Billy Power's death. Very neat.

'It wasn't Clarke who took Billy Power's clothes, by the

way. It was the Iraqis. Once they had them, they went looking for Clarke to put them on him.'

'Funny that the woman found Clarke before any of the heavies,' de Burgh said. 'Funny that she was out looking for him at all.'

McCadden shook his head, while keeping his eyes locked on the road. 'Don't think of women in conventional ways in relation to anything, Liam,' he advised, 'not even assassination. Whoever Vera Dunne is, she's no call girl, no escort. I've no doubt it was she, not the others, who was sent in to rub Clarke out. She came over Saturday, after the others. From England, I'd say. Met up with Sayed Salman at the greyhound track that night for instructions. Their only contact. She's gone now, of course. Left the country as soon as she discharged herself from hospital. Wouldn't mind seeing her again some time, would you, Liam?'

'Hmm.'

'Anyway,' McCadden said, 'Clarke gave his position away again, of course, probably by another phone call to Tom Byrne. He wasn't much good at what he was trying to do, really. But the woman, Vera Dunne, she was good. Is good. Wherever she is now. But she was unlucky. She'd just reached the door of the house where Clarke was hiding when the cops turned the nearest corner, also looking for Clarke. Consider the problem, Liam. She has to kill Clarke, and yet she can't kill him in full view of the police and get away with it. What did she do?'

'Well, she — '

'It was very good, Liam,' McCadden went on. 'Very clever. She pushed her way in past . . .' McCadden tailed off.

'Past Clarke,' de Burgh supplied. 'And then she — '

'No, no, wait,' McCadden said. 'I wonder did Clarke say to Tom Byrne on the phone, no tricks this time, send a woman in broad daylight, send one of your daughters?'

'Byrne's daughters are blonde,' de Burgh objected. 'Vera Dunne didn't look like either of them.'

'Three years had passed, Liam,' McCadden pointed out. 'Tina Byrne was, what, then? Twenty? She was away in college in Dublin. Did Clarke ever even see her since she was in her early teens?

'It would explain it, though, wouldn't it? Why Vera Dunne didn't disguise herself. Why she didn't push in. Clarke opened the door to her because he already had her description, he knew she was the messenger.

'She might've hurried in, all right, but she was expected. She said to Clarke, look, this has nothing to do with me, they weren't following me, but there are two cops out there, watching the house.

'The two of them settled down, waiting to see what was happening. What happened was that more cops turned up, more and more cops turned up, until they were into a siege.

'Vera Dunne then said to Clarke that his only chance of getting out of this was to call Tom Byrne in there, pretend to take the two of them hostage. Clarke asked, why do I need two? She told him, walk out of here with me in front of you and they'll shoot you in the back. And Clarke wants to talk to Tom Byrne, anyway.

'So, Tom Byrne came in. Watching him, even Clarke must've wondered why the Alderman was ducking with his hands raised in the air. Because even Clarke didn't know at that stage that there was a gun in the house.

'The only possible way Vera Dunne could get away with murdering Clarke while surrounded by a hundred cops was to get a reputable third party in there to tell it the way she wanted it told. And that's exactly what she did.

'They talked for a while afterwards, Clarke, Vera Dunne, Tom Byrne. They had to. They had to give the impression that Byrne was negotiating.

'And then Vera Dunne gathered Clarke and Byrne in close. She drew the Beretta and shoved it into Clarke's body and fired. She went behind Clarke and fired from where he'd been standing, with Byrne's hand cupped around the muzzle.

'That's what fooled the old experts, Liam. It looked as if Byrne's hands were cupped around the muzzle for the shot that killed Clarke. But the slightly muffled shot must've come before the loud shot. Was it like that? I was sleeping.

'Vera Dunne wiped the Beretta. They must have a contact in Italy. Italian watercolours, Italian guns. Anyway. She got Clarke's and Byrne's fingerprints all over the Beretta. She got Byrne to drop it to the floor, talking to him all the time, getting his story straight. She came out hysterical. She was rushed to hospital. She made a rapid recovery. And she vanished. Very good. Eh, Liam?'

But de Burgh was fairly quiet for the rest of the journey.

When they reached Byrne Plastics, McCadden went in with de Burgh, telling the squad car to wait until he called. On the stairway to Tom Byrne's glass-walled office, he looked down over the factory floor and saw more than twenty pairs of eyes glancing up at him and one pair that didn't look upwards at all. He faltered for a second, then skipped a step to catch up with de Burgh.

With all the old confidence and bounce, none of the recent fear and a little of the new cockiness, Tom Byrne came out from behind his office desk to greet them. Byrne came grinning all the way, the hand extended, the hand of the victor extended in reconciliation to the vanquished.

De Burgh blinked as McCadden accepted that hand.

And then he stared as McCadden said, 'Eddie Hayes. Is he in today?'

'He is, yes,' Byrne said. 'I've made him permanent, you know.'

'Always better to take on someone that's been recommended to you,' McCadden offered.

Byrne nodded. 'Yes, I find it is, actually.'

'Could I use your office to have a word with him?'

'Certainly, certainly. Nothing wrong, is there?'

'A few loose ends I've got to tie up in the Billy Power case,' McCadden said. 'And when they're all neatly tied up, by the way, I won't be seeing you again for a long while after.'

Byrne, on his way out the door, turned to face him again, not doing much to hide the little smirk on his face. 'I'm sorry to hear that, Inspector. Been transferred, have you?'

McCadden shrugged. He said, 'You'll have to ask Chief Superintendent Cody about that.'

When they were alone again, de Burgh whispered urgently, 'I thought we were going to search the place?'

'We will, Liam,' McCadden assured him. 'We will.'

'Why do you want to talk to Hayes?'

'It just struck me on the way up the stairs,' McCadden said. 'Should really have seen it a lot earlier, though.'

'What?' de Burgh asked.

'I didn't make the connection,' McCadden said. 'I've never been there. Think of all the trouble I would've saved if I'd seen it earlier.'

'What?' de Burgh demanded. 'What?'

McCadden walked across to the glass partition and looked down. Eddie Hayes was coming slowly up the steps, like a condemned man mounting a gallows. Tom Byrne was in the centre of the factory floor, smiling and waving happily at McCadden.

McCadden took the search warrant from the inside pocket of his jacket and used it to wave back, smiling through clenched teeth.

De Burgh asked suddenly from behind him, 'Why did he do it, I wonder?'

'Who?'

'Tom Byrne,' de Burgh said. 'Why did he rip off the collection, get stuck in shady dealings with the Iraqi? Was his business in trouble or something?'

'I don't know,' McCadden said again. 'But we're going to find out. We're not having any more mysteries with this lot, any more unexplained — '

He broke off as Eddie Hayes came mournfully through the office door without knocking. Hayes' legs and hands were shaking and he seemed to be on the point of tears.

'Sit down, son,' McCadden said to him. 'Sit down.'

But then, catching another glimpse of Byrne swaggering on the factory floor, McCadden suddenly changed his mind, thought of a better approach.

He said to de Burgh, 'Get Byrne back up here, will you?'

And when Byrne returned, a concerned look on his face, McCadden gestured him into his own chair, behind his own desk, and said, 'I thought you should hear this as well. As his employer.'

Byrne sat. 'Of course,' he said soberly. 'Yes. Of course.'

McCadden stayed by the glass partition, standing, adding nothing. In the silence, Eddie Hayes, sitting the visitor's side of the desk with his head bowed, struggled to stop shaking. And Tom Byrne's self-assurance started seeping a little. In his eyes, behind the official interest and concern, there were flashes of doubt, of irritation.

McCadden turned to Byrne, 'You told me just now that Mr Hayes had been recommended to you by someone.'

Byrne, staring at Eddie Hayes, expecting the questions to be shooting in that direction, started slightly. 'Did I?'

'Didn't you?' McCadden enquired.

Could've stayed there all day, swapping questions.

Byrne stuttered. 'Well, I — '

'Who was it?' McCadden asked. 'Who recommended him to you?'

Byrne laughed nervously. 'To be honest with you, I don't really know. It might be in the files. I just don't remember.'

But he did. He remembered all right. You could see it in his ashen face, greyer now than it had been in hospital the previous week. You could hear it in his quick breathing. And you could see it in his hands, locked together on the surface of the desk, but still trembling a little.

He remembered. And as he remembered, he started making dangerous connections, jumping to wild ideas, chasing down his fears. McCadden told him all that.

McCadden said, 'I wouldn't bother trying to think it through, Tom. You'll get there much quicker if you listen to my questions.'

He turned to Hayes. 'You live in Poleberry Street, don't you, Eddie?'

Hayes nodded, without looking upwards.

McCadden said, 'And — let me see, one, two, three, four, five — five doors down, the other side of Poleberry Street. That right, Eddie?'

Hayes muttered, almost inaudibly. 'Yes.'

'You know who lives there, Tom?' McCadden asked Byrne. 'Lived, I should say. Five doors down from Eddie, the other side of the street.'

Byrne stared at him, trying to swallow down his dry throat. What to do? What to say? Where was this going if he admitted the knowledge. Where was it going if he denied it? Which was the trap? Which the exit?

Finally he cleared his throat twice. 'Peter Clarke.'

'That's right,' McCadden said. 'Peter Clarke. And who recommended Eddie to you?'

Byrne said drily again, 'Peter Clarke.'

'*Now* you remember,' McCadden applauded. 'Was that when Eddie left school this year?'

'Yes.'

'And you couldn't refuse Peter Clarke's request, could you?'

'He was an old friend. Of course not.'

'Yeah,' McCadden said ironically. 'An old friend. Yeah. Did you ever wonder, Tom, why Peter Clarke escaped from prison at precisely the time he did? What information did he have? Who fed him that information? Who was in a position to gather that information here in Waterford? Who scouted hideouts for him while he was on the run? Who had a change of clothes ready for him? Who muddied the waters with stories about Billy Power's attack on your daughter, Tina?'

McCadden turned to Hayes. 'Eddie?'

And Hayes, crying openly now, finally lifted his head.

It wasn't the boy's tears, though, that McCadden wanted to see. He gestured to de Burgh to take Hayes away and turned again to Byrne as the pair were leaving the office behind him.

Byrne had the telephone receiver in his hand, his forefinger poised over the buttons on the panel.

McCadden said, 'That verse of the ballad I recited in the pub on Friday. The last line. *For the saying of our captain was that a dead man tells no tales.* You thought I already knew it, didn't you? I didn't. You thought for a while I was playing on your nerves. But I wasn't. I am now, though. So, tell me. What are you going to do about it, Tom? Arrange to have Eddie Hayes go as quietly as Peter Clarke?'

246

Byrne had dialled his number and was staring at McCadden while waiting for an answer to the call. The look warned McCadden that he'd gone too far. The look promised a transfer to some place uninhabitable. The look asserted that its owner wasn't just a punk who could be easily intimidated. But underneath it the hand holding the receiver wasn't quite as steady as the look itself.

Byrne shifted his gaze then and said suddenly into the receiver, 'Chief Superintendent Cody, please.'

He waited.

He said, 'Yes, I know, I know. Tell him it's Tom Byrne.'

And he waited again.

And he said, angrily, 'Look, my dear girl! This is Alderman Thomas Byrne — '

McCadden walked from the glass partition to the desk and lifted the receiver from Byrne's shaking hand.

'This is Inspector McCadden,' he said. And then, 'Hi, Rose. How are you? Would you put me through to the chief superintendent's office?'

After an effort, a little concentration, he put the receiver back in the moving target of Byrne's hand.

Byrne got as far as, 'Dan? Tom here. I — '

What Cody was saying didn't carry to McCadden. It was delivered in whispers. It was brief and didn't last more than thirty seconds. But it broke Tom Byrne, back to the shattered man who'd staggered from the house where Peter Clarke had been murdered in front of him.

Murder. Something he'd wanted done. But not something he could stomach seeing.

And it wasn't remorse that was bothering him now, McCadden knew. Just self-pity.

McCadden took the search warrant from his pocket again and unfolded it and said ruthlessly, 'We're only starting, Tom. Thomas. So let's get moving.'

thirty-five

Six o'clock that Monday evening, McCadden was told he'd
lost the Iraqis.

His response seemed indifferent. Unconnected.

'Paul Hyland around?' he asked.

'No, he's out,' he was told. 'He's on sick leave.'

'*Still* on sick leave?'

'He reckons he'll be back Wednesday, Thursday at the
latest.'

'You got a number for him?'

'Well, there's his home, I suppose.'

'Anything else?'

'I don't think so, no. No other number.'

'Hmm. Right.'

McCadden himself had been nosing around. And getting
close to nailing the Iraqis in Passage East. And they'd obviously decided to cut their losses and abort the deal. Abort it
for the moment, anyway. Maybe they intended coming back.
But the reason they'd left in such a hurry this time round, on
a flight from Dublin to London, as early as the previous Saturday evening, maybe only five hours after McCadden had tailed
Tom Byrne to the car ferry and back, had as much to do with
Paul Hyland as it had with McCadden.

At least it explained why Byrne was so relaxed, so confident
at the dinner that night. He thought he had nothing to fear
any more. No more dicey phone calls to make. No more risky
meetings to organize. No trading that might set him up for a

raid. He thought there was nothing more for McCadden to see.

If Byrne was clever, he would've let McCadden waste a lot of energy chasing him over the next few days, would've kept McCadden too busy covering unexpected moves in front and too anxious covering his back. But Byrne wasn't clever. Not in the intelligent sense, anyway. He wasn't a strategist. From the time Peter Clarke escaped from prison, through Billy Power's death, the siege and the death of Clarke himself, he hadn't been doing anything more than reacting to a move at a time.

So what was he, then? Greedy? Addicted to expensive vices? Was he in financial trouble with his business?

It took McCadden three days to dig out the answer.

Right after the premises of Byrne Plastics were searched and he was taken into custody, Byrne bought in some pricey legal advice whose talent was for asking rather than answering questions. You could see Byrne's point. All right, his basement was crammed with art treasures and antiques he had no receipts for. But there was no one left around to definitely say he'd stolen them. George Brockenshaw was dead. Theresa Cheasty was dead. Peter Clarke was dead. Even Billy Power was dead. And the Iraqis weren't going to toddle back to Ireland and incriminate themselves. The State was kind of short of witnesses. So McCadden and a team of detectives spent Tuesday plugging that particular gap, interviewing anyone who'd ever been in George Brockenshaw's house. The old man McCadden had bought the Scotch for at the fund-raising dinner. One or two contemporaries of his. Doctor Kearns in Woodstown.

Even then Byrne wouldn't talk.

Wednesday, McCadden interviewed the members of Byrne's family again.

Byrne's wife, Georgina, was too shamed, too shattered by it all, to even listen. How could she possibly remember anything from the autumn of 1989? For nearly thirty years her life had been even and comfortable and unquestioned. One summer was as crowded as the next, one winter as cosy as the last. Now it had all suddenly blown up in her face and she was simply bewildered. For her, 1969 was much the same as 1979, just different parts of a careless past that was now lost to her.

Tina Byrne, too, was stunned and lost and confused. The source of all her self-doubt and her lack of confidence had just been exposed as a cheat. So she didn't even have her neuroses to believe in any more.

Catherine Byrne, characteristically, looked to her husband for an answer. Any answer. Not knowing he had the real one.

Wednesday afternoon, less than an hour after seeing him in his home in Glenview, Robbie Hearne called on McCadden at the Garda station.

Hearne said, 'You're talking about the autumn of 1989, aren't you? That's when Tom Byrne started, isn't it?'

McCadden nodded. 'Any time after September of that year.'

Hearne lowered his head. He said, 'I've never mentioned this to anyone. Not even to Catherine. Especially not to Catherine. I'd better go back a bit first, before what you already know. When we were first married, myself and Catherine, I worked for Tom Byrne in Byrne Plastics as a sales rep. I was a fool. That's what Byrne wanted, to have us under his control, to own me the way he thought I owned Catherine, and so to still own her like that. You remember I told you the way he'd undermine you without you being able to put a finger on it? He was doing that to our relationship. I had to get out. But I left Byrne Plastics at a bad time. Catherine was pregnant with our first child. And the company I changed to went out of business in six months. So it was either back to the begging bowl with Tom Byrne or take our chances out on our own. There weren't many jobs, and what there were Tom Byrne made sure I wasn't in the running for them. But I'd always fancied myself as a bit of an entrepreneur, to tell you the truth. I borrowed and put our own savings with it and opened up a little café in the centre of town. That was May 1989. You know the place, don't you? It was mostly for the young people in the evening, the type of place they went to. But it really started taking off when it became popular for lunches with people working in town. And that's when the trouble started, too. Every second night you'd get guards in there, looking for drugs, looking for stolen goods, responding to complaints. Any excuse. Tom Byrne must have a few friends among your colleagues, does he?'

McCadden said, 'I suppose he must have, yes.'

Hearne said, 'Except the idea backfired. It only added to the colour of the place for the kids. October that year, another café opens up a few doors down the same street. Everything we had, they sold cheaper than we could. Everything we hadn't, they made sure to get it. You won't find Tom Byrne's name connected anywhere with that business, but that's whose money was behind it. I often wondered where he was getting that kind of money to throw away, and now I know. It was a bitter struggle, that was.'

'But you won,' McCadden said. 'Your place is still open. The other isn't.'

'I was blessed with a cook,' Hearne said. 'It doesn't matter if you're cheaper, if the food's not good enough people won't eat it. You know who the cook was?'

'Who?'

Hearne laughed. 'It was Catherine,' he said. And then he was suddenly serious again. 'That wasn't the end of it. When I opened the first mini-market, eighteen months ago, Byrne tried every trick in the book. You have to understand the way he did it. He wouldn't leave himself open. He wouldn't say, I don't want you supplying that fellow. He'd say, the son-in-law, Robbie, he's opened a mini-market there. Will you supply him with what he asks for. As a favour to me. I'll see you all right if there's any trouble. I'll see you won't lose on it if the business goes down. That's the way Tom Byrne was, Inspector. Always trying to be helpful. There's an awful lot of people in Waterford don't believe what you say about him. Me, I feel for Catherine, all right, because whatever Tom Byrne was, he was her father, after all; but as for myself, I haven't felt as free since I was a kid.'

McCadden sat on in the interview room for about ten minutes after Robbie Hearne had left, until Paul Hyland, all smiles and songs and shuffles, shoved his head round the door and said, 'Hear you've been looking for me.'

'That's right, Paul. I have.'

'I've only just got back. Couple of hours ago. What the hell are you doing hiding away in here all by yourself?'

'Among other things,' McCadden said, 'trying to remember the slogan Tom Byrne's party had in the last general election. The law and order one.'

'*When was the last time you felt safe in your home?*' Hyland supplied instantly.

Still shuffling in the doorway, he laughed, inviting McCadden to join him. If Hyland felt the weight of any irony on himself, he wasn't really showing it much.

McCadden said, 'So. Where've you been the last ten days? Not in Liverpool, right? We'll by-pass all that shit.'

'Come on, Carl,' Hyland snorted. 'You met the travel agent at the dinner last Saturday. Use your imagination.'

'OK,' McCadden said. 'OK. Sometimes my imagination runs a little wild, though.'

'That's the way I like it.'

'OK,' McCadden said again. 'One Sunday night, after a not very productive case briefing, you rang the reception at Jurys Hotel and found the Iraqi, Sayed Salman, was staying there with a few friends. So you either had a chat with Mr Salman or sat on his tail for a while. One or the other. Either way you sniffed something odd. How much did he pay you to keep off his back? Enough to clear your debts?'

Hyland was smiling. Still smiling. You never really knew with him.

'I turned a corner,' he said. 'I'm on a roll. It happens. Even to gamblers.'

'Yeah,' McCadden said. 'Yeah. What happened last Saturday that they ran away? Did you lean on them again? Too much? Were you breathing too closely down their necks while they were on their way to meet Byrne in Passage? Did they think you'd betrayed them to me, playing both sides against the middle?'

'Wild,' Hyland exclaimed. 'Like you said. Wild.'

McCadden shook his head. He said, 'Not really. Wednesday last, Cody threw me off the case and told me to pull you off as well. It didn't make any sense at the time. But it might now. If Tom Byrne heard it from the Iraqis, for instance, that you were leaning on them, and if Byrne passed the word on to Cody, thinking you were working with me, Cody would assume I was stringing him along when I told him you weren't . . .'

Hyland shrugged. 'Cody,' he said dismissively. 'Cody's judgement was off the wall last week.'

'Fuck you, Paul,' McCadden said quietly then, without animosity. 'We could've taken the lot of them. Together. The redhead. You saw her at the greyhound track that Saturday night. No one even knows who she is, where she came from. All the Iraqis. We could've taken them.'

'Hey, hey,' Hyland protested, not smiling any more. 'I wasn't the one who kept me off the case, was I? I wanted in. You reckoned you didn't need me.'

'You weren't being straight.'

'You said I was gambling.'

'That, too.'

'You went for de Burgh.'

'You weren't around, man. Saturday night, we found Billy Power's corpse in a cargo container, you weren't around. Liam was. Remember?'

'And like I said at the time, with average help, you get average results.'

'Solid.'

'What?'

'Solid,' McCadden said again. 'Solid and reliable. What you actually said was that with solid and reliable people, you get solid and reliable results.'

Hyland shrugged. 'Solid. Average. What's the difference?'

'Anyway,' McCadden said. 'When was the last time *you* felt safe in your home?'

Hyland frowned. 'Hah?

McCadden got up and left the interview room and went back to his desk. Not even knowing himself exactly what he'd meant by the question. Thinking more about the loss of the Iraqis and Vera Dunne, about the relative merits of Hyland and de Burgh as detectives, as friends, as husbands . . .